Pretending
Shanna Clayton

For Perla
My friend, my beta reader, and my beauty guru.
Love you, girl.

CHAPTER ONE

DOLL

Anyone who thinks living in a mansion is a dream come true has never been alone in one at night. Hearing loud noises, trying to figure out where they're coming from and what's causing them—trust me when I say the glamour and glitz goes straight out the window. First thing tomorrow I swear I'm buying a dog. A big ferocious one. With fangs.

I bet Harland is laughing his ass off somewhere from the other side. I loved that man like he was my own dad, but sometimes I wonder what he was thinking by leaving me here in his rustic Victorian. Payback for giving him hell as a teenager? Possibly. He did have one twisted sense of humor. No college dormitories for me, oh no. That would've been far too conventional for his tastes. If he thought my life was anywhere bordering normal, I would've become his unfinished business. I glance at the ceiling.

Go ahead and cross into the light, Harland, you jackass. I'm scared shitless.

I inhale, trying to get a handle on myself so I can listen. A few seconds of silence tick by, and I figure I must've dreamt the noise. Either that, or it was just an eerie nighttime sound. Kent House is known for those, the air clanging through its pipes, wood expanding and contracting, crackling pops in the attic—all testaments to its old age. This place was built before the invention of cars and most modern technology. It's bound to make a few weird noises. Or have a few ghosts…a possibility that makes me shudder. When Harland was alive, these things never bothered me. His presence alone made me feel safe.

My phone flashes from the nightstand. It's three a.m., meaning I've only been asleep an hour. This is what I get for studying with Gwen. I should know better by now. Those late night study sessions include one too many margaritas and little to no actual studying. She must've just gone to bed even later than me, because there's a text from her.

Got us white shirts 4 Graffiti Bash. Don't care if Princess Bitchface is hosting. We're still going.

She's referring to Charlotte Hart. They've hated each other for as long as I can remember, but it's anyone's guess as to why. Both of them change the subject whenever I bring it up. Being stuck in the middle isn't easy, but I've gotten pretty good at staying neutral. Taking sides isn't a good idea when your best friends don't get along. Chances are I'd lose one of them if I did.

A long sigh escapes as I lay back down. Going to that party is the last thing I want to do. Professor Barakat is hosting a seminar tomorrow night discussing new insights into evolution. Wanting to go screams lameness but hanging out with the Greek elite doesn't compare. I'd rather be lame.

A thud booms from downstairs.

I bolt upright in bed, now very much awake. I did *not* dream that up.

Obscure noises and shuffling ensue, each sound making my heart pump a little faster. Throwing my sheets aside, I rush to the closet and grab the first robe I find. Then, keeping my steps light, I creep into the dark hallway outside my bedroom. My cell phone is tucked to my side, 911 already punched on the keypad. I'm ready to press the dial button at a moment's notice.

Why don't I own a gun?

Charlotte told me to get one after seeing this place. "Guns are loud and dangerous," I said at the time, inflecting my very liberal, collegiate stance on weapons. "Besides, there's plenty of staff at the house. What do I need a gun for?"

Clearly a dumb call.

Should've listened to her.

Muffled voices come from up ahead. I listen to them closely, trying to figure out who they belong to. Can't be staff. Gwen and the few staff members who live here sleep on the third floor. Everyone else should be long gone.

The voices grow louder as I reach the balcony overlooking the front entranceway. On both sides are wide mahogany staircases leading down into the foyer. Instead of turning to either side, I crouch into the shadows, pretty sure it's a good idea to stay unseen, at least until I figure out who's down there. Peeking out from between the banister's wooden legs, I focus in on the dark space at the end of the stairs and catch the outline of three shadowed figures.

Oh God. Are they here to rob the place?

There are plenty of valuables in the house. I should call the police now. But I'd probably be safer calling from my room. I don't want to think about what they'll do if they hear me.

Just as I'm about to take off, someone switches on the light. I blink, my eyes adjusting, and focus in on the guys in the foyer. My breath catches in my chest.

He's back.

There's no mistaking that dark shade of hair or tattooed-covered biceps for anyone other than Wesley Kent. He stumbles into the foyer, dressed in a grey shirt and dark jeans. He looks the same except his hair is slightly longer, and his skin is tanned.

Well, damn.

Now I feel stupid.

My roommate. Of course. Most people would've come to that conclusion long before now, but Wesley and I aren't your average roommates. I haven't seen him since the beginning of summer. That's one of the stipulations in Harland's will. We're allowed to leave town for the summer—and Wesley always does—but we have to stay here during the fall and spring semesters. That part wasn't added for me. Harland knew I was content living here in Kent

House, and I promised him long before he died I'd go to college.

Harland added that stipulation for Wesley. They weren't speaking at the time of his death, but he knew his son well, and he knew Wesley would never stay if he weren't given some time off. Exploring is in the Kents' blood. If it weren't for the inheritance, I doubt he'd be here at all. Harland knew he was dying. I think he created the will to push Wesley and me together, possibly to create a friendship between us. That's far from what happened though. I see Wesley during the school year just as much as I see him during the summer. This house is big enough to get lost in, and it's definitely big enough to keep us out of one another's way. Whatever his reasons, Wesley doesn't want anything to do with me or with his dad's plans.

"Take his arm, Chase, before he passes out here on the damn floor."

Wesley's friends hold him up, one on either side of him. They're both tall, and they look like they're in good shape, but they're struggling to keep Wesley upright.

"Jesus, Tyson," Chase hisses. "Did you have to get him so drunk?"

"Whiskey masks the pain," Tyson says, looking offended. "I've kept him this way since we landed. It's called friendship."

"More like alcohol poisoning."

I recognize them from campus. They're both anthropology majors, and by the sound of it, they also went to Egypt over the summer. Just thinking about the Egyptian dig makes me stiffen. It killed me to let it go. Opportunities like that don't come along often, especially for students. I wanted to sign up but knew better once I saw Wesley's name on the info packet. He'd been chosen to lead the team. It was crushing, but working alongside a guy who can barely stand to live with me stole the trip's appeal.

"I don't understand you, bro." Chase, the bigger of the two guys, hefts Wesley to the staircase. "You knew when you took that beating they'd make it worse for you than for Hayes."

Beating? Did he just say that Wesley was beaten up?

And Hayes? It had to be our neighbor Hayes. This town isn't tiny, but it's hard to imagine that many people with the same name.

Wesley doesn't say anything, and Chase continues to yell at him. "Why did you do it? And right after you got the cut to your stomach. Did you know you almost *died*?"

I bite my lip.

He's exaggerating. He's got to be exaggerating.

"I don't think that's helping, Chase."

Wesley stumbles forward, swaying so much he loses his balance. My chest tightens right before Chase catches him mid-fall. He slides to the floor, collapsing on the first step. "S'kay. I think I'll stay right here..." he mumbles, closing his eyes. "Just leave me the bottle of whiskey."

"Like hell," Chase yells. "You've had too fucking much to drink already."

Tyson's voice is less impatient. "We can help you to your room, Wes. Doesn't a warm bed sound nicer than the hard floor?"

"Yes, but the bedroom is so...far."

That isn't the alcohol talking. This place is a maze of hallways and rooms. It's the reason Wesley and I have only been in each other's presence a few awkward times. We both stick to our ends of the house.

"Just point us in the right direction," Chase snaps.

Wesley tries to focus his vision. He starts to lift his arm, but it falls slack, and so does the rest of his body. Looks like his bed is made for the night.

"Oh that's just wonderful," Chase says. "Now we'll have to wake up the staff."

That's my cue to leave. None of this has to do with me, and the last thing I want is to get involved. I should get out of here before Wesley's friends come trudging up the stairs and find me.

Using the banister as support, I pull myself up when a loud creak gives way. The noise grinds against my eardrums, freezing my body into place. Oh God. As far as creaks go, that had to be the loudest one ever made in the existence of time. They had to have heard it. I can't look back though. I don't want to bring more attention to myself. Maybe if I stay perfectly still, I'll blend into the shadows. My only other option is to break out into a run.

"Wait there, miss! We need your help!"

Guess running is out, dammit.

I stand, glaring at the wooden rail like it's out to get me. Tyson marches up the stairs while my mind runs rampant constructing a plan to get out of this mess. Wesley and I live our lives pretending the other doesn't exist. If he were sober, he wouldn't want me talking to his friends. He wouldn't want me having anything to do with them. This is what I get for letting my curiosity get the best of me. Never again will I inspect a noise in the middle of the night—serial killers and thieves be damned.

Thanks again, Harland.

I turn and nearly smack into Tyson's chest. When I look up, the guy is smiling at me and giving me a look I haven't gotten in quite a while. "Well what have we here?" he asks no one in particular, eyeing me from head to toe.

Guys haven't looked at me this way in so long I'm not sure how to react. It completely throws me off. I sort of have the urge to laugh, but at the same time, I feel like rolling my eyes.

"What the hell is going on?" Chase calls from the foyer, sounding irritated.

Tyson doesn't tear his eyes from me. "Nothing." His smile widens. "Just admiring some of Kent's artwork. This piece is in-fucking-credible."

Oh Jesus. He's really working that seductive appraisal thing. Tyson is a good-looking guy with blonde hair and dimples, and he's got a certain swagger about him. I'm not swooning at his feet or anything, but even so, I can't help the laugh that bubbles up in my throat because:

1. I'm a girl.
2. Flattery works on me every time.

"Well stop eyeballing her, and ask her to point us in the direction of Wesley's room."

"I may ask her more than that," Tyson says so only I can hear.

I'm more than amused at this point, but not the least bit intimidated by the heated look he's giving me. Back home, I dealt with guys like Tyson all the time. Waitressing at the local sports bar meant serving guys who came on too strong once they had a few beers in their system. I can handle him.

"Tell me, beautiful, how much does Kent pay to keep you on his staff?"

A grin tugs at my lips. I can't really blame him for that assumption, considering Wesley probably never mentioned me before.

I decide to have a little fun with it. "Why are you asking?"

"Because I want to offer you double his price."

Now I know he's drunk. Either that, or he's teasing me. I'm not sure which. "You're making me think I'm underpaid."

"I assure you, I'll pay more. My house could use a maid."

"I'm not a maid."

He shrugs as if he couldn't care less what my job is. "Cook. Clean…whatever you want to do." He winks, and there's a suggestive cadence to that last part.

I purse my lips, pretending to consider his offer. "Gee, what's the going rate these days for a roommate? Because I can assure *you*, Kent pays me nothing."

Tyson's jaw drops. The look on his face is priceless, and I laugh again.

"You've got to be shittin' me," he sputters. "You're Wesley's *roommate*?"

"Dahlia Reynolds," I say, sticking my hand out. "But most people call me Doll."

"You live here with Wes? In this house?"

"Yep, that's how the whole roommate thing works."

"How come I've never seen you before?"

"We had Biological Anthropology together. You've seen me before."

Tyson rubs his hand over his jaw, trying to place me. "You sure about that? I don't remember you being in that class."

"You probably never noticed me because…" I look down at my body, catching the way my tank top and boyshorts peek out of my robe. Readjusting the fabric, I pull the strings tighter to cover myself up. "Well I don't usually look like this."

That's something of an understatement. I usually go out of my way to look as unnoticeable as possible. Tonight I look like myself.

"That's hard to believe." Tyson's sexy rasp reappears. "'Cause I don't think I could ever forget you."

Oh geez. He's back to flirting. Better change the subject now before Wesley wakes up and realizes what's going on.

"You're looking for Wesley's room, right?" Glancing over the balcony, I spy my roommate's limp form sprawled across the stairs. "What exactly is the matter with him?"

As soon as the question leaves my lips, I feel like banging my head into the nearest wall. I shouldn't have asked.

"He's uh…got a bit of a gash across his stomach," Tyson says. He turns, looking back at the lifeless Wesley and tilts his head. "Among other problems."

"What other problems?"

Crap—I'm curious now, especially since it sounded like there's a story behind those words. But I really shouldn't be asking. His problems, whatever they are, have nothing to do with me.

"Never mind," I say before Tyson can answer. "I don't want to know the details."

The problem is I *do* want to know. What did Tyson mean Wesley has a gash on his stomach? A gash could mean something as small as a scratch or something as big as a gaping flesh wound. It's on the tip of my tongue to ask, but I swallow it down.

No more questions. I can't involve myself in Wesley's business any more than I already have.

"Go help your friend," I say to Tyson. "I'll show you where his bedroom is."

Wesley's friends end up carrying him, Tyson holding his arms and Chase in charge of his legs. When I hear Wesley groan—an agonizing sound—I stop.

Chase catches my look of horror. "Don't worry about it, babe. Just keep going. He's not exactly light."

"That's easy for you to say." Tyson grunts, breathless. "You're not carrying his upper body."

I continue to lead them down the hallway, ignoring every painful sound Wesley makes. When we finally get to his side of the house, I have to stop and think about where to go. The first room I check is a bedroom. The only other bedroom on this floor is mine, so this one has to be his.

They lay Wesley on top of his king-sized bed, then take a moment to catch their breaths.

"You should take off his shoes," I suggest from the doorway.

I don't know why I said that. Wesley's comfort doesn't matter to me, but it's too late to take it back now.

Looking tired and aggravated, Chase and Tyson each wrench a shoe from Wesley's feet. Before I can ask them to do anything else, they both turn to leave. Chase nods on his way out by way of a goodbye, and Tyson pauses at the doorway. "Thanks, Doll. Maybe I'll see you on campus."

He sounds hopeful. Tyson is one of Wesley's friends. It's not like we can be buddy-buddy or anything, but I don't think he realizes that he's playing for Team Wesley just yet. Once he understands how divided this house is, it will be the end of us knowing each other. "Night, Tyson. Drive safe."

With one last wink, he's gone. I suddenly find myself alone in the dark bedroom.

With *him*.

I shuffle my feet. I've been in this room before. Once. I hadn't been prying…

Okay, maybe I was prying a little bit.

So what. I'm curious. I've lived with the guy for the past three years, and I barely know him. Besides, it's not like he keeps anything personal in here anyway. Not unless you count the drawer full of condoms or the set of dumbbells in the corner. I shake my head, remembering my disappointment. I always held a starry-eyed image of Wesley Kent, figuring he'd be one of the most fascinating, adventurous, intelligent people to walk the planet. If he had any of his dad in him, he should've been all those things and more.

Sadly the most noteworthy item in this room is the picture Wesley keeps of his brother, Sam, buried in the back of his closet behind his clothes. From what Harland told me, they were inseparable. Sam died in a car crash a few years back, and Wesley never recovered from the loss.

I can relate. Loss and I are old friends. Harland and my mom were all I had, and now they're both gone. That picture of Sam is the only thing that makes sense about Wesley Kent. It's the type of thing you stuff in the back of the closet to make their absence easier to deal with. All my mom's things are tucked away in a drawer somewhere too.

Daring a glance at Wesley, I decide to move closer. I know I should turn and walk away, but I can't help myself. An overpowering need to look at him up close takes over my body and propels me to the edge of the bed.

Whenever we cross paths, I usually avert my eyes and go about my business as if he's not there. Ignoring him is the easiest way to deal with him ignoring me. But he doesn't know I'm here, and I can't let this chance go to waste.

Moonlight spills in from the window, giving me just enough of its glow to take in his face. I let out a small breath; he's so damned gorgeous it's a shame. Everything about him is lean and chiseled, and it makes me wish things were different between us.

Sleep softens the hard lines of his face. The squareness of his jaw becomes a little less rigid. His eyes aren't open, but I remember the color vividly. It's a dark shade of blue, almost black but not quite. Like the night sky.

I'm not sure why, but I lean even closer, until my face is only inches from his. He smells like alcohol mixed with a clean, intoxicating scent that sparks a desire to grab his shirt and nuzzle my face against his neck.

This is crazy.

I keep waiting for someone to barge in and stop me, but no one does. Maybe it's my curiosity again, I don't know, but something draws me to Wesley. There have always been two versions of him—the one Harland told me about and the one I've been living with. It doesn't matter that we have no involvement in each other's lives. Part of me still holds out hope the boy in Harland's stories will come to life. I feel like I'm waiting for that day to happen, sitting on the edge of my seat in suspense, always on the lookout for a flicker of the real Wesley to appear. There's got to be more to this guy than an empty shell of a bedroom.

Again, this is crazy.

This is the real Wesley. He's drunk, sleeping, and pretty beat up. I should leave.

Steely fingers grasp my arm, wrenching me back. I gasp, and my heart slams against my chest. Wesley is awake. His blue eyes lock onto mine. They look wild, like he doesn't know where he is or who I am. I stare back at him, not sure what to do. Should I say hello and ask him how he's been? Because I doubt that'd go over very well. Thankfully his hand goes slack, and he falls back onto his pillow.

I run from the bedroom, not bothering to shut the door behind me. I don't slow down until I'm far across the house. After several seconds, my heart rate returns to a steady pace. I'm not sure what the heck just happened.

One thing's for sure. Next time I hear a strange noise at night, I'm staying in bed.

CHAPTER TWO

DOLL

"Gwen, please don't do this to me. Not today."

This isn't the first time I've chased after Gwen Hubbard, begging for her help. It's irritating and embarrassing, especially since we've had this same fight too many times to count. Keeping up with her stubborn pace makes me want to scream. I hold it back and remind myself that she means well.

"You are a waste of my talents!"

"Come on, Gwen. You're being ridicu—"

"A waste of my training!"

I'd love to remind Gwen she's on the clock right now, but it would no doubt send her into a blind rage. This is a prime example of why one should never hire best friends. Boundaries disappear completely. Seriously, what made me think this would work?

Let's see, Gwen needed a job, Kent House needed a maid, and it *is* nice having a friend around.

Most of the time.

Now, not being one of those nicer times.

Gwen quickly makes her way through the main hall, tossing her long dark hair over her shoulder with a huff.

"Gwen, wait!" I call out, staying fast on her heels.

"Why?" she sneers over her shoulder. "Talking to you is a waste of breath."

I stop in the middle of the hall.

Ouch.

That was low, even for her. "You don't mean that."

She turns towards the library and shoves the doors open. I follow her inside.

Shelves upon shelves of endless books tower from the floor to the ceiling. Renowned for their explorations, the Kent men filled this library with a massive collection of artifacts and treasures, most of which were discovered before treasure laws. Some I think were found later but were brought here to Gainesville in secret and then passed off as having belonged to the family for centuries. They sit in glass cases all around the room, an array of world history tucked away in the middle of nowhere instead of some big-city museum.

I stop by the fireplace, placing a hand on my hip. "Gwen," I plead, breathless. "I really don't want to argue with you today."

She turns to face me, her dark brown eyes glaring beneath perfectly arched jet-black brows. "I know exactly what you'd like, Doll. You can forget it. I'd like nothing more than to throw all that crap out the window." She crosses her arms and taps her foot against the carpeted floor. Apparently she didn't mean the "waste of breath" comment; the foot tapping is a sign her rant has only just begun.

Wonderful.

"First of all, you know my momma is an amazing hairdresser. She took pains to teach me her skills."

"Yes, yes. You're very talented. This isn't news to me." Gwen and I went to the same high school back in Savannah. We've known each other since we were kids.

She points a finger at me and narrows her eyes. "I'm not finished."

I manage not to groan. "Go on then, of course."

"I'm old school southern, babe. I can sew a stitch like nobody's business, and when it comes to makeup—I'm a freaking artist."

"Can you get to the point?"

"My *point* is that everyone knows we're best friends. But when they see you…" She eyes me up and down, shaking her head disapprovingly. "It's bad for my image."

I can't believe she just body-checked me—and with that disgusted look on her face! My hands curl into fists at my sides.

Making myself look this way has become so routine I don't even think about it anymore. My old hoodie that does a good job of hiding everything suddenly feels much heavier. I adjust the bulky fabric over my hips. I'm hiding beneath it, and we both know it.

"Does it really matter?" I ask Gwen. "No one knows you help me."

"Yes, it matters," she says matter-of-factly. "People who know me know I would never allow one of my friends to look like this, much less my *best* friend. If that isn't bad enough, I'm helping you make yourself look like something you're not. Well, no more. I'm done with all that craziness."

For a second I think she's bluffing. Then she squares her shoulders and angles her chin. The girl means what she says, dammit.

"Fine," I grind out through clenched teeth. "Just give me back my glasses. I'll do my hair and makeup myself."

"Your vision is twenty-twenty, Doll. You only wear those hideous grandma lookin' glasses to look like a googly-eyed freak."

"That's not true."

I wear them because they round out the almond shape to my eyes.

She cocks her head to the side, giving me the *I'm not stupid* look. "Before we moved here, you wore sundresses and shorts centimeters away from landing you in detention. Your hair was always down, a smile always plastered to your face. When I first started this, I thought it would be a one-time-only thing."

It was supposed to be a one-time-only thing. It just didn't work out that way.

"Is this about your dad?" she asks me point blank. "Is he back in town?"

I flinch at the mention of my dad. Most of the time I don't acknowledge I have a father, much less say it out loud. He chose to walk out of my life, and that's fine with me. The world is full of dead-beat dads. I was just unfortunate enough to land one of them. It didn't matter what he wanted though—he wasn't going to deny me the chance to meet him. That's how this whole thing started, to give me that chance. Even though it was from a distance, it suppressed the need I had in me to see his face and know what kind of person he was. It made me invisible.

"This isn't about him, Gwen."

"Then why, Doll? Seriously, give me a reason. Maybe if you explained yourself—"

"No."

Her shoulders slump. She pulls my glasses out of her pocket and stuffs them into my hands. "Whatever."

I beat myself up a little as she walks away. Why can't she just let this go? She doesn't need to know how reliant I've become on the way I look. Somewhere down the line, looking this way has become my shield. People don't notice me now, and when people don't notice you, they can't hurt you. Trying to explain that to Gwen wouldn't do either of us any good. She would just try to fix me, and as weird as it sounds, I don't want to be fixed.

"Gwen, stop." I follow her behind a bookshelf.

She stops and looks back, waiting for me to speak.

"You have your secrets too," I point out.

"Like what? We've been friends since we were ten. I tell you everything."

"If that's true, why do you hate Charlotte Hart?"

At the mention of Charlotte's name, Gwen tenses up and breathes through her nostrils. "Charlotte Hart is a bitch. That's all there is to it."

I roll my eyes. I won't buy that crap for one minute, and she knows it.

"Listen," she sighs. "It's a little hard for a chubby girl like me to understand why you would want to keep all the goods hidden away. You're beautiful, Doll. Why do you try so hard to look ugly?"

I look over at a glass case a few feet away, unable to meet her gaze. Chubby is not how I would describe Gwen, and it's not how I thought she saw herself either. She's curvier than me, but in an enviable proportioned way. Her hip to waist ratio is the stuff video vixens could only dream of, but more importantly, she exudes confidence. It's hard to believe the word chubby ever came out of her mouth.

Maybe that's why it's hard for me to look at my situation from her point of view. She thinks I'm acting crazy. Okay. I can admit my behavior *is* sort of crazy, but everyone has personal stuff.

Still…this is Gwen. If I don't give her some insight soon, it's going to impact our friendship. "I'm not trying to make myself look ugly. It's not a self image thing." I make sure to clarify that part because it's the truth. "I just want to stay...unnoticed."

"Why?"

"Can't we just leave it at that? For now?"

Or forever. Forever works even better.

Gwen watches me closely, thinking. I shuffle my feet, waiting for her to say something. "All right, I give in. We don't have to talk about it *today*," she adds. "Just…know that I'm here if you ever need me."

Nodding, I let out a deep breath. Good friends say that sort of thing. It really is the most perfect thing to say. I'll probably never want to bring this subject up again, but it's nice knowing I have the option.

Gwen's eyes light up and she grabs my arm. "I've got an idea." She pulls me towards a case we've spent a lot of time gawking at in the past. Locked away beneath the square of glass is a necklace glittering with diamonds and rubies. At the base is a stunningly brilliant ruby in the shape of a heart.

The *Zumina-al-Shimaz*, or the Heart of the Beloved in English. It's my favorite of all the Kent House pieces. I researched the necklace, searching online and through all of Harland's old books, obsessively trying to find more information about it. When I couldn't dig up anything, I invited the curator of a local museum over to visit. The curator recognized the ancient piece right away, a gleam in his eye, because the Kent men had uncovered a precious gem.

The necklace had been passed down through generations of sultans in ancient Arabia only to be lost sometime during the sixteenth century. It was tradition for each Sultan to give his favorite wife the necklace, claiming her as his beloved. Symbolically, it meant she who wore the *Zumina-al-Shimaz* held the sultan's heart.

Gwen thinks the sultans were all pigs. When I told her about the tradition, her reply was, "Polygamy is a bullshit excuse for men to sleep around. Favoritism does not make it better, Doll. Think about how the *other* wives felt."

She's got a point, but I don't care. It's sort of romantic. According to legend, the creation of the necklace came about by a sultan who wanted to prove his loyalty to his fourth wife. The sultan's previous marriages had been arranged, but it was the fourth he chose for himself and fell in love with. So he carved the ruby himself, letting the fourth wife know she was his heart's true mate. It's said that Allah was so moved by the sultan's gesture, he blessed only the fourth wife to bear his children—which is the nicer way of saying she didn't let the sultan mess around on her after that. Nothing says romantic like kicking your culture's customs to the curb for love.

"So what's your idea?" I ask Gwen, my eyes still roaming over the necklace.

Bouncing on the balls of her feet, she says, "I think you should wear it."

I have to look her in the eye to see for myself if she's really serious. "Are you crazy? I can't wear that thing."

"Why not? You could wear it to Charlotte's party!"

"Graffiti Bash?" Okay now I know she's lost it. "Yeah, let me go ahead and take a priceless necklace to a party where everyone vandalizes each other. Awesome idea."

Gwen scrunches her lips to the side. "Good point. Didn't think of that," she admits. "Wait! What about that formal thingy you go to every year?"

She means the Pretty in Pink Ball, which helps raise money for breast cancer research. I never saw myself going to charity balls, but I go every year. I'm not even sure why; I'm extremely skeptical about cancer research. Bitter might be the appropriate word. It seems like the research never ends. No one ever finds a real cure. Even if they do, it's too late to save my mom. It's too late to save Harland.

I think I go as a sort of tribute. My two hundred bucks might not help find a cure, but it helps me remember my mom. It helps me honor her.

"So?" Gwen asks again. "Will you wear The Heart?"

"No," I say, emphatically shaking my head. "It's not mine."

"Of course it is. Everything in this house is half yours."

"It's not half mine *yet*. Nothing is until Wesley and I both complete our bachelor's degrees. Those are the terms of Harland's will."

Harland wanted Wesley and me to earn his fortune. As long as we both complete our degrees, we split everything equally, and then we can go on our merry ways.

The thing is, I don't want Harland's money or this house. Gwen would flip a switch if she knew, but I plan on handing all of it over to Wesley once the four years come to an end. It's the right thing to do. Wesley is his son. Harland had only been dating my mom for seven months before she passed away. He didn't owe me anything, and he's given me far too much already. The only reason I'm here is because I promised him I'd finish school, and this is my only means to pay for it.

"For once, take something you want, Doll," Gwen says, still eyeing the necklace with awe. "It would look amazing on you."

"No way." I steer her away from the case. "I'm not wearing it. End of story."

She opens her mouth to say more but stops as the door to the library clicks open. The cook, Hannah, slinks inside the room, adjusting the straps of her bra that's showing through her skin-tight tank top.

"Since when does she ever come in the library?" Gwen asks me, her tone laced with insinuation. Hannah doesn't do anything without ulterior motives. I've never seen her pick up a book, so I seriously doubt that's what she came here for.

She chooses this moment to glance up at us, faking a display of surprise. "Oh I didn't know anyone else was in here."

It's such a bald-faced lie that I almost roll my eyes. She followed us, and I have a pretty good idea as to why. Tormenting me is on that girl's list of favorite hobbies, and I think she feels more comfortable doing it now that Wesley is back in the house.

"Fancy seeing you about, Hannah," Gwen says, the twang in her southern accent more pronounced. "Shouldn't you be preparing Mr. Kent's lunch at this time of day?"

"My, my, you're right, Gwen. Must've lost track of time."

"Glad to remind you." There's a sweet smile on Gwen's face I recognize as anything but sweet. The two of them have been known to get into it over the messes Hannah leaves in the kitchen. Their arguments have gotten so heated, they can be heard across the house.

Although I haven't said a word yet, Hannah gives me her attention anyway. Sharpening her green eyes on me, she looks like she's up to something. Great. I can only imagine what it is this time.

"That reminds me, Miss Reynolds. Wesley is having a party this weekend. Make sure you and your," she looks pointedly at Gwen, "friends stay out of the main rooms downstairs. Unless…did he invite you? He invited everyone on staff."

My face and chest grow extremely hot. Hannah knows Wesley never invites me to his parties. She once caught me peeking in on one of his rowdier keggers. I'm not sure what made me stop to look in, curiosity maybe, but Hannah saw me spying behind the doorway. She brushed past me and shut the door in my face, and I swear she did it just to be spiteful. I don't know why she feels it's her responsibility to keep me out of Wesley's way, but she sure takes pleasure in doing it.

"Hannah, you would do well to remember *Mr. Kent* is not your only boss," Gwen says to her. "Miss Reynolds lives here too, and if she wants to go into the main rooms, that's her prerogative."

Hannah purses her lips into a pretty pout. "My bad. It's just that *Wesley* asked me to take care of this for him."

Gwen snorts. "I doubt he asked you to do that," she says, looking about two seconds from snapping. "And to you, his name is Mr. Kent."

"I'm not lying." Hannah says, all innocence. She achieved what she sought out to do, so she saunters away from us. Before she leaves, she looks over her shoulder and smirks. "Excuse me if I prefer to use Wesley while I'm screaming his name later tonight."

Both Gwen and I gape as she slips out the door. For several seconds I stand there like that, wondering whether I heard her correctly.

"What a little ho-bag," Gwen mutters, shaking her head.

Nausea twists inside my stomach. I'm completely disgusted. "You have no idea how much I would love to strangle that girl."

Gwen waves that aside. "I have a better idea. Why don't you fire her instead?"

"For what reason?" I scoff. "Because she's banging the boss?"

"Her food tastes like shit," Gwen says, smiling. "Half this household will vouch for you on that one."

Although I know I won't actually fire Hannah, there's something about knowing she's an awful cook that's really funny. This is why I love Gwen. She can pull me out of a bad mood faster than anyone.

"As tempting as that sounds, I'm not embarrassing myself like that."

"Fine. We'll figure out another reason." She taps her fingers against her chin, thinking. I can practically see the wheels in her head churning from here.

"Wesley would be pissed," I remind her. "We don't get involved in each other's business."

It's still hard to believe Hannah knows Wesley better than I do. I mean, Jesus, he'll sleep with the cook, but he won't even talk to me. It bothers me more than I'd like to admit.

"Let me fire her for you." Gwen looks truly excited by the idea. "Trust me, I'll have no problem doing it in your place."

She's ridiculous, and I don't have the patience to argue with her anymore today. After dealing with Wesley and his friends last night, and then taking two finals this morning, all I want to do is curl up in my bed and sleep. Gwen isn't letting me get out of going to Graffiti Bash either, which means I'll be up all night again.

"I think I'm gonna take a nap, Gwen. Do me a favor. If you see Wesley, tell him we'll stay away from his party."

Gwen nods. "I'd rather tell him to kiss your ass, but you're the boss."

That must be her selective memory talking, because she completely forgot that earlier while she was yelling at me.

I take one last look around the library. Harland and I used to spend hours in here researching. Memories of him are everywhere in this room, from the sound of his voice, to the spicy old-man cologne that I loved, to everything he taught me about reading hieroglyphics and studying ancient artifacts. Spending time in here isn't the same without him. This room makes me wish for some of that old magic back.

What's even sadder is that it's obvious no one comes in here anymore. This place is in desperate need of a good cleaning. We usually keep the library locked up, which is why it's been overlooked. Dust is caked on the shelves, and it smells a little musty too. Maybe later I'll come back and work on getting this place back to its former sparkling self.

Gwen's voice rises from out in the hall, catching my attention. "Hannah, pack your bags—you're fired!"

Holy crap, I didn't really believe she'd do it!

The two of them argue in the next room, their voices growing louder by the second. I could easily go put an end to it by telling Hannah she can keep her job, but my feet refuse to budge. Instead I quietly head the opposite way towards my bedroom, a wicked smile pulling at my lips.

I'll probably go to hell for this. But right now I don't seem to care.

~ ~

When I walk inside my bedroom, my cell rings. There's an unknown number on the screen. It could be important. I guess.

"Hello?"

"Hey, baby, it's Styler. You have no idea how good it is to hear your voice."

Gah!

I pull the phone away from my ear to look at the screen again. Why didn't the damn thing warn me he was calling?

"Dolly?" His voice reverberates against my hand. "You there?"

I place the phone next to my ear again, inwardly groaning.

"How did you get this number, Styler?"

"Hayes gave it to me."

Mental note to self: strangle Hayes.

I changed my number since the last time Styler called. I never gave him my new one, and there was a reason for that.

"I still don't get how you two became friends."

Styler is part of my past. We dated in high school, back when I lived with my mom in Savannah. I wish he would stay part of my past, but one could only be so lucky.

"We met on Facebook, remember?"

"You mean do I remember how you maniacally stalked all my guy friends to make sure I wasn't dating anyone new? Yeah, I remember."

A snorting noise comes from his end. "I didn't do any such thing."

I roll my eyes. As far as exes go, he's the delusional kind. "So what do you want?"

"Can't I just call to see how you are?"

"No, you can't just call to see how I am. Styler, we broke up." I've told him this before. I hate constantly spelling it out for him. He's not that stupid. Actually, he's kind of smart. Book smart, anyway. It's what attracted me to him in the beginning. Emotionally, on the other hand, he's the biggest idiot ever.

"Like you have more important things to do," he says, mocking me. "If you weren't speaking to me right now, I bet you'd be going through Harland's old books. Or watching documentaries on the History Channel."

"Hypocrite. You like those documentaries too."

"Yes, but unlike you, I enjoy doing other things. Like having a life."

This time I'm unable to stop from groaning out loud. "Okay. I'm done."

"No, don't hang up. Dolly, wait—"

"I've asked you not to call me that."

"Sorry. Just stay on the phone for one more minute. I need your opinion."

I sit down on the foot of my bed. Might as well hear him out at this point. "About what?"

"What if I told you I may have found your map?"

I suck in a breath. He's messing with me. I know Styler, and he always has tricks up his sleeves. This is one of them. "I would say I don't believe you."

I should've never told him about the map. It was mine and Harland's thing. Something we researched together for fun. It leads to an ancient sword covered in gemstones. I dream about finding that sword almost every night. Most people think it's a legend, but I happen to know it exists. Harland had already found one half of the map before he died. If I can just find the other, I could get to the sword.

"What would you do if it were true?" he asks me curiously.

"It doesn't matter. You're lying, and I'm not feeding into your games, Sty."

"I always said I'd find it for you, Doll."

"Yeah, well, I'm pretty sure I've spent more time than you researching. There's no way you could've gotten to it before me."

"That map is everything to you. What would you do if I actually found it?"

"I don't know."

"Humor me."

I let out a breath, still wishing I'd never answered the phone. "Probably anything short of selling my soul."

"That's what I thought." His tone lightens, and he says, "I've decided to come to Gainesville, Doll."

He's told me that before. The first time it scared the living bejesus out of me. Now I take everything he says in stride. All the talk of winning me back, of coming here and sweeping me off my feet—it never happens, thank God.

"Yeah, okay, Styler. Listen, I've gotta go."

"I'll see ya soon, babe."

"Okay then. Bye."

I click the end button before he can say anything else. Stupid phone. I need to figure out how to block him.

CHAPTER THREE

WESLEY

Fucking treasure hunters.

They can try every tactic they know, but they won't beat me through intimidation. Fear is something I let go of a long time ago. Why let some baseless emotion stand in my way? It didn't take me long to figure that one out. There's too much to gain, and I have nothing to lose. Seeing things from that perspective kills the fear pretty quickly.

I'd never even heard of Black Templar up until last year. Sounds like some boy scout secret society, if you ask me. I doubt they're affiliated with the Knights Templar. Probably just fame seekers looking for the next great find.

Well they aren't getting it through me—and they sure as hell aren't getting a hold of my sword. It took me years of research and dead ends to find it. The only thing their threats manage to do is piss me off. They can come after me if that's what it takes.

I log out of my email and slam my laptop shut.

The effects of my hangover come back in full force, and I groan. This headache is nothing short of a pounding hell.

Alka-Seltzer dissolves in the glass of water sitting in front of me, foaming around the outer ridges, popping and sizzling. I don't reach for it though, just continue to sit there on my barstool, rubbing my temples. Yesterday is a blur, but not so much that I don't remember how I ended up this way. Images of Tyson handing me shot after shot run through my head, each one hazier than the last. Later I'm going to kill him.

I shift in my seat, and my stomach lurches in response.

Yeah. *Kill* him.

Francisco breezes inside the kitchen through the swinging door, surprising me. I didn't expect him to be here today. "You won't get rid of your hangover that way," he says, nodding to my glass on the counter. "How about I fix you up something better?"

"Sure. Why not." At this point I'm willing to try anything.

He opens the cupboard and takes out the blender. He's always doing these kinds of things, checking up on me, making sure everything is okay around here. He's just my dad's old attorney. Technically he doesn't have to do shit except to make sure the stipulations in my dad's will are carried out. He's supposed to verify that Dahlia and I get our bachelor's degrees and that neither of us move out of the house, but those are the only things he's required to do. Everything else he does because he and my dad were good friends.

"I learned this recipe in the islands," Francisco says. "Ancient cure—only the locals know about it."

I fold my arms over the counter, watching him concoct his island remedy. Francisco is Puerto Rican, but he grew up in New York, and then moved down to Florida three and a half years ago when my dad passed away. The Spanish accent is genuine, but I think he thickens it on purpose.

Throwing several tomatoes into the blender, Francisco casts a look in my direction. "You look bad, Wes. Rough morning?"

"You have no idea."

Aside from the email those bastards from Black Templar sent me, I'd been cornered by Hannah, a pretty cook I use to mess around with. She'd been crying hysterically, barely sustaining enough breath between sobs to tell me what was wrong. I've never been able to deal with emotional girls before, but this was a thousand times worse, because every tearful wail made my head feel like it was being split open.

When she finally got around to telling me what happened, I was mad as hell.

"Miss Reynolds—she f-fired me! I d-didn't do anything wr-wrong, I sw-swear!"

Kent House doesn't keep that many employees to begin with. Firing the few that are here is crazy. My roommate doesn't have the right to get rid of Hannah or anyone I hire, so I don't know why she thinks I won't be pissed. Up until now, she's never gotten in my way. Three years of living together, and aside from the occasional formalities, this is the first I've heard from her. It's okay though, because I've been itching for an excuse to make her life miserable since my dad died. She'll regret it—that much I can promise.

Francisco presses a button on the blender, pulverizing the questionable ingredients he placed inside. I cover my ears, hoping to God the noise will end soon.

"Are those the photos from the dig?" Francisco pours the brownish-colored liquid into a glass.

Photographs are strewn across the counter, but they're not from the Egyptian dig he's talking about.

"No—well, yes." I slide one of the photos toward him. "This was my own personal project."

Francisco sets the glass in front of me. I take a whiff. It smells like sewage. "Just drink," he says, picking up the photograph. "Trust me."

I don't know how I get the slimy liquid down my throat without vomiting all over the place, but I manage to drink the entire glass.

"Is this what I think it is?" Francisco asks. He leans back against the refrigerator, running a hand over his bald head.

I nod, unable to keep from grinning from ear to ear. "The *Saiful Azman*."

"The Sword of Dreams." He lets out a deep breath, still staring at it. "I can't believe it actually exists...it's beautiful."

Seeing the scimitar in person was even more incredible. The gold hilt is encrusted with hundreds of glittering jewels worth a small fortune. I remember holding it, thinking I was imagining the whole thing. My family spent lifetimes looking for that sword—and there it was. In my hands. I couldn't fucking believe it.

Sam would've cried. My brother was emotional that way, and he cried over everything he found. He once got teary over a damned Mesozoic rock. "This existed during the time of dinosaurs, Wes," he said, holding it up to show me.

My brother was good at finding the exceptionality in ordinary things. More than anything though, he wanted to find that sword. Some guys fix up old cars with their dads. Sam and I searched for treasure, the *Saiful Azman* our holy grail of all treasures. When he died, I promised I'd find it for him. He would get his dream, even though he wasn't here to live it out.

Years from now, after Black Templar stops watching my every move, I plan to take the sword out of hiding. I'll bring it back here, to Sam, and bury it with him. Then he can rest knowing he got his dream. Hell, maybe I can rest too.

"Does anyone know about this?" Francisco's question is edged with worry.

I shake my head. "Only Tyson and Chase."

"Are they trustworthy?"

I nod. The three of us have been friends for years. There's no way they would rat me out.

"Did you hide it?"

"It's in a safe place."

Francisco rubs his chin, smoothing out his goatee. "If you get caught—"

"Not gonna happen. Besides, most people think the *Saiful Azman* is a myth. No one will believe it's real, or that it was found by some random college student."

"Maybe not." Francisco hands me back the photograph. "But people would believe a Kent found it. You better get rid of these."

He's right. I need to burn the evidence. It's going to suck ass. These pictures are all I have to prove I'm not dreaming, and I'm the owner of a priceless relic.

"How are you feeling?" Francisco asks. "Did my remedy work?"

Now that I think about it, my head isn't killing me anymore. "Yeah, actually it did. Thanks, man."

"Anytime," he says, smiling. "So what are your plans for the rest of the day?"

"Just some stuff for school…maybe later I'll hit up the gym." Exercising sounds like a good way to blow off some steam. I'm still pissed as hell over that email and how my roommate tried to fire my cook. "Do you wanna come?"

"Wish I could, but I've got stuff going on." He walks toward me, resting his hand on my shoulder. "Your dad would be proud, Wes."

"Yeah, well…" I shrug, clearing my throat. "It doesn't really matter."

Francisco eyes me, as if he's trying to read something between the lines. I wish he wouldn't. The way I feel about my dad—it is what it is. I just don't give a shit. Even when he was alive, he was dead to me.

"Well *I'm* proud of you," Francisco says, clapping my back. "Hopefully that matters." He reaches for his keys, but pauses at the door. "We'll catch up more soon. I want to hear more about your trip."

"Okay," I say, relieved the awkward moment is over. "See you later."

I sit there in the kitchen for a few moments. My headache is completely gone, and I'm grateful I didn't have to chug that drink for nothing.

Someone's voice in the hall catches my attention. I glance up, noticing Dahlia's maid pass by the door.

"Hey, you—" What the hell is her name again? "Dahlia's friend."

She doesn't stop, so I jump up to follow her. Up close, I notice she has earphones attached to her head. She's bobbing up and down, humming along to the music and twirling the feather duster in her hand.

"Hey!" I call out louder. "Hobble...Hummus?" Man, I can't remember her name to save my life.

She hears me and turns around, pulling the buds from her ear. "My name's Gwen," she says, narrowing her eyes on me. "Gwen Hubbard."

Hubbard, that's right.

"Do you know where Dahlia is?"

She arches a brow, giving me a funny look. "I think she's in the library. Would you like me to give her a message for you?"

"No, it's okay. I'll find her myself."

She nods slowly. "You'll...find her yourself?"

"Yeah, thanks."

I don't regularly seek my roommate out. Most times I forget I even have one. I guess it doesn't go unnoticed around here.

Weaving in and out of the library's bookshelves takes forever. Row after row, they never seem to end. I'd forgotten how huge this place is. The windows are all open, and the curtains are drawn back. Lint particles swarm around in the sunlight, the only movement in an otherwise lifeless room. In a way, it's depressing. The greatness it used to hold is gone.

Looking for Dahlia becomes frustrating after a while. This place is a fucking maze. Worse, it reminds me too much of my dad. I'm over this. I should've left a message with her maid.

A faint rustling comes from the back corner. Circling around the last shelf, I thought I'd finally find Dahlia, but it's not her. Just another maid standing on the top of a wooden ladder, organizing the books.

I give up.

It's almost as if that girl knows I'm pissed at her, and she's gone off the radar. Oh well—probably a good thing anyway. The resentment I carry for Dahlia goes beyond her firing my cook. I would've ended up saying things I'd regret.

The maid stretches her arm far above her head to reach a stack of books. Grabbing one, she brings it down to her eye level and blows across the top, scattering dust everywhere. "Nope, you're not the one," she says solemnly to the book.

I'm not sure why, but I grin. Who the hell talks to books?

She steps down the ladder a few legs, tossing the dusty old book into a box on the floor. As she lowers herself, she steps directly into the sunlight, her features coming into view. I freeze.

She's fucking *gorgeous.*

I can't tear my eyes away. All I can do is stand there and stare, immobile in my spot across the room. Every movement she makes, every small gesture has me captivated. I've never been struck by a girl like this, and I'm not sure why, but something about her keeps me frozen in my spot.

Loose reddish-brown waves frame her perfectly oval face in a chaotic way. She's wearing a snug pair of jeans that hug her hips nicely and a T-shirt with…wait—is that Yoda on it?

It is.

I'm in love.

Climbing back up the ladder, the maid takes each step slowly, as if she's afraid of heights. Although she's unaware, she's giving me a great view of her ass. I lean against the bookshelf beside me, no longer in a rush to leave. I'm good right where I'm at.

When she gets to the top step, she raises her arm, intent on reaching the stack of books on the highest shelf.

The ladder sways.

My body tenses up, knowing she's about to fall. She grasps the shelf for support, but her hand slips. I break out in a run, but she falls backward before I can get to her, landing on the floor with a hard *thump*. Dozens of books topple around her, smacking against the carpet loudly.

"Ow," she groans, rubbing her back.

She starts to cry, and I hurry to her side. "Are you okay? Did you break something? Do you need me to call an ambulance?" It all comes out in one huge breath.

She looks up at me, and there's a huge grin on her face. She's not crying…she's laughing.

I don't believe it.

"I'm fine," she says, pushing her hair out of her face. "I mean, I think I'm fine…oh God." She laughs again, and falls back against the carpet, holding her stomach.

Amazing. Any other girl I know would be screaming bloody murder. The fall alone had to be at least fifteen feet. Hell, *I* would be screaming bloody murder.

She lets out a deep breath. "Yeah, I'm okay. Physically—and mentally—just in case you were wondering about that too."

I yank her up by the arm in one swift motion. "That was a huge fall."

"Yes, but…" Her sentence trails off as she locks eyes with me, the humor disappearing from her face. "Oh…wow…you."

Up close she's even more gorgeous. Her eyes are a warm amber color that glow beneath a ridge of the longest, thickest lashes I've ever seen. She's not wearing any makeup, but still looks like something I've dreamed up. I'm so mesmerized, I just stand there staring.

Until what she said hits me. "What do you mean *you*?"

"Oh, I um…" She takes a step back. "I just didn't expect to see you here."

I don't like the way she squares her shoulders or the way her body tenses up. She obviously recognizes me, and I seem to make her uncomfortable. Fucking hell, I think she's another one of Dahlia's maids. Gwen didn't seem comfortable around me either.

"Something *is* wrong," I say, calling her out on it. "You stopped smiling the moment you recognized me. Tell me why." I cross my arms over my chest, letting her know I'm not giving up any time soon.

CHAPTER FOUR

DOLL

I wish I could smile right now. I really do. Smiling would prove I'm taking this all in as if it's just another ordinary, everyday thing. As if Wesley taking notice of me for the first time in three years doesn't matter at all.

The truth is, here in this moment, I'm incapable of smiling. I'm also incapable of talking, moving, breathing, or making any verifiable sign to my claim as a fully functioning human being. Instead I become a statue. A very awkward, inarticulate statue.

"Tell me," he says again, softening his voice. "What did I do to take the smile from your lips?"

Is that an attempt at charm? I'd heard he could be charming. I've just never been around him long enough to find out.

A million questions spin around inside my head, firing off one after the other. Why's he here? Why's he speaking to me? Why's he being nice?

Relax, Doll. Breathing in through my nose, I try to calm myself. Whatever his reasons are, it's important I get some composure. Harland had hoped his son and I would become friends. I can't think of another reason he pushed us together. Deep down it's always bothered me that he never got what he wanted. Or that he probably never will. However, I can be nice enough to speak to Wesley. Out loud hopefully. If I can manage to get a grip.

I start by clearing my throat. "Sorry, one of those books must've hit me on the head."

Wesley's face breaks into a grin, ending the awkward moment. "You sure you're okay?"

"Yes." I look up at the stack of books I'd been trying to reach and then back at him. He looks like he's around six feet tall or so. Perfect height for what I need. "Actually, I was just wondering…well, I was wondering if you could—"

"Anything," he cuts in with devastating seriousness.

This time I'm able to smile with no problems. He is sort of charming.

"Good thing I'm only asking you to get that stack of books up there. What if I'd asked you to buy me expensive jewelry or something?"

He climbs the ladder with ease, making me feel like a dumbass for falling from the thing. Over his shoulder, he says, "Too bad you didn't. I would've asked if you prefer diamonds or sapphires."

I roll my eyes. "Yeah right. I'm sure that's exactly what you would've done. I'll have to remember that for next time."

He grins down at me, but doesn't say anything. Reality sinks in as I realize what I said. I stupidly assumed there would be a next time. I'm not sure what made me jump to that possibility. Aside from the reading of Harland's will, this is the longest we've been around each other. Chances of next times aren't all that good.

Wesley climbs back down the ladder, then hands me the stack of books.

"You made it look so easy," I say, taking them from him. "Thank you."

"Like I said, anything for—"

"You're bleeding!"

I didn't mean to shout, but there's a crimson circle soaked onto the front of his gray shirt, expanding by the second. That must be the gash Tyson told me about last night. It wasn't there before, which means Wesley opened it while climbing the ladder. Guilt claws at my insides. Asking him to get those books was stupid.

He looks down to see where I'm pointing, then simply waves it aside like it's no big deal. "That's nothing compared to what it used to be."

My mouth drops—is he for real? It's not like there's a few speckles of blood on his shirt. It's the size of freaking donut.

"Hey, do you know how to change a bandage?" His eyes brighten. Dark blue, just like I remember. Except now there's something different about them. They're weightless. Intoxicating. Smoldering. Beautiful.

I swallow. "Um…" What the hell did he just ask me?

"Come on. It will only take a minute."

Oh, yeah. The bandage. I start to tell him no, but he grabs my wrist. By the time I'm able to say anything, he's already pulling me across the library. *What is going on here?*

All I'm aware of is the way he's holding my hand. Tingles soar up my arm as he links his fingers through mine. This doesn't feel like type of handholding that happens between strangers.

Coherent thought returns only after he's pulled me halfway through the main hall of the house. "Um, I think this is a bad idea."

"You'll be fine," he promises. "I'll walk you through it."

I groan, but he doesn't hear me. Either that, or he's pretending not to.

We pass by Gwen in the hall, who does a complete turnabout when she sees Wesley tugging me alongside him. The feather duster in her hand falls to the floor, and her eyes widen. She gives me a look as if to ask me what the hell is going on. I shrug. I'm just as confused as she is.

Before long, we're both in Wesley's bedroom. He leaves me standing by the door while he goes to get a first aid kit. I wait there for him, feeling completely out of my element. Being in Wesley's bedroom while he's passed out drunk is one thing; being here while he's wide awake and sober is another.

He returns a moment later with a fresh bandage, alcohol, gauze, and some water. He sets everything down on his nightstand and motions for me to join him. "Why are you hiding out by the door?"

I suppose it does look like I'm hiding, standing halfway in the room, my body veered to go back the way I came. I can't help it though. Talking to Wesley like we're old friends, it's setting me on edge. This isn't the way things work between us.

Wesley pulls his shirt over his head, tossing it aside. Swallowing, I take a step forward. His chest is covered in painful looking bruises, cuts and scrapes. Imagining what he'd gone through to end up looking like that makes my stomach clench.

"I'm a little beat up," he admits.

"A little?"

"It was three to one," he says, removing his bandage. "They had the advantage."

I notice the muscles contracting beneath his battered chest. There's a ruggedness about him; the combination of his bruises and muscles look downright lethal. This dangerous version of him could be the real one—and if the frat guy personification could all be an act. After all, he wouldn't be here right now if Harland hadn't made college a stipulation in his will. But if that's the case…who the hell have I been living with all these years?

Wesley tosses the rest of the bloodstained bandage away, revealing a jagged cut lined by black, uneven stitches. The cut stretches from the right side of his abdomen across his upper torso, ending right below his ribs. Seeing it makes me place my hand over my own stomach. It looks like it could have been fatal at one point.

Wesley notices. "Increased feelings of empathy?" he asks, amused.

"Blood and violence was never my thing." Looking away from his stomach, I meet his gaze. "Aren't you in pain?"

"Not like before. The worst part was when Chase stitched me up. Let's just say his hands aren't the steadiest."

"You let your friend do this to you?"

"Yeah, why not?"

I'm about ninety percent sure he's one of those thrill-seeking deranged people, the kind that go skydiving, run with the bulls, and shoot themselves in the leg just to see what it feels like to take a bullet.

And I'm living under the same roof as this lunatic.

"I'm not sure if you know this, but there are these places people go to when they get hurt. They're called hospitals."

"I'm not a caveman. I know what hospitals are."

There's a cocky smirk plastered to his face. I get the feeling he's not taking me seriously.

"Then why didn't you go to one?"

He shrugs. "I don't like the smell."

"You don't like the smell?" I gape at him, trying to read his face to see if he's kidding in any way whatsoever. He's not. "So you're telling me you'd rather risk dying than go to a hospital because you don't like the way they *smell*?"

"If the last thing you want to inhale before you die is a combination of vomit and disinfectant, that's your business. I prefer not to."

"So you'd rather let your friend do some crap stitch job on you, what, in a bed of roses? Next to vanilla scented candles?"

He walks toward me, closing the distance between us. "Technically we were in the desert." He places a cloth in my hands. "No candles or roses around. Now are you gonna help me out or not? According to you, I'm dying over here."

I look down at his stomach again, feeling dizzy. "I'm not sure I should be doing this."

"You can't do any worse than me."

That's probably true. It's easy to see why he asked for help. The cut is long and rises to areas he would have trouble reaching on his own. Part of me still wants to refuse in hopes that he'll seek some actual medical assistance, except I think he is genuinely too stubborn to do that. If I don't help him, I'm not sure he'll get the proper care he should.

Taking a deep breath, I press the cloth against his stomach. My hands feel awkward and stiff. Immediately, I look up at him. He has no reaction.

Some of the tension in my body releases; I think I was expecting him to scream, shout, curse me out, I don't know—something. Since none of those things happen, I set to the task of cleaning his wound, trying to be gentle so the stitches won't come loose.

When I apply the alcohol, I tense up again, certain this time it will hurt. He doesn't even hiss. His jaw stays relaxed. He's either silently suffering through the pain or impervious to it. I sniff the alcohol—did he switch it out for water?

"Seriously?" he asks, catching me in the act. "You think I'm trying that hard to impress you?"

Heat creeps into my cheeks, and I set the bottle down. "If it were me, I'd be screaming my head off by now."

"Somehow I doubt that." He lifts his arm and turns slightly, so I have better access to his side. "Especially after watching you fall from the bookshelf and then laugh about it."

I wince at the reminder. "I hate that you witnessed that."

"Don't worry. I won't tell." He makes a little cross over his heart. "And if it makes you feel any better, that stuff stings like a bitch."

I raise a brow, surprised to hear him admit he's in pain. "Well you had me fooled. I was convinced you had superpowers."

"Maybe I am trying to impress you."

I catch him grinning from the corner of my eye. He continues to watch me as I go back to bandaging him up. He really is handsome—too handsome. It's unnerving. And knowing he's watching only makes me more uncomfortable. I fumble with the gauze, wishing he'd stop.

A piece of my hair brushes over his forearm. He picks it up, twirling the strands between his fingers. "You have pretty hair," he says. "Soft, too."

My stomach does a little flip-flop. As soon as it happens, I stiffen, straightening my shoulders. I'm not usually so nervous around guys. This only happens when I'm…oh God. It hits me like a bomb going off inside my head.

I'm attracted to Wesley.

My heart rate picks up, beating wildly beneath my chest. Is this really happening? The realization isn't something I can deal with right now. Not while I'm in the same room with him. The only thing I can think of to do is to distract him—and myself—until I can get out of here.

"So what happened to you?" I try to sound interested instead of being nosy. "Or do I even want to know?"

"I took the beating for a friend. It was a beating that should've been mine in the first place."

"How so?"

"Because my friend was in trouble for helping me."

"And that makes it your fault?"

Wesley's jaw tightens. "It damn well means I should shoulder some of the blame."

"But instead you shouldered it all."

He opens his mouth, then closes it again. Several long seconds pass before he speaks. "He's just a kid. Getting beat up would've humiliated him."

I finish wrapping his bandage, pretty sure now that Tyson and Chase had been referring to my friend Hayes last night. He's a senior, but he's only eighteen because he skipped two years of high school—one of those genius types. I wonder what Hayes did to help Wesley, and why he almost got his ass kicked for it. I can't even begin to guess, so I make a mental note to ask him later.

Whatever it was, Wesley definitely proved he is capable of compassion. Hayes looks like a string bean, all gangly skin and bones. He probably wouldn't have been able to withstand that beating.

I get the choking feeling I may have misjudged Wesley. Maybe there is a lot more to him than this shell of a bedroom and the stories I've heard. Maybe I've been wrong about him all along.

"Sounds like you're a good friend to have around," I say.

He shifts uneasily, like he's shaking off my comment. Compliments make me uncomfortable too, but mostly because I like being recognized in more subtle ways. With him, it's different though. Like he doesn't believe it's justified. I don't say anything else, sensing it would make things more awkward.

"There." I pat the last of the tape into place. "All finished."

Wesley catches my hand, trapping it there against his stomach. He draws it up across his chest, startling me, and pulling me toward him.

"What are you doing?" My voice comes out whispered even though I'm screaming that question inside my head.

"Getting closer." He pulls me until I'm flat against him. I feel every ripple of muscle, every inch of his body against mine. For a second I imagine how it would feel without my clothes separating us, and the thought makes me panic even more.

What is going on with me?

What is going on with *him*?

"This isn't a good idea."

"Why not?" he asks, tilting me back.

"Um…" Why shouldn't I kiss him? What could it hurt? "You're going to reopen your wound."

There. Valid reason.

"Good," he says, grinning. "It'll give me a reason to keep you here longer."

I stare at his lips, losing all train of thought. My curiosity begins to outweigh any reservations I have about kissing him. This could be a mistake, but nothing in me seems to care.

Wesley leans in before I get the chance to back away. Sparks of heat ignite inside me as he presses his lips against mine. He tastes me at first, lightly, each stroke of his tongue sending a wave of electricity through my body. My brain doesn't work anymore; it's like it just switched off, not allowing room for thought.

I've kissed guys before, but I've never felt like this while kissing guys before. It's exciting and frightening all at the same time. He's like a magnet, molding my body into his and making me feel like I'm losing control over myself. My hand involuntarily reaches around his neck, pulling his head closer to mine, deepening the kiss. That one small movement makes Wesley groan, and it vibrates through me, warming me straight through my core.

Part of me wonders if this is real. Two people can't fit together so perfectly—can they? It seems impossible, especially with someone I barely know. Touching and kissing Wesley feels easy though, like I've known him forever. Like we were both split from the same atom.

I feel him lift me up, pushing me onto the bed. He takes over completely, running his fingers through my hair and kissing me like he can't get enough. There's an intensity surrounding him that's so strong I can feel it. Probably because I feel the same way. I can't get enough of him either.

The buttons on my shirt come undone. Not sure how or when that happened. His kiss becomes several little kisses, his mouth moving hotly down the length of my jaw, across my neck, and down the center of my chest. I never knew skin could feel this way—so alive. So tingly and warm.

"Tell me your name, beautiful."

The question doesn't register; I'm too distracted by the way Wesley is making me feel to focus on what he's saying. Then he asks a second time, his hand sliding behind my back, reaching for my bra clasp.

This time the words hit me with the force of a semi-truck. I open my eyes. "What did you say?"

"Your name," he demands. "I can't do this without knowing your name."

Buckets of invisible ice water flush over my body, prompting my brain to work again. I can't think straight with him hovering over me. I shove my hands against his chest. Space. I need space.

"What's wrong?" he asks in a ragged breath.

"You don't know who I am?" I can sense that he doesn't, but I have to be sure.

"Believe me when I say I could never forget someone like you."

Unlike myself, his desire hasn't cooled at all. He grasps at my waist, ready to go back to where we left off. This time I punch him in shoulder. Hard.

"Ow." He stares at me incredulously. "What was that for?"

I slide off the bed, feeling more humiliated than I've ever felt in my life. The night Tyson and Chase were here plays over in my mind like a bad case of déjà vu. They mistook me for a maid. I look up at Wesley, sensing he did the same thing. I can't believe it. Three years together, and he doesn't even know who I am.

Wesley fists the sheets on the bed in what looks like an attempt to keep his emotions under control. "Why don't you just tell me who you are, babe? I promise never to forget again."

Seeing his frustration surprises me. He usually appears so calm and collected; I never picked him for the type to have a temper.

Still, mine outweighs his.

"Say something," he pleads, looking helpless. "Fuck, is this really not happening anymore?"

"No, it's not happening, you ass!"

I immediately place my hand over my mouth, shocked to hear that much anger come out of me. I screamed at him. Actually *screamed*. That's never happened before. Sure, I get annoyed as much as the next person, but screaming is for toddlers throwing temper tantrums. Getting that worked up is beneath me. Until now, apparently. Because right now I think I could scream until my heart comes out of my chest. Since being around Wesley is the cause of all this, I march towards the door, determined to get out of his bedroom as soon as possible.

"Wait," he calls, veering in front of the door just as I'm reaching for the handle. "I'm sorry. That was so fucking insensitive, and I'm sorry."

"Doesn't matter." I cross my arms over my chest, refusing to meet his gaze. "Just move so I can leave."

"Offending you was never my intention."

I keep my eyes trained on the floor as I wait for him to get out of the way. Offending is putting it way too nicely. I know I go out of my way to stay unnoticeable, but we've lived together for three years, dammit. He should know who I am!

"Look, I'll give you some time to cool off." He reaches for my chin, forcing me to face him. I give him the coldest, harshest look I can manage, hoping he'll get the hint. "But I *will* figure out your name. Eventually."

"Good luck, buddy. Now can I please pass?"

After a long moment, he lets out a sigh and grudgingly steps to the side. I swing the door open, practically running down the hall to get away.

"Something amazing happened before I pissed you off," I hear Wesley call out from behind me.

I ignore it and pick up my pace. Over my dead body will he find out who I am.

"You know I'm right."

"Doesn't matter," I say again over my shoulder. And it *doesn't* matter. Or at least it shouldn't. "I'm already over it!"

The sound of his laughter echoes down the hall. He doesn't believe me one little bit.

God, I can't believe I came so close to…no, I don't even want to think about what I almost did with that conceited jackass. I don't want to think about how easily he got me in his bed, or the way he kissed me, or the way my body acted as if it practically belonged to him. I don't want to think about any of it.

It occurs to me he can follow me, so I race down the twisting hallways, not stopping for breath until I reach my bedroom.

I need my makeup. I need my glasses, and one of my sweaters. I need to be completely unnoticeable again. A sense of urgency takes over. He can *never* know it had been me.

I lock the door and lean back against it, taking several breaths. Gwen is in my room, using my laptop. She doesn't even look up, too focused on whatever she's typing. "I've been talking to this guy online forever, and he still won't commit to meeting me. You think he's a catfish?"

"Quick, Gwen!" I say breathlessly.

She looks up, her mouth parting a little. "Goddammit, what did I miss? Did Kent finally try to kill you off so he can hold the majority of the will? I knew when I saw the two of you together something big was going down. Did you use the tae kwon do moves I taught you? Did you kick him in the balls?"

I hold my hand over my throat as if the action will help me breathe normally. "I never want to speak about what happened with that-that *person*." I can't come up with something else to call him—there's got to be better insults than person—but I can't think clearly right now. "We've got to get ready for Graffiti Bash. Help me with my makeup?"

"Fine," she grumbles, closing her laptop.

"I want my hair pinned back in a bun. And I want to wear my biggest, rattiest hoodie. Oh and my glasses. I'll need those too."

"So much for the idea of you wearing The Heart then," Gwen mutters.

I pretend not to hear her.

She does my makeup, applying pale concealers that wash me out, giving her a blank canvas. Gwen is trained in theatrical makeup, and she's got a talent for changing faces. She uses shadows to make my eyes appear smaller, my nose wider, and my lips less full. I just sit there staring at myself in front of the mirror, trying not to think about what happened moments earlier.

"Distract me," I say to Gwen. "What's going on with Internet Guy?"

"Oh him." She shakes her head. "He's getting super annoying. Every time I suggest we meet, there's always an excuse."

"Why don't I know about him?" I ask, pushing for more. "Give me details."

Anything to get my mind off of the guy a few halls down from here.

"His name is Luke." She holds her phone in front of me. There's a picture on it of a guy wearing sunglasses and a Florida State ball cap. "He's an engineering student in Tallahassee."

"FSU isn't that far. Why doesn't he want to meet you?"

"No clue." Gwen gathers my hair into one hand, brushing back the bumps with the other. "Last time he said he had car troubles, so I offered to go up there—and you know how old school I am about wanting the guy to me pick me up on the first date."

Gwen always makes the guy chase after her. If she offered to drive all that way for someone she's never met, she must really like him.

"Anyway," she continues, "after that, he came up with some lame excuse about needing to study for his midterm."

"Maybe he really needed to study for his midterm."

"I could buy that, but this isn't the first time something like this has happened."

"Do you think he has a girlfriend?"

Gwen shudders, and her hands go still. "I've got to admit, it's crossed my mind." She lingers a second before pushing a bobby pin into the back of my scalp. "That's why he's getting annoying. I want to drop him completely, but he makes my days so interesting, and then there's his voice—"

"You've spoken to him on the phone?"

Her cheeks redden, a grin tugging at her lips. "His voice is so sexy, Doll. I can't get rid of him if it means never hearing that voice again."

"You should mess with his head, do something to get a rise out of him."

She holds her hand over my forehead while spraying the top of my head with hairspray. "What do you mean?"

"I don't know…" I press my lips together, thinking. "Tell him you're dating someone new. See how he reacts. If he really likes you, it's going to bother him."

"Hmm. I've never thought of that before. What if he has no reaction?"

"Move on. Find someone else with a sexy voice. Preferably someone who lives here."

That gets a scowl out of her, but she knows I'm right. "Fine. I'll give it a try."

"Let me know how it goes."

"I will." She hands me my glasses. "There you go. Your sad little look is complete."

I put the glasses on, then turn my head back and forth in front of the mirror, checking everything out. Air fills my lungs, and I let out a relieved breath, my shoulders noticeably relaxing before my eyes.

I'm invisible once again.

She hands me a plain white shirt. "If you wear anything else, you're going to stand out."

I take the shirt, frowning. How am I supposed to fit in and be invisible at the same time? "I'll wear my zip up hoodie over it."

I pull off my Yoda shirt and replace it with the white one, careful to avoid messing up my hair and makeup.

Gwen studies me carefully, tapping her foot against the floor. "So why are you using my love life to distract yourself from whatever happened with Kent? You sure you don't want to talk about it?"

As soon as she speaks his name, I feel his lips pressing against mine again…and hear him asking what my name is. Bastard. "I'm sure."

"Maybe I can help."

Gwen's brand of help would be prying every last detail out of me, and only after that, she'd try convincing me to sneak into Wesley's bedroom later tonight to finish what we started.

"No, thanks."

She holds up her hands, surrendering. "Okay. I'll leave it alone, but just so you know, I haven't seen you this wound up in a long time."

"What are you trying to say?"

"I'm just guessing here, but I think something other than talking went down."

"Gwen—"

"When you walked in, your hair was a mess and your lips looked pretty swollen. If I didn't know any better, I'd say you made out with him."

"*Gwen.*"

She shrugs, smirking. "But again, I'm just guessing."

CHAPTER FIVE

DOLL

"Doll!"

Charlotte Hart screeches my name *à la* Carrie from *Sex and the City,* catching the attention of everyone within a five-mile radius.

"Hi, Charlotte." I gasp for breath as she envelopes me in an extra-tight hug. "Can't…breathe."

Her blue eyes are glassy; she's already buzzed. "I knew it was you when I saw those hideous glasses, and what is this?" She picks at the back of my bun, twitching her nose. "Is this a hair piece?"

Sometimes I wish Charlotte and I didn't go to the same high school. The way I look bothers her more than it does Gwen, and that's saying a lot. She never fails to give her opinion on it.

I veer my head away from her fingers and change the subject. "You did a great job on the party, Char. This place looks amazing."

Located in the heart of sorority row, this house is bigger and grander than most others with its large white columns and sleek marble floors. Tonight it's decked out in the theme of the party. Large graffiti art canvases the walls, lit up by black lights and rotating glowing orbs. When Charlotte throws a party, she goes all out. Mediocre is not in her vocabulary.

"Why, thanks," Charlotte says, her proud smile growing wide. "The girls and I stayed up late last night decorating."

Gwen walks up from behind us, smoothing out the short black skirt she's wearing under her white T-shirt. "Jesus, it looks like a rainbow threw up in here."

Inwardly I cringe, preparing myself for the worst. The lighthearted mood instantly shifts. "I see you brought a guest," Charlotte grumbles, then gives me the *look*. "Doll, didn't I mention this party is for students only?"

"Technically, Gwen *is* a student." We both know I'm reaching here. The truth is Gwen dropped out of the university last year to study at a cosmetology school a few blocks from campus.

Right on cue, Gwen looks up and plasters on the biggest, phoniest smile she can manage. "Whaddup, Char?" she drawls in a high-pitched voice. "How've you been, girl?"

"Gwendolyn." She nods stiffly. "I was great, until you showed up."

"You know I just *love* these little soirees you throw," Gwen says, smacking her lips. "The food, the drinks, all the frat guy eye candy. It's a real treat. Thanks for inviting me."

"I didn't invite y—"

"Looky there, I think I see chips and queso. Ya'll know that's my favorite." Gwen sashays away, heading toward the food table in a hurry.

"Really, Doll?" Charlotte snaps as soon as she's gone. "Did you have to bring her?"

Shuffling my feet, I try to think of something to say. I hate when they do this. Both of them always make me feel like I'm betraying the other one. "Aside from you, she's the only person I know here. I need someone to talk to tonight."

"Why can't you make new friends?" she asks, and she's dead serious. "I've got an idea! Let me give you a makeover. Your confidence will skyrocket." She starts to pick at my hair again. "We can go shopping, get you some new clothes and makeup—and of course you'll have to let me get this hair under control."

I swat her hands away. "No, Char. There's nothing wrong with the way I look—"

"There's nothing right about it either."

"—so stop it with the Gwen thing. You know I refuse to get involved in ya'lls drama."

"Ugh, fine," she huffs, her lips forming a pout. Someone from across the room shouts her name. "Great. I gotta go," she says, sounding annoyed. "Hostess duties."

"I understand."

She reaches around me for another hug. "Seriously though. Despite your plus one, I'm glad you came."

"Me too."

"Leave space on your shirt for me." She points at the front of it. "And not the sleeve or some shitty, less noticeable part. You're my best friend, so I better get the boob or the stomach—promise?"

Laughing, I motion to my invisible crowd of admirers. "Sweetie, you'll have to get in line."

"I mean it. Save me a spot." She smiles before slipping back through the crowd.

I look around to see if I recognize anyone through the sea of white T-shirts. These parties are usually pretty tame, basically a chance for students to make new friends or catch up with the ones who were gone over summer. Charlotte's crazier drunkfests happen midsemester—those being the kind I'm more reluctant to attend.

I weave through the mass of bodies, politely tapping on shoulders to get them to make way for me. Blocking my path, a guy with stringy black hair shoves a can of spray paint in my face. "Want me to draw you a dragon?"

"Uh, no thanks," I say, circling around him.

The girl in front of me steps aside. I catch a glimpse of dragon guy behind me moving on to his next victims, shoving his can of spray paint in their faces. Weirdo.

Gwen is just up ahead, standing next to the refreshments, but there's a group of guys in my way. "Excuse me."

"Sorry," one of them says, moving to the right.

"No…worries."

A pair of dark blue eyes freeze me into place.
Wesley.

Thankfully those eyes pass over me quickly, barely taking in my presence. He goes back to talking to his friends without recognizing me. I breathe a small sigh of relief, then dart toward Gwen in a hurry.

"Don't get too excited by the fancy umbrellas." She waves at the table, pouting. "These are all *mocktails*. Ugh. School regulations, probably. I swear these mixers aren't as fun as they used to be."

"Charlotte always keeps a bar upstairs," I remind her. "Wanna head up there?" I try not to seem like I'm itching to get out of this vicinity.

She links her arm through mine. "Course I do. I knew there was a reason why we're such good friends."

Sneaking a peek over my shoulder, I check out Wesley again. Only his side profile is in my line of view, and he's engaged in conversation. The tightness in my chest releases, and I breathe normally again.

For a few seconds, I watch him out of curiosity. Wearing a shirt heavily covered with girl's handwriting, I'm guessing from all the hearts and swirls, he appears much better suited to this type of atmosphere than me. I figured he'd be here—he and Charlotte are in the same circle of friends—but I never thought I'd run into him.

He seems so casual and so at ease, inhabiting the relaxed and somewhat cocky quality that comes so naturally to the preppy Greeksters. The thing is, it's all an act. I know that now. Whoever Wesley Kent really is, he isn't a self-absorbed rich kid.

Since I'm not sure how I feel about what happened in his bedroom earlier, I'd like to steer clear of him for a while. I still can't get over him mistaking me for an employee. I mean, yes, I keep a low profile, but *really?* It's not like he's never seen me in normal clothes before. We've been around each other countless times—at Harland's funeral, one year at Christmas—he should know what I look like by now.

God, and the worst part is knowing how differently he would treat me if my name wasn't Dahlia Reynolds. Earlier today he was *nice*. Seeing that side of him took me by surprise; he's always been cold and devoid of emotion. Talking to him without all the family stuff hanging over our heads was refreshing. I needed to know that side of Wesley, for Harland's sake…and I think for mine too.

"Champagne?" Gwen says, sounding surprised. "That seems fancy, considering how casual this party is."

Green and gold bottles line the table. There aren't any flutes or glasses though, only red solo cups—but I'm not surprised. Charlotte does things by her own standards.

"It is random," I agree, shrugging.

"Here's a toast to a great year." She holds up her cup and takes a sip from it.

"Our *last* year," I add.

Saying that out loud hits me pretty hard. I should be excited. After all, I've been waiting for the chance to get out of this town. Harland never required us to get our master's degrees, so I plan to work on that somewhere else. Still…my experience here feels incomplete.

"Hold this for me." I push my cup into Gwen's hands, spotting a bathroom down the hall. "I'll be right back."

I beeline for the bathroom, ducking into one of the stalls before someone else comes in. Communal bathrooms are the one thing I'm glad I missed out on when it comes to college life. Sharing the same toilet space with other people can't be sanitary.

Outside the stall I hear a group of people shuffle in. Doors open and close, metal locks clanging as they enter the stalls beside me.

A squeaky, ultra-feminine voice fills the bathroom. "Her name is Dahlia, but everyone calls her Doll."

What the—they're talking about me? I've never heard that voice before. I peek through the crack in the stall's door. No way am I walking out there now.

A group of girls check themselves out in the wall mirror, adjusting their hair and tugging on their clothes.

"And she *lives* with Wesley?" one of the girls ask—a tall blonde wearing the tiniest pair of denim shorts I've ever seen.

"Yep, that's what Charlotte told me. Apparently they were friends in high school or whatever."

We're still friends, I want to growl, but I stay quiet inside my stall. Their curiosity doesn't surprise me. Not many people know Wesley and I live together, and the ones who do know think it's strange. I would too, if I were on the outside looking in.

"Are they like…?" Blondie cocks a brow. "You know, *living together*-living together?"

I roll my eyes. It's amusing how she arrives at that conclusion when in reality there's an ocean between Wesley and I inside the walls of Kent House.

The girl with the squeaky voice slides her lipgloss wand across her lips. "No," she says, chuckling. "Come on, Lauren, have you *seen* that girl? If you were a guy, would you want to go home to that?"

My nose twitches.

Okay.

I can't even get mad about that one. The way I look is self-inflicted. But still…no reason to be catty.

"The way she looks doesn't matter," says a new voice.

Thank you, whoever you are.

"Because she's super annoying."

My mouth drops open.

"She's in one of my classes. The professor is always calling on her, saying, 'Dahlia, explain this to the class' and 'Dahlia, tell us your opinion on that.'" She groans out loud, clearly aggravated. "The professor should just let the little genius teach the class so the rest of us won't feel like a bunch of Neanderthals."

I suck in my breath, feeling like someone struck me in the stomach. I know exactly which class she's talking about. It's not my fault the professor likes to call on me; he was one of Harland's good friends, and he knows about the research we did together.

"Oh God, Amy," says squeaky-voice. "How can Wesley stand to live with her?"

Amy shrugs, tying the front of her T-shirt in a knot so it pulls closer to her body. "It was arranged by his father. Otherwise he wouldn't be there."

"Wow, that sucks."

All the girls shake their heads, sharing matching looks of pity.

"Yeah, but he gets to move out when he graduates," Amy tells them. "He said to me, and I quote, 'I can't fucking wait to get out of that house.'"

"Wow," Lauren shakes her head. "He must really hate her."

"That's the general consensus."

A lump forms in the back of my throat, choking me. At least the girls don't stick around, filing out of the bathroom just in time for me to let out a whimper.

Stupid, nasty gossips. Their opinions shouldn't affect me like this. It shouldn't hurt to hear how pathetic they made my situation sound.

Nonetheless, tears well up in my eyes, threatening to spill. Cursing at myself, I grab a wad of tissue. Letting someone see me this way will only make things worse. I need to become presentable again—and quick—before everyone thinks I'm a mess because Wesley can't stand me. Ugh, I still can't believe they said that. Or that *he* said that.

Somehow knowing it came from him directly makes it even worse.

I stand up and flush the toilet, heading to the sink. Cold water rushes out of the spout. I splash it over my neck. Trickling droplets stream over my skin, and it helps. A little.

I look into the mirror. Some of my powder is coming off. Grabbing a paper towel, I pat my face and neck dry, hoping I won't remove too much of it. From what I can tell, the girl staring back at me is still unrecognizable. Since I can't stand to see my own reflection, I gravitate away from the mirror and out of the bathroom.

Squaring my shoulders, I take a deep breath. I'm determined not to let what I overheard ruin the rest of the night. Harland used to say that living in fear of what other people think is the same thing as living in a cage. I agree with him. What they think doesn't matter. I know the truth, and the truth is I've never given Wesley one good reason to hate me.

The first place I head toward is the champagne table. Gwen is still there, chatting up some guy in the corner. "Hey, is everything okay?" she asks, handing me my cup.

"Yeah. I'm fine."

"You were gone a while."

"There was a long line."

I tip the cup and down the entire thing, pouring myself another right away. Gwen clicks her tongue and pushes away from the guy she's talking to. "I'll see ya later, boo. This is gonna be a *great* party."

She leaves him standing there looking confused, and we make our way back downstairs. "Dahlia Evelyn Reynolds," she says, grinning. "That is one full cup you got there."

"Don't be ridiculous, Gwen. I didn't want to keep going upstairs for refills."

"Whatever you say. So does this mean we're dancing on the tables tonight?"

Unable to help it, I bust out laughing. "There's no way I'm doing that, but you can if you want. I'll even cheer you on."

As I'm laughing, I feel lighter, all the stuff I heard in the bathroom fading away. Thank God for Gwen. She's makes me feel better, even when she doesn't realize she's doing it.

"Hey, it's the dynamic duo."

Gwen and I look up to see Miles, Charlotte's boyfriend, walking toward us. His white "T-shirt" is a perfectly pressed white polo, but it fits in line with his personality. He's the clean-cut, all-American frat guy, with the classic good looks: lean build, blonde hair, and big green eyes. He and Charlotte were pretty much made for each other.

"Charlotte told me to make sure you two knew where the drinks were, but it looks like you found them." Miles smiles at us, showing off years of good dentistry.

Gwen places a hand on her hip. "Twenty bucks says your little girlfriend never once mentioned my name."

Miles's cheeks turn slightly pink, giving him away. "Well *I* wanted to make sure you both had something to drink."

"That was nice of you, Miles," I tell him.

"Yeah, yeah." Gwen shoves my shoulder, moving me along. "Thanks, Smiles, but we're good. You can tell your little girlfriend I'm having fun drinking all her booze."

We make our way down the hallway leading back into the front room. "That was rude, Gwen," I say once she stops pushing me. "Just because you and Charlotte have issues doesn't mean you have to take it out on him."

People are standing around chatting with their friends and signing each other's T-shirts. She's not paying any attention to what I'm saying, already distracted by someone in the crowd. "Kent's here."

Trying not to frown, I glance in the direction she's looking. Wesley is on the other side of the room, laughing over something one of his friends said. Seeing him like that, happy and smiling, and knowing that gorgeous smile was centered on me earlier today makes every muscle in my body tense up. It was all a lie. Every kind word, how he helped get the books from the shelf…that kiss. If he'd known it was me he was kissing, it would've never happened.

"I saw him earlier." I swallow another sip of champagne.

"You gotta admit, the guy is hot," Gwen says, devouring him with her eyes.

I place a hand on my hip. She's supposed to be on Team Doll. It goes without saying that praising Wesley in any way whatsoever is not okay.

Catching the look I give her, she clears her throat. "Ah, that is if you're attracted to his type."

"And what type is that?"

Gwen taps the rim of her cup and scrunches her lips to the side. "You know. He's just aiiight. The rugged, bad-boy thing he's got going on isn't anything to write home about."

She's trying so hard to lie I can't help but grin. "It's okay, Gwen. He's the kind that makes girls go weak in the knees. I get it."

"Uh huh, and do you know from experience or…"

"I'm not going into that."

"Why not?" she whines. "You didn't give me details the first time."

And I never will, if I can help it. Erasing what happened today from my mind is number one on my priority list. If there were a button that could wipe that memory away forever, I would press it in a heartbeat.

"I'll promise you this," I say, thinking of a way to appease her. "The details are yours when a guy actually remembers my name."

"Really? I'm holding you to that," Gwen says, pointing a finger at me. "When the time comes, you better keep that promise."

I pull out my marker, uncapping it. "Here, hold my drink and turn around."

"Oh, I love this," she says, her eyes brightening. "Are you putting it in writing?"

"Sure am. I, Dahlia Reynolds, swear to provide Gwendolyn Hubbard explicit details of all my romantic affairs, conditional to a guy remembering my name, and therefore preventing me from hanging my head in shame."

"Aw, how cute. You rhymed. Make sure you sign it."

I sign my name at the bottom. "There. I've sworn my privacy away to you."

Gwen bounces on the balls of her feet. "Now all we've got to do is find you a man."

The excitement in her eyes both amuses and terrifies me. "Hold your horses, cowgirl. There will be no man shopping on my behalf."

She purses her mouth into a pout. "How the hell am I supposed to get my details if there is no guy in the picture?"

"You'll just have to wait for fate to present that opportunity."

"Oh, Jesus," she grumbles. "Fine. But you better believe I'll be there waiting when the right one comes along."

"Don't doubt it for a second." I'll probably end up regretting this later, but the damage is already done.

CHAPTER SIX

WESLEY

They never suspect a thing.

The fake smiling, the fake laughing—it fools everyone. They think I'm genuine, and most of the time I'm trying to be genuine, but the truth is I really don't give a fuck about this party or most of the people in it. I come to these things out of boredom, to fit in, and mostly because I hate being in my dad's goddamn fortress of a house for too long. This is the world he wanted me to immerse myself in, the world he put his fortune on the line for. So I come. I laugh, I smile, try to blend in with university life. And tomorrow night, I'll repeat the process over again.

The Black Templar's email still weighs on my mind. I don't know who they are or how much they know. That eerie feeling that someone is watching me has me constantly looking over my shoulder. It was the same in Egypt. Someone followed me then, and they're following me now.

"Hel-looo." Christine waves her hand in front of my face. "You know, Wesley, it's kind of hard to flirt with you when you're not paying attention to anything I'm saying."

I like how straightforward Christine can be. We've never hooked up, but she's let me know several times she's interested without playing games. "Sorry," I tell her. "What did you say?"

"Am I boring you?" She asks me in a way that lets me know to be careful when answering that question.

"You could never bore me." I fake-smile again, slipping back into my social mode. "I just have a lot on my mind."

"Like what?" she asks. "Anything I'd be interested in?"

"Probably not." Talking about old artifacts is the fastest way to lose a girl's interest; I know from experience.

She narrows her eyes on me. "It's a girl."

"No, it's not."

"You're lying."

I am lying. Sort of. I hadn't been thinking about the library girl when Christine asked, but I've been thinking about her almost every second since she left my room.

"I swear it's not a girl, Christine."

She rolls her eyes. "What a load of crap. If there wasn't a girl, you'd be more interested."

"Christine—"

"I'm losing patience with you, Wes. Maybe it's better if I put it this way: My room is upstairs, the third one on the right. If you want to have fun without games or strings attached, you know where to find me."

With that said, she walks away. I can't say I'm surprised. Christine has never been one to beat around the bush. She is lonely, though, and trying to play it off like she isn't. Freshman year, her boyfriend died in a car accident. She hasn't seriously dated anyone since.

One of these days I might take her up on her offer. She's a pretty girl with silky brown hair and legs that go on for days. She knows it too, which is probably why she doesn't play hard to get. But most importantly, she's not looking for more than I'm willing to give. Not that I'm irresponsible or anything. I don't strive to fuck every female whose willing like the way Chase and Tyson do. God knows dealing with one is more than enough. Right now I just don't want anything from Christine. It wouldn't be fair to her—I'm entirely distracted by someone else.

The library girl.

Everything that happened this morning replays inside my head. I haven't been able to stop thinking about how amazing her lips tasted, and the way her hair and skin smelled like fucking heaven. All of it still feels like a dream.

There's just that annoying problem of me not recognizing her. Remembering the way she stormed off frustrates me all over again. For the life of me, I don't know who she is. Not that I have any doubt I'll find out. If I can find an ancient sword in the middle of the desert, finding the girl from the library will be a piece of cake. Because I need to find her. There's something about her that's…different. In a good way. She would be worth the chase, as Sam used to call it.

"Finding the right girl is like playing your favorite video game," he once told me. "Some games you'll play for a little while, then put them away. But your favorite video game will keep you up all night trying to figure out a way to get to the next level. You know, like Call of Duty. There's just something about it."

I think I finally understand what he meant.

Sighing, I run a hand through my hair. Staying at this party when I can't focus isn't a good idea. I need to go home and get some rest.

I say goodbye to few friends, then head for the door. A familiar black hoodie catches my eye as I reach for the handle. Turning, I recognize the girl inside of it.

Seeing Dahlia always makes me want to bolt. My dad would hate me for ignoring her—I'm pretty sure he put us together for a reason—but I've never felt guilty about it. Neither one of us wanted this. As much as I've avoided her, she's avoided me too, so there's nothing to feel bad about. We have an unspoken agreement based on a lot of distance. It works.

A white T-shirt peeks out from Dahlia's hoodie, but it's not covered with much writing. Apparently she doesn't care about the point of Graffiti Bash. Then again, neither do I, but it's a good icebreaker.

A few sorority girls hover close to Dahlia. They're up to something. She's oblivious to them, and they're giggling and pointing at her. I know those girls. They're your typical, catty mean girls. Whatever they're up to, it isn't innocent fun and games.

I turn away. Not my business. Getting involved with Dahlia is the last thing I want to do. I should leave.

An irritating sense of dread washes over me. I reach for the door handle and pause.

Dammit.

I'm not going to be satisfied until I figure out what those girls are doing. I move toward them, noticing a can of spray paint in one of their hands. It looks like she's writing on the back of Dahlia's hoodie. I take a few more steps, then stop abruptly, seeing a giant red letter C.

I shake my head, sighing. Part of me wants to turn around and pretend I don't see this happening. It would be so much easier to look the other way; I don't give a damn about Dahlia's life. But it doesn't matter what girl is inside of that hoodie. Walking away would make me the biggest asshole in the world.

The giggling girls disappear just as I approach. Placing my arm around Dahlia, I cover up the four-letter word on her back and guide her toward the back door. "Come with me."

"What are you doing?"

She's clearly confused, with me all but shoving her through the French doors leading out into the courtyard. She tries to push away from me. "Let me go."

The muggy night air hits us, and I close the door. No one else is outside. Good thing too.

I pull the right sleeve of her hoodie and slip it off her arm.

"Hey! What the—"

Spinning her around, I grab the left sleeve. The hoodie is so big, it comes off with one swift yank.

"Give that back!" she squeals angrily.

"You don't need this. We live in Florida."

She grabs a handful of the fabric, and we begin to play tug-of-war. "Have you lost your damn mind?"

It's a possibility, considering I'm out here trying to save her ass, and she's giving me hell for it.

Jerking the hoodie out of her hands, I hold it high over my head. She jumps up and down, reaching for it, but I'm almost a foot taller than her. She doesn't stand a chance.

Spotting a trashcan on the side of the house, I go there and toss the hoodie. "You don't need this one," I say, blocking her path. "I'll buy you a new sweater. One that's not so old and frumpy looking."

"What's gotten into you?" she asks me, and for the first time, I take a good look at her.

Whoa.

There's something familiar about the curves of her face, something unsettling about her slender shape. But I can't figure out what it is.

She *should* be familiar. We've lived together for three years. But then again, she isn't. I barely know the girl.

The motion detectors activate the outside lights. The entire courtyard brightens. There's a soft glow to her eyes watching me beneath a thick fringe of lashes. Amber eyes. Eyes that slice into me like a knife.

Holy fucking shit.

Her?

My moment of clarity gives her the advantage. She circles around me and grabs the hoodie before I can stop her. "I like old and..." She straightens out the fabric, her fingers slowing over the bright red letters. "...frumpy."

I see the small rise and fall of her chest, and the way her eyes twist around the word. She looks up at me. There's so much pain and accusation in that one look; I can't breathe.

"I had nothing to do with this, I swear." I reach for the hoodie, shoving it back into the trashcan, as if making the thing disappear will somehow make it not exist. "It was stupid, juvenile girls that never should've been let out of high school."

"I'm pretty sure I know who did it." Averting her gaze, she stares at the trashcan.

If I had a lighter, I'd light the damn thing on fire. That's how much I want to destroy those four red letters.

"Well I guess it's ruined now." She shivers and wraps her arms around herself, even though it's a million degrees outside. "Thanks for saving me the embarrassment of wearing it."

She starts to leave, but I grab her arm. "Wait."

She looks down at my hand and then up at me. "Yes?"

"We should catch up."

"Catch up?"

"You know, have a conversation." God, I sound like an idiot, but I need a reason to keep her around a little while longer. I need to know my mind isn't playing tricks on me. I've got to be sure.

Metal benches are scattered through the courtyard. I steer her toward one of them.

"I've been fine. Completely fine. You?" She's edgy, like she's itching to get out of here. I'm not surprised, since she thinks she's keeping a secret from me.

"Exhausted. Jetlag," I explain. "I should tell you about Egypt sometime."

"Yes, yes, you should. Sometime. Well, glad to hear all is well. If you don't mind, I'd like to grab a glass of champagne—"

"I do mind."

I frown. The voice, the way she speaks—it's the same. Dahlia Reynolds is definitely the girl from the library. It's hard for me to process. Mostly because I don't want it to be true. I hate that they're the same girl. The girl from this morning was obtainable. This one, I've never wanted anything to do with.

I force my tone to sound calm. "Can't you spare a few minutes?"

She looks at me, and then at the door leading back inside. "Sure," she sighs, sinking into the nearest bench. "What do you want to talk about?"

Sitting down next to her, I watch her fidget with those ridiculous over-sized glasses, which I suspect she can see perfectly fine without. Speaking to her is going to be difficult. This whole conversation is going to be difficult. I feel like a fool, but I don't want to take it out on her after what she just went through. The hoodie thing was bad enough. And although I'm furious, it's not entirely directed at her. I think I'm angrier with myself. It's no wonder she stormed off earlier. She probably thought I was the biggest ass in the world for not knowing who my own roommate is. I sure as hell feel like one.

On the other hand, she's the one parading around dressed as two completely different people. Why would she do that anyway? The beautiful girl I met this morning is nothing like the girl I've come to recognize as my roommate. I suppose I've never really looked at her the way I am now. Because the longer I stare at her, the more I see through her disguise.

Dahlia shuffles her feet, picking lint off her jeans that isn't there. The silence seems to bother her. "Didn't you want to talk?" she finally asks. "Why don't you start by telling me about Egypt?"

"Egypt was awesome," I answer carefully. "But I would rather talk about you."

She watches me out of the corner of her eye. "Is this about Hannah?" she asks. "Because I told Gwen to give her back her job. She probably hasn't done it yet. I suppose I'll have to do it myself—"

"This isn't about Hannah."

"Oh." She twitches her nose. "Okay. Well what's it about then?"

I should keep her guessing, just to torture her, but I'm tired of playing games. "Why don't you start by telling me why you look like that?" I lean in close to her ear. "Especially since I know how sexy you are underneath your little costume."

Her eyes fly to mine and her mouth falls open. She knows I know. What?" I ask innocently. "You didn't think I'd figure it out? Told you I would, babe. Now, now, there's no reason to burn me with those eyes of yours, which just so you know, were a dead giveaway."

She presses her palms flat against the bench. "Figuring it out wouldn't have been necessary had you known who I was all along."

"And how was I supposed to know when you make yourself look like two different people?"

She opens her mouth to say something, but changes her mind and stands up. "Catching up was a blast."

"Where do you think you're going?"

"I need a drink."

Dammit, I stayed calm the whole time—and *she's* the one who ended up pissed off?

"Don't you think you owe me an explanation?"

"No." She says it so simply, then turns around and walks away.

I jump up and rush to move in front of her, but she sidesteps me. "Listen, whether you think you owe me one or not, I'd still like to hear it." My voice is sharper now. Everything I tried to hold back is slipping through.

"It's not my fault you can't recognize your own roommate."

"Come on, Dahlia, you can't blame me when we've barely spoken."

"Yeah, well that's not my fault either."

The door slams behind her, making me flinch. What the hell did she mean by that? As far as I can remember, she's never attempted a conversation or tried to create any kind of relationship whatsoever.

So she's angry. Well, she can just get over it. No matter how much of an ass I may have been, she is still the one that deceived me.

CHAPTER SEVEN

WESLEY

There's no doubt in my mind. Dahlia is wasted.

I've been watching her for an hour now, and after that last conversation, I have no idea how to approach her. So I just stand here across the room, watching her lift glass after glass of champagne to those full pink lips, a dreamy alcohol-infused smile plastered across her face.

No one else is paying her much attention. Every now and then she'll dance with Gwen. The two of them look more like toddlers learning to walk, but they're having fun doing it.

That smile is amazing.

I've never noticed it before. It brightens her entire face, the weird makeup and awkward glasses fading into the background, and I can't seem to take my eyes off her. It makes me wonder what else my roommate is hiding.

Charlotte Hart passes by me, catching my attention. "Hart, wait up."

"Hey, Wes," she says cheerfully. "How've you been?"

"I need to talk to you about something."

"Okay," she says, frowning at the seriousness in my voice. "What's up?"

I tell her about the girls who vandalized Dahlia's hoodie, giving her the names of the ones I could identify and describing the ones I couldn't. As I'm speaking, the muscles in Charlotte's throat work to swallow a lump, and I can tell she's having a hard time processing everything. I assume she's upset because it means her sorority sisters could potentially be in serious trouble. This school doesn't take bullying lightly; they could be facing serious consequences. Expulsion, possibly.

"I need to find Doll," she says, looking like she's on the verge of tears.

"Doll?"

"Yes, I need to find her and make this right. I can't believe those bitches did that to my best friend." She stands on her tiptoes, peeking over the crowd. "Do you know where she is?"

I'm not sure if we're talking about the same person. "Are you saying Dahlia Reynolds is your best friend?"

She nods, still looking around the room frantically. "We grew up together."

It's hard to imagine my roommate and the president of Alpha Delta Pi as friends, much less best friends, but whatever. I'll go along with it.

"Listen, Hart, I don't think you should bring it up again. Let her enjoy the rest of the party." Falling-down drunk is better than that look Dahlia gave me when she saw her hoodie. There's no reason to ruin the rest of her night. "I told you so you can deal with the ones responsible."

"You're right," she says, biting her lip. "I just feel so awful about this."

"She's over it," I say, thinking of her and Gwen's chaotic dancing. "Trust me."

"Okay…I guess." She turns to leave, but pauses. "Hey, Wesley?"

"Yeah?"

"Thanks for looking out." She said it almost like she can't believe I would bother.

"It's nothing."

Once she's gone, I search for Dahlia again. She's in the corner, sprawled across one of the stuffed chairs, her wrist holding up her chin and her elbow resting against the arm of the chair. Her glasses sit skewed on the bridge of her nose, and when she tries to correct them she only manages to unbalance them some more. Gwen isn't with her anymore, and seeing her alone bothers me. There's no way she's driving home like that.

One of the football players, Miles Cahill, approaches Dahlia and says something that makes her smile. He reaches for her hand and pulls her out of her chair. Twirling her under his arm, Miles guides her to the dance floor. I can't believe it. The girl can barely walk, much less dance at this point.

I stand there for a second, debating whether or not I should intervene. Dahlia stumbles, catching herself on Cahill's arm. Every muscle in my body lurches. He doesn't notice how close she is to falling on her ass.

I clench my fist; I want to go over there and do something about it. But it's none of my business. What I should do is go home and get some sleep. I should forget about this whole night.

Dahlia's shoe catches on the floor, and she stumbles again.

Yeah, fuck that. I'm going over there.

~ ~

DAHLIA

"Sorry to cut in, Cahill, but Dahlia and I have to go."

The abrupt way Wesley removes Miles's hand from my side takes me a few seconds to register. My entire body tenses. I didn't expect to see him again this soon; I figured once he realized who I was, he would go back to ignoring me. Why hasn't he gone back to ignoring me?

"Sorry, Wes," Miles says. "Charlotte asked me to keep Doll entertained."

Why is Miles apologizing? We were just dancing. There's nothing to apologize about.

"I didn't know you two came together."

I start to tell Miles we definitely did *not* come here together, but before I get a word out, Wesley says, "Last time I checked, I was living with the girl." He stares Miles down, daring him to push the issue.

Miles smiles sheepishly, then looks at me. "Oh right. I should check on Charlotte anyway. See you later, Doll."

He takes off, leaving me standing there gaping at Wesley. By the casual look on his face, he has no idea how rude he came off. "You are the most…" I'm so worked up, I can't seem to finish my sentence. This is all the champagne's fault. Thinking clearly is impossible.

Oxygen. That's what I need. Lots and lots of oxygen.

Taking a deep breath, I start over. "Is this about getting your stupid explanation?"

"Why does everyone call you Doll?" He asks, totally oblivious to my irritation.

"What?" I clench my hands into fists. "My name is Doll. Short for Dahlia. And Miles can call me by name, if that's okay with you."

"Is that sarcasm? Because I know your name, babe. I'll admit I don't know much else about you, but I do know your name."

"Then why did you ask?"

Wesley shrugs and says, "I figured maybe you have separate names for each personality—"

"That's not funny."

"—and if that's the case, your friends are only making the situation worse. Mental illness shouldn't be taken lightly."

Part of me realizes he's teasing, but my mind is foggy, and I can't get around how overbearing he's acting. He has no say-so about my life in any way whatsoever, joking or not. "Well I don't think your cook should call you by your first name or talk about all your sexcapades, but you don't hear me complaining, do you?"

Except for right now, of course. But I don't feel the need to point that out.

"Are we talking about the same cook you had fired?"

"I did *not* fire her!"

Wesley reaches for my hand, unlocking my clenched fist and tucking it beneath his arm. "Let's not cause a scene, okay?" One corner of his mouth curves up. He doesn't seem like the type to care about causing scenes, so I get the feeling he said that for me. Looking around, I notice there are a few people staring.

Oh God.

Nausea churns my stomach, sending goose bumps down my arms. The room slowly spins around me, a whirlwind of people, music, and voices.

"Are you all right?" Wesley asks me, sounding alarmed.

"I don't think so." My skin feels clammy, and all I want to do is go lie down somewhere. Even the floor isn't looking so bad. "I think I might be sick."

I really don't want to be sick in front of all these people. Being the invisible girl is better than being known as the girl who gave Graffiti Bash a new meaning.

Wesley's face turns serious. "Let's get you home then. There are a few cabs out front."

My stomach twists painfully. "I'm not sure I can make it that far."

"Yes, you can." He tugs me toward him. "Lean against me, and I'll walk you there."

I'm reluctant to do it, but can see no other option. Resting my weight against him, I lay my head on his shoulder and allow him to lead me out of the sorority house. He does it in a way that makes it look like he's simply walking beside me, not practically carrying me like he's actually doing. As soon as the outside air hits me, I feel a little better.

While we wait for the cab, I breathe in his spicy cologne. "You smell really good." The words just kind of slip out without shame. I blame the champagne for that too. Hopefully I won't remember this come tomorrow.

"Thanks," he says, chuckling.

"Just so you know, I don't usually drink this much."

"I didn't think you did, but either way, I wasn't judging." The cab pulls up, and Wesley opens the door.

"Guess we're even now. Chase told me you helped out when they dropped me off last night."

He helps me inside, then shuts the door behind me and gets in on the other side. The cab driver asks where we're going, and it occurs to me there's just one address to give him. Our address. That seems weird to me right now. It's always been just my address.

Wesley gives him the directions, and then we pull out onto the street. I hold my stomach like it's about to detach itself from my body.

"Easy on the gas, man," Wesley says to the driver. "Your tip will be worth five trips as long as you slow it down."

The car slows, and the ride becomes smoother.

"Thanks," I whisper.

"No problem."

"All I did was show them to your room."

"Huh?" he asks, confused.

"Your friends. I didn't really help them. I just showed them the way to your room."

"Oh." He leans across me and grabs my seatbelt, buckling me in. "How did you know where it was?"

I think about the times I've snuck in there while he was gone, snooping through his lackluster belongings, which I'm beginning to see never shed any real light on his personality. "Easy. I followed the scent of women and cheap booze."

"You're funny."

"Or maybe it was booze and cheap women. Either way, I suppose."

"You could be a comedian."

Resting my head against the seat, the swirling in my head and stomach calms. Sitting down makes me feel so much better. "Oh no, Gwen!" I pat the pockets of my pants, feeling for my cellphone. It's not there. "Oh no, *my phone!*"

This night keeps getting worse and worse.

"It's okay," Wesley assures me, pulling out his cellphone. "What's her number? I'll text her."

Thankfully Gwen has had the same phone number since seventh grade, otherwise I wouldn't have been able to remember it in my current state. Wesley sends her a text, letting her know I took a cab home. Then he calls my phone, but it goes straight to voicemail. Not knowing where my phone is gives me an uneasy feeling, but there's nothing that can be done tonight.

I relax against the seat again, feeling my eyelids droop. Kent House is about twenty minutes from campus, more remote than most of the old Victorians in this area. That's what Harland loved about it though. He said it gave him room to think, whatever that meant.

"He used to talk about you all the time," I murmur sleepily.

"Who?" Wesley asks.

"Harland."

The cab stays quiet, and I keep my eyes closed. In the dark of my mind, I see Harland's dark hair tinged with gray on the sides, and his blue eyes, a few shades lighter than Wesley's. I hear his laughter, remembering the way it filled the halls of Kent House. The sound of it warmed the whole house.

"When he spoke about you and Sam, it was like listening to a fairytale." My voice sounds dreamily faraway. "His whole face lit up, his voice changed, and he would go on and on about your adventures together…in my mind, you guys were heroes. Like Indiana Jones or something."

Wesley doesn't say anything. I get the feeling I may have treaded onto a sore subject. Over the years, he's made it pretty obvious he harbors some deep resentment for his dad. I'm not sure why; Harland never spoke about it, and I never asked.

It bothers me though. Harland was a genuinely good person, the kind the world doesn't get enough of, and he adored both of his boys so much. Sure, he liked to play pranks on people—maybe sticking Wesley and me together was his biggest prank of all. And sometimes it was hard to pry him from his research. The man truly loved to work. But aside from that, I can't imagine why Wesley could hate him so much.

It shouldn't bother me.

But it does.

CHAPTER EIGHT

WESLEY

The moment I'm positive Dahlia is sleeping, I snatch the crooked glasses from her face, stuffing them in my pocket. They look uncomfortable to wear while sleeping anyway. Holding onto them for a while isn't such a bad idea. As far as I'm concerned, I'm doing her a favor. At least until she starts banging into walls and falling down stairwells.

Even without the glasses, tension lines her brow. Sleeping with her hair tied into that knot doesn't look comfortable. I need to do something. Seeing her looking so stiff is bothering me.

Carefully, I work my fingers into her hair, prying out the pins latching her bun to her scalp. She stirs slightly, then relaxes into my side, giving me better contact. Soft locks absorbed in a flowery smell fall from the loosened bun, slowly bringing back the girl I met earlier today. I continue pulling the pins out, one by one, until a sharp one pricks my finger.

"Son of a—"

Dahlia stirs again, and I close my mouth. Blood seeps from my index finger. I press it against the bottom of my shirt, narrowing my eyes on her sleeping figure. Does she realize she's wearing miniature weapons in her hair?

"You are forbidden," I whisper while throwing the pins out the window, "to wear these again."

Tossing out the hairpins stirs up old memories. Images of my mom reading *Snow White* to Sam and me at bedtime when we were kids flood into my head. We didn't like the fairytale much, preferring dragons and robots to dwarves and poisoned apples. But it was our mom's favorite. After she left, we'd make up our own stories and act them out. Our twin beds became pirate ships, and we'd chase each other around the room with plastic swords.

I lean my head against the seat, pushing all those nights from my mind. Getting over his death has been the hardest thing I've ever had to do. I don't know if I'll ever get over it, or get over the unfairness of him dying so young. I thought finding the *Saiful Azman* would bring us both peace, but it hasn't yet. As soon as it's safe, the sword is going in Sam's grave. Where it belongs.

You have to rest, brother. Your treasure is in Kent hands now.

I'm not sure he'll get my message, but it makes me feel better to think it's possible.

Outside the trees and stars rush by in a blur. The pain is still there in my chest, and it's suffocating. Desperately, I try to think of something else. Anything else.

Dahlia draws her arm across my chest, laboring a sleepy sigh. It startles me for a second, but then I notice how relaxed she is. Seeing her like that, with all the tension gone, is nice. It's a sign of trust. A subconscious one, anyway. I wrap my arm around her, cradling her against me, and she buries herself into my shoulder.

This is Dahlia.

The same girl I've ignored for years.

Why does it seem so unreal?

~ ~

DAHLIA

"Are you carrying me?"

I'm half awake when I feel Wesley scoop me up into his arms and carry me up the porch steps.

"Nope. You're only floating. Go back to sleep."

I blink several times, then wipe my eyes groggily. "You *are* carrying me."

He fumbles with the keys. The lock clicks, and he uses the side of his body to push the tall wooden door open.

"Kind of ironic," I say with a yawn.

"What is?"

"That you're just now carrying me across the threshold. You're sort of late, you know."

"Uh, that's for newlyweds," he says, chuckling.

I wince, catching what I just implied. "Right...I meant it in a metaphorical way."

He glances down at me. "Metaphor or not, you're right. I am late." He begins to climb the wide staircase leading to the second floor. "I am very late concerning you entirely."

"You do realize I can walk, don't you? And what do you mean by 'concerning me entirely?'"

"I'd rather carry you." He turns a corner, veering toward the east wing. "And I mean there are things I should've done long ago."

"What kind of things?"

He shakes his head. "We'll save that conversation for later."

I wish I hadn't asked. Waiting to understand the meaning behind that cryptic reply sounds exasperating. I'm not sure what Wesley suddenly wants from me, but I know I don't want to play this game. Before this morning, he never acknowledged my presence. Knowing his motives are based off the way I look pisses me off.

"Put me down."

"No."

"Why not?"

"Because we're almost to your bedroom...fucking hell." Wesley pauses and swings around, and my head to spins. "Where is your bedroom?"

He's so frustrated and lost that I forget my anger. Laughter bubbles up inside my throat. I cover my mouth to stop it, but it comes out anyway.

Wesley stares at me like I'm a crazy person. "You think this is funny?"

Slowly, I peel my hands away from my face, keeping my lips even. "Not at all." The corners of my mouth curve despite my struggle to stay straight-faced. "But I'd rather go to the kitchen anyway."

"Are you hungry?" he asks. "I can have some food sent for."

Sending for food means sending for Hannah, and although I'm not sure if she still works here, I'd prefer not to risk dealing with that girl ever again.

"No need to wake the staff. I'm perfectly capable of making my own food."

"Fine. I'll make you something."

"And have you get lost on the way to my room?" Another giggle escapes. "I don't think so. Put me down."

Wesley obliges me, effortlessly standing me upright on the floor. When my feet touch the carpet, my stomach violently swirls. I grab onto his arm, not expecting the nausea to rush back so quickly.

"Whoa," he says, steadying me. "You're not walking. And you're definitely not cooking. I'll make you something to eat."

He draws me back up into his arms with ease, making my weight seem feather-light. Arguing is pointless. Everything around me is spinning, or my head is, I don't know which. Closing my eyes, I rest my head against his shoulder. Now I understand why he wanted to sleep on the stairs the other night. If it weren't for him, I'd probably end up on the ground too. For one long moment, I'm intensely grateful for Wesley. Or his shoulder at least. Either way, the feeling is…unexpected.

When we get to the kitchen, he gently sets me on a barstool behind the counter. "So what are you in the mood for?" He opens the fridge, sticking his head inside, then shuffles stuff around in there.

"Breakfast." I lay my head against the countertop, liking the way the cool marble feels against my cheek. "It's after midnight, so I think it's acceptable."

"Breakfast it is," he says, pulling out a carton of eggs. "You're in luck because I make a mean omelet."

Harland was good at making omelets too. No matter how hard I try, I can't get my eggs to turn out as fluffy as he could.

Wesley slides the cutting board to the same counter I'm perched at and begins chopping veggies. I watch his biceps shift as he chops, almost in a daze. It makes me a little mad. Why does he have to ooze sexuality all of the time? Seems unfair.

"Do you like mushrooms?" he asks, startling me out of my daze.

I lick my lips, thinking about the question. Something about mushrooms…

"Yes." I'll go with that. Yes or no answers work most of the time.

He lowers his arm for a moment, studying me. "So are you ready to give me an explanation?"

"An explanation for what?"

He draws his finger across my cheek, then holds it up to display the makeup residue.

"Oh that." I scoot the barstool back a few inches and sit up straighter. "That's just how I do my makeup."

"Care to tell me why?"

"Not really."

He arches a brow, giving me a look that says he won't be brushed off so easily. But what am I supposed to say? I have deep-rooted issues that no one could possibly understand? Somehow I doubt that will go over very well.

I cross my arms over my chest; my defenses going up. Wesley can stare at me like that all night, but it won't matter. Spilling my guts to him isn't going to happen. And who does he think he is anyway, coming out of nowhere and invading my privacy like he has the right—

"You're beautiful, you know." Dark blue eyes meet mine, and my mind goes blank. "Underneath your disguise. Why would you want to hide that?"

Breathing is…difficult. The air in my lungs is depleting. Good God, and why am I so hot all of a sudden? He hasn't even turned the stove on yet. I fan my hair away from my face. It's down. That's weird. Last I remember, it was secured on the top of my head in a tight bun…

Those eyes continue to stare me down. Like he's figured me out.

I don't like it. "I'm not hiding anything."

"That's bullshit," he says, not breaking his stare. "And you know it."

He's doing it again, working that same magical spell he used on me this morning. His heated gaze, the warmth of his lips drawing closer and closer…wow he's good.

I push against the counter, scooting the barstool back several more inches. Being in the same room with him used to feel like being miles apart. Now I feel the need to put up a freaking barrier.

Wesley only grins, that same cocky grin that makes me want to smack him. He knows he holds some kind of force over me, and he's clearly gloating about it. Ass.

"What's the matter, babe? Afraid to be near me?" At first it looks like he's cracking up, but as soon as he gets a good look at my face—and I'm going for murderous—he lets out a long sigh. "Don't worry. That's not what I want from you." He sets down the knife. "Tonight, anyway. I won't pretend I'm not interested. Obviously, you can tell from this morning I am *definitely* interested. It's just well, tonight…all I want is to talk. Get answers and stuff."

He's rambling, which puts me at ease. It's nice to see him a little nervousness. Especially after that disgusting display of conceit a second ago. God knows he makes me more nervous than anyone I've ever met; it feels good to know I can provoke a similar reaction.

Wesley runs a hand through his hair, then walks to the sink and rinses his hands. He turns a dial on the stove and places the frying pan over one of the burners. "I'm not giving up until you tell me, you know."

He can't be serious—can he? "Are you really that stubborn?"

"When I need to be." He looks up at me. "Being stubborn isn't always a bad thing. It's how I managed to hunt down most of the treasure I've found. When I want something, I don't give up until I have it."

He's talking about things other than treasure, and I believe him. He's the type of person that always gets what he wants.

"I already told you I'm not hiding anything. This is the way I normally look."

"You didn't look like that in the library."

"That's because I was wearing old clothes. I was cleaning, in case you didn't notice."

He cracks an egg and pours it into the pan. "Oh I happen to notice just about everything about you, babe. Now that I can see through your disguise."

Thank God it's dark in here, because I can feel myself blush. I want to stay unaffected, but I can't. Wesley has his own brand of paying someone attention.

"Why do you care how I look anyway? You've never bothered before."

He stays silent for a long time, stirring the eggs. The pan sizzles as I watch him. I'm usually good at reading people, but figuring Wesley out is impossible.

He sets the spatula down on the counter. "No, I haven't."

I wait for him to say more, but he continues to stay silent. I'm fishing for something. I don't know what that something is, but it definitely isn't "No, I haven't."

I look out the kitchen window. Stars shine brighter out here, one of the good things about living in the middle of nowhere. But it's the same scenery I see every night, and it does nothing to keep my mind off the guy behind the stove. Maybe if I try counting them…

One. Two.

Nope. Not working. They sparkle and blend together into their dark blue background, reminding me of Wesley's eyes.

"How's your cut?" I ask, trying to find some neutral territory between us.

"Would you like to change the bandage again?"

Of course he would go there. Should've seen that one coming. "You could've popped a stitch by carrying me up the stairs."

"Concerned? For me? I'm touched."

The corners of my mouth pull into a frown. I don't like how unconcerned he is about his health. I've never seen anyone that beat up, not in real life anyway.

"I'm fine," he says, glancing at me. "I'm not bleeding, and I didn't rupture anything by carrying you up the stairs."

"Good."

I feel guilty enough for making him bleed once today already.

Wesley sets a plate down in front of me. The omelet looks and smells delicious, covered in cheddar cheese and chopped tomatoes. "Thanks," I tell him.

"The grease should help your stomach," he says. "Your hangover won't be as bad."

I pick up my fork and dig in. It tastes just like Harland's omelets. "So about your trip to Egypt," I say between bites. "You never did tell me about it."

"I didn't think you really wanted to hear about that."

He's half right. At the time, I was only thinking about getting away from him, but that doesn't mean I'm not extremely curious. "Are you kidding me? I live for this kind of stuff."

He takes two glasses out of the cupboard and fills them with water from the fridge. "That's right. I forgot you were studying archeology. My dad told me you used to help him with his research."

I nod, thinking of all our late nights together. "I loved helping him. I wanted to go on that Egypt trip, but…" I bite down on my lower lip.

Wesley sets a glass of water in front of me. "But what? Why didn't you go?"

"There were things I couldn't get out of." I chew my eggs, shifting uncomfortably on the barstool. "You should tell me about it though," I say, trying to move on.

Leaning against the counter, Wesley looks into his glass, a distant smile tugging at his lips. "Have you ever been to a Bedouin wedding?" he asks me.

"No." I scoot closer to the counter, getting the feeling a good story is in the works.

"Well they take place during a full moon," he begins. "And they last anywhere from two to five days."

"Sounds like one heck of a party."

"It is." He grins. "But in order to go, you have to bring the bride a goat or a sheep."

"And where exactly did you get one of those?"

"The desert isn't full of goat stores," he says, scratching his chin. "Tyson had to steal one from a nearby tribe."

"He did *what*?"

"And the people from that tribe ended up at the wedding, which is a whole other story."

I place my hand under my chin, listening quietly as he talks. He tells me all about the wedding, the expedition, and other adventures he had while he was in Egypt. I could sit there and listen to him all night, enjoying the sound of his voice. It's deep and a little rough, but he builds excitement in just the right places, and there's something lyrical about the way he talks.

I try to dig for information to find out how he came by the cut on his stomach, but he dodges my attempts. Finally, I just come out and ask him.

"You know that saying, 'If I tell you, I'd have to kill you?'"

"Don't tell me you're about to use it," I groan.

He smiles, then looks down at his stomach, placing his hand over his cut. "One day I'll tell you that story, babe. But not tonight."

I'm disappointed, but I don't push for more. I can't get past the way he said *one day*. As if it were imminent. My heart pumps a little faster. I study Wesley closely for a minute, really seeing him for the first time.

"Do I have something on my face?" he asks, noticing my intense stare.

"You're beautiful, you know," I tell him, my voice turning serious. "Underneath your disguise."

Wesley stills, holding his breath. He looks at me as if he isn't sure he heard me correctly.

Blood rushes to my face and neck, my words surprising me too. What made me say something like that?

I hop off the barstool. Apparently I'm way too tired to keep from speaking my thoughts out loud, which means I should probably leave.

"Thanks for the omelet." My eyes drift to the stairs behind me. "I should head up to bed."

Wesley circles around the counter, moving in front of me. He stands there for a long moment, making me question what he wants. Then, lifting his hand to my cheek, he traces the side of my face. Every inch of skin he grazes comes alive beneath his fingertips.

"You're welcome," he finally says. "Do you need help getting to your room?"

No. Bad idea. If he follows me to my room, I may not want him to leave. "I'm good now, but thanks."

There's a hint of regret in his eyes, thrilling me even more. I need to get out of here before I change my mind.

His hand drops away from my face. "See you later, Dahlia."

"Good night, Wesley."

I turn around, quickly heading for the stairs. A huge smile spreads over my face as I'm climbing them.

See you later.

Why do those three little words make me so deliriously happy?

CHAPTER NINE

DOLL

"Come on, Doll. Wake up."

Someone is prying at my eye mask and lightly slapping my face. Whoever it is, I hate them.

"*Wake up.*"

I open my eyes. Resentfully.

It's dark. My curtains are sheer, which means if it were time to wake up, the room would be bright and sunny. My blurry vision focuses in on a narrow face shaded by unkempt pieces of blonde hair. He pushes his glasses up the bridge of his nose and stares me down.

"Hayes?" I croak out in a voice that doesn't sound like my own.

"Oh good, you're awake."

I glance at the window, seeing it's been left open. Telling Hayes about the ladder I keep perched outside was clearly a mistake. This is what I get for being lazy; it's easier to park my car by the side of the house and use the window than to go through nine thousand square feet to get to my room. Now I'm learning it's more trouble than it's worth.

"Go away," I groan, turning over on my side. "I'm tired and hungover."

"You'll be glad I woke you up once you've heard what I have to say." His weight lifts from the bed. I hear him shuffling around, but I don't care what he's up to. As long as he does it quietly.

Light floods into the room, feeling like the power of a thousand suns burning through my eyelids. "What the crap," I screech, furrowing my head beneath my pillow.

"I'm sensing some adversity from you."

"No kidding," I say, but it comes out muffled. He always uses intellectual words like adversity, and right now I don't feel like translating Hayes. Listening to him speak can be as difficult as deciphering hieroglyphics.

"I'll get right to the point," he says. "Styler has the other half of the map."

I sit up too quickly, my head spinning from the movement. When I swallow, my throat feels scratchy and dry. "Hand me that water bottle," I say pointing to the dresser next to Hayes.

He tosses me the water, then quietly waits while I drink the entire thing. "Thank you," I say, feeling a million times better.

"Next time you should intersperse your drinks with water," he tells me in his monotone, know-it-all voice. "Alcohol is a diuretic."

"I'll keep that in mind. Back to what you were saying about Styler." Just saying that name makes me cringe. "Is it true?"

He nods, looking around my slightly messy room. Clean by most people's standards, but Hayes has OCD issues. His eyes drift over clothes I left strewn along the floor, his fingers practically itching to tidy up.

"It's true. I saw it with my own eyes."

"Did you take a picture?"

He lets out a small snort. "Styler's not *that* stupid, Doll."

No, he isn't. Styler is a conceited jackass that I wasted a year of high school dating, but by no means is he stupid. He knows I've been looking for the other half of that map, and I told him myself I'd do anything to get it.

"First of all, how and why did he show you?"

"We're both in an ancient collectibles group online." Hayes picks apart my closet's beaded curtain, separating all the strands until they're in perfect order. "He's kind of an Egyptologist. Did you know that?"

"Yes."

It's one the things that attracted me to Styler in the beginning. Shame he lets his ego get in the way of his good qualities.

I sit up straighter, sliding my legs off the bed. "You said you saw the map with your own eyes. How?"

"He showed it to me." Hayes sits in my desk chair, swiveling it around to face me. "Styler's here in town, Doll."

My hands drift to my temples as I try to grasp everything. He was telling the *truth*? How is this even possible?

"He only showed me for a few short moments," Hayes adds. "Just to validate the map's existence. It's the real deal."

My heart speeds up. If anyone could identify an ancient treasure map, it's Hayes. He is literally a boy-genius, and the most versed on ancient artifacts out of everyone I know. If he says it's real, it is.

"My God," I whisper. "What does he want?"

"You."

"Excuse me?"

"He was very clear about that. If you meet a few stipulations, he's agreed to give you the map."

Meet a few stipulations? What the hell does Styler think this is—a business transaction? I stand up, shaking with the need to hit something. At the same time my heart is still racing. The possibility of finally getting my hands on that map thrills me beyond anything I could ever dream up. I've never been this close before. I'm not sure if I hate Styler for finding it, or if I want to hug him until he can't breathe. He always said he knew where he could find it. I never believed him. For years, I've thought the other half of the map was lost forever, destroyed over time. Now to know it's out there within my grasp…incredible.

"What're the stipulations?" I ask, my voice skeptical. It almost seems too good to be true.

Hayes looks up at me, his eyes worried. "Remember I'm just the messenger."

"Just tell me what he wants."

"Well…he's here. In town."

"You already said that."

"Yeah, but I didn't mention that he transferred schools. Or that he moved here."

I nearly choke on my next breath and have to cough a few times before I can speak. "Please tell me you're joking."

Hayes shakes his head, looking like he's going to be sick. "He's rented a condo close to campus. Real nice place, too. Three bedrooms, two bath—"

"Out with it, Hayes. What does he want?"

"He wants you to move in with him."

The words ring in my head, but I want to push them out, pretend like I can't hear him. This isn't happening. Styler's playing a prank on me. A sick, evil prank. Something to grab my attention. That's all it is.

"Is he serious?" I say, afraid to ask.

Hayes nods, and looks at the floor. He doesn't want to tell me this anymore than I want to hear it. "Afraid so. Moving here, finding the map—it was all for you."

All for me.

Me.

"It doesn't make sense," I say between short, uneven breaths. "He cheated on me in high school by hooking up with some softball player—Frankie something or another in the girls' locker room. I don't remember her name. My point is that he didn't care about us then. Why does he care so much now?"

Hayes shrugs, looking helpless. "I don't know."

My knees go weak, and I clutch the bedpost. It feels like a tidal wave is crashing over me, and I'm struggling to stay grounded. How can Styler do this to me? Doesn't he know what he's asking me to give up?

Hayes crosses the room to where I'm standing. "Breathe, Doll," he tells me. "Take a few deep breaths."

I do what he says, inhaling through my nose. "If I leave, I'll have to break the agreement in Harland's will." I'd have to leave Kent House forever. I mean, it's not as if I've lived here long. We didn't move here until the beginning of my senior year. But still...

This is the only home I have.

This is where Harland helped me finish up my last year of high school. It's where we researched ancient texts together. It's where we both healed over the loss of my mom. I always thought I'd be excited to get away, but I'm not sure where else I belong.

I never cared about the money. But there are things here Harland knew would entice me to stay, things Wesley wouldn't care about...like the library. Although, I planned to give up my share of the money, I'd hoped Wesley would let me have a few of the books. Something to remember Harland by.

Ugh. This is all his fault. If Harland didn't spend those last few years of his life teaching me how to analyze artifacts and read hieroglyphics, I never would've become so interested in archeology. I spent my rebellious teenage years complaining to him how I couldn't care less about "all that old crap." He wouldn't let it go though, and over time, I fell in love with his work. The more he taught me, the more passionate I became. All that old crap transformed into priceless treasures.

After I graduated high school, we were planning to go to South America on a real expedition. We would grow famous together, the next Howard Carter and Gertrude Bell. But then his cancer came back...destroying everything. Just like it destroyed the plans my mom and I made together.

"Did you make copies of the other half of the map?" Hayes asks me. "The one Harland left you?"

I nod, staring at the carpet blankly.

"It's a big decision, and it kills me to tell you this, but you have to make that decision now." He runs a hand through his hair, looking helpless. "Styler doesn't want you sitting on this for long. He said if you have too much time to think about it, you'll never agree. He's out front, Doll. He's giving you an hour."

"He came here in the middle of the night?"

"We were here earlier, but you were out. He's been waiting at my house."

I walk to the window, searching the grounds for Styler's car. Sure enough, it's parked a few feet away from my window, the same black Mustang GT he had in high school.

"How long do I have to live with him?"

"One semester."

"And then he'll give me the map?"

"Then he'll give you the map." Hayes lets out a breathy sigh. "I'm sorry, Doll. I tried to explain your situation to him, but he doesn't care."

I'm not surprised. Styler never cared about anyone except himself.

"You don't have to do it, you know. You could still find the treasure on your own. I'll help you. I'll do everything I can to help you find it." Hayes wraps his hand around mine, surprising me. He's not big on affection or touching people in general. "We'll research together."

"The two of us have been researching that map for years, Hayes. I can't pass this chance up."

"I figured you'd say that." His hand releases mine. "I almost didn't come over here because of it."

"I would've hated you for keeping it from me." I want to hug him, to let him know this isn't his fault, but he's not the hugging type. So instead I pat him on the arm.

"What about Wesley?" he asks, nodding toward the door. "Do you need to speak with him?"

I stare at the door wistfully, thinking about the amazing night I spent with him. There's so much that could've been, so much that will never be. I try to tell myself it doesn't matter.

Any relationship that could've happened between us, friendship or otherwise, seems entirely based off of him believing I was someone else. I can't get around the fact that he might never have spoken to me if he hadn't mistaken me for a maid.

Maybe it's too little too late. I mean, we graduate this year. What's the point of trying now?

"I'll write him a note." It's a little impersonal, but it's not as if I can go wake him up in the middle of the night to give him the news. I scribble a few lines down in a notebook on my desk, letting him know I'm leaving and how I understand it exempts me from the will. I don't tell him where I'm going.

Partly because it doesn't matter. But mostly because I'm embarrassed.

If I know Styler, and I do, I'm walking into a bachelor pad with kegs in every corner.

"He knows I'm not giving it up, right?" I look Hayes directly in the eye. "I'll live with him, but we're going to be in separate rooms."

"He knew you would say that too." Hayes winces. "He thinks he can win you over."

Hearing that makes me want to gag. "There will be no winning me over," I sputter out, holding up a finger for emphasis. "I can promise you that."

"Again. I'm just the messenger."

Shaking my head, I go into my closet to get my suitcase. Styler is delusional if he thinks anything will come of me living with him. The only reason I'm doing it is for the map. I wouldn't leave for anything less.

Hayes helps me pack. Since we only have an hour, I run around the room, throwing and stuffing clothes into my suitcase, only to have Hayes go back and fold them into neat, organized stacks.

As we're finishing up, there's a knock at the door. My body freezes into place. I have no idea who it could be.

"Doll?" Gwen's voice comes from the other side.

I let out a breath and direct Hayes to the window. "Will you take my suitcase down for me?" I whisper. "I need to tell her what's going on."

"Sure." He swings over the windowsill, and I hand him the suitcase. "You've got five minutes," he reminds me as he climbs down.

"Doll, please say you're in there." Gwen knocks again, louder this time.

I open the door to find her standing there, mascara running down her face. She throws her arms around me. "Thank God," she breathes. "I've been calling you all night. What happened?"

"I lost my phone," I say in a rush. "Gwen, there's something I need to tell you, and I don't have much time."

She scrunches her lips to the side, studying me. "Is everything okay?"

"I'm fine." I'm lying. I'm not fine at all, but I don't have time to go into that. "Sit down. You're going to need to sit for this."

I tell her about Styler, about the map, about his conditions, everything. She listens quietly, but I can see all the questions in her eyes. She doesn't understand.

"Why do you want that stupid map anyway?" she asks. "What's so important about the treasure?"

I think about how I should answer. How can I say it in a way she'll accept? "It's the life-changing kind of treasure, Gwen." I press my lips together and look toward the window. "It's my Luscious."

Luscious is the name of the salon Gwen and her mom plan to open once they save enough money. It's Gwen's dream, and the only thing I can think of she can relate to.

"Okay," she says, nodding, and I can see she's trying to accept it. "What about Wesley? What am I supposed to tell him?"

I grab the note off my desk, folding it up. "Give him this." I hand it to her. "Don't tell him where to find me. Just tell him he can have everything. I'm okay with it."

Gwen eyes me closely. "Are you sure that's true?" Her voice is slightly whiny. "What about The Heart, Doll?"

"He gets *everything*," I stress.

"I think you're making a mistake. It feels like you're quitting a few feet from the finish line."

I swing one leg over the windowsill. "It doesn't matter. This isn't a race I ever cared about winning."

I climb onto the ladder carefully, wary of the last time I was on one of these things.

"Harland wanted more for you than this," Gwen says, shaking her head. "What would he say now?"

She's digging the knife in deep, but I'm actually glad she asked. I need to say this out loud. "Harland wanted me get my degree. That's the only promise I made to him, and it will still be met. I'm not planning to drop out now."

"But he wanted you to have the ability to research. To do what you're passionate about without money getting in the way. If you leave now, you may not ever find that for yourself."

"He made those choices when I didn't know what choices to make for myself. I'm an adult now, Gwen. Making mistakes is a part of life."

Hearing myself say that is strangely reassuring. It lets me know I'm making the right decision.

Gwen leans out the window, and I give her a hug. "What about all your stuff?" she asks me.

"I'll get it later."

"Am I allowed to visit?"

"As long as Styler isn't too much of an ass." I start climbing down, unable to avoid thinking of Wesley as I do. Every time I see a ladder I'm going to think of him now.

"He was always an ass," Gwen groans and turns her lips down in a pout. "I still can't believe he's taking you from me."

Her expression makes me smile. "I'm kicking and screaming on the inside."

I hop down from the last leg and wave bye to Gwen. "Be safe!" she shouts. "And call me as soon as you find your phone!"

"I will," I promise, and then turn around to face the car. Memories of Styler trying to feel me up inside of it make me want to turn right back around. He is the part of my life I want to be over, and yet here I am, back at square one.

This map better be worth it.

CHAPTER TEN

WESLEY

My phone rings. I see my mom's picture on the screen, and I don't answer right away. Each ring pierces my eardrums with guilt. She told me to call her as soon as I landed, but I never did.

"Hey, Mom."

"Hi, sweetie." She lets out a relieved sigh. "It's good to hear your voice. I thought by now you would've called. I was worried."

"Yeah, um sorry about that. Things have been hectic here." It's a weak excuse, but it's the best I can come up with.

"You should always make time for your mother."

Running a hand through my hair, I stare up at the ceiling and try not to groan out loud. Guilt trips are my mom's specialty. No one can bullshit their way around that woman. "I swear I was just about to call you."

"Mmm hmm. I bet," she says dryly. "So how was your trip?"

"It was a success."

Something is shining on my bedroom floor. I kneel down, realizing it's Dahlia's glasses. They must've slipped out of my pocket sometime last night.

"Find anything?"

"Actually, yeah. We excavated a lot of old bones and artifacts next to the town's river. Everything we found predates the Roman Empire."

"That sounds amazing, sweetie. I'm happy for you."

That's all a lie. Anything that reminds her of my dad and Sam upsets her, so I don't go into many details about my trips or my classes. I love her for saying it though. She's trying to be happy for me. Trying is more than I'm used to from her.

"How's everything in Nashville?" I idly twirl the pair of glasses between my fingers. "Are you and Mandy doing okay?"

"Oh we're fine." Her voice softens at the change of subject. "Mandy starts kindergarten next week, and Paul got a promotion at work. Life is pretty great right now. No complaints."

"That's good to hear."

She deserves the life she has now, and the ability to say she's doing great. There was a time she was anything but. When Dad left, our family fell out of balance. We didn't think it could get much worse, but I guess the adage is true. It can always get worse. And when Sam died, it crippled us. Any family we may have been shattered with his death. My mom and I walked around like zombies for months, purposeless. We were living, breathing, functioning people, but we died right along with Sam.

Not long after, Mom met Paul, and she found direction. Life for her had meaning again. I'll always be grateful for that.

"I hope you're coming home for Thanksgiving," she says cheerfully. "We're all excited to see you."

Home.

That word doesn't ring true for me in the same way she means it. Everything about my mom feels separate from me now. My family was the one we shared with Sam and Dad. That family doesn't exist anymore.

"I'll be there," I promise.

"Good."

"Hey, Mom?"

"Yes?"

I pry open the glasses and look through them. Just as I thought, they're not prescription. "When Dad was alive…did he ever talk about Dahlia?"

That name rolls off my lips with new definition.

Dahlia. It's never sounded this way before, never had so much energy attached to it.

"Why do you ask?"

"He never spoke about her to me. Then again, we barely spoke." I stare at the glasses, trying to dissect my own thoughts. "It's just...she must've been important to him."

The line goes quiet for a long moment. I shouldn't have mentioned Dahlia to my mom. This is a mistake.

"She's the daughter of his girlfriend, sweetie. That's all I know."

"What happened to her, his girlfriend?"

"I'm not sure. You know I don't like to talk about them."

Talking about the other woman can't be easy. My mom avoids the subject entirely. Avoidance is something I've learned from her over the years. Instead of demanding to know why my dad chose to do what he did, I ignored him. He wanted to walk out on us? Fine. I'd cut him off like he was no one to me.

Now I wonder if I should've asked more questions. If nothing else, someone should've forced him to admit what he did was wrong.

"Why the sudden interest in her anyway?" My mom asks a little too sharply. "Did something happen?"

"I thought you wanted me to shut up about her."

"I did—I do, but you've never asked about her before. I'm curious."

I could tell my mom I never really saw Dahlia Reynolds before. I could tell her my roommate was hidden beneath the cloud of hate and bitterness I held for my dad. I could also tell her that cloud is stripping itself away, little by little, and now I am so fucking fascinated by the person I once overlooked.

But I don't say any of those things.

"I don't know, Mom. Just making conversation."

She doesn't press me for more, thank God. All she does is ask a few more questions about school, and then we hang up.

Setting the glasses down on my desk, I leave my bedroom, feeling restless. Without thinking about what I'm doing, I weave through the hallways towards Dahlia's bedroom. Since I'm still not sure where it is, it takes me a while to find it.

I knock on the door, but no one answers.

"Dahlia?" I call out.

Still no answer. Only silence.

"She's not here."

I turn around, finding Gwen behind me.

"Do you know where she went?"

She studies me for a moment, frowning, then digs inside the pocket of her apron. "Here, she asked me to give you this."

She hands me a folded up piece of notebook paper. I open it up to see a few lines scrawled across it.

Sorry for the short notice, but I've decided to move out. I understand this exempts me from Harland's will. – Dahlia

I have to read the words several times before the meaning sinks in. "What the hell is this?" I ask Gwen, still staring at the note as if it's written in another language. "She moved out?"

Fidgeting with her hair, Gwen nods. "Yeah...this morning."

I crinkle up the note and open the door to Dahlia's room. Seeing is believing, and I need to see this for myself.

There's no one inside.

I look around, my mouth parting in disbelief. The room is tidy, except for random pieces of clothing lying on the bed and floor. I peek inside the closet, finding a bunch of unused hangers and a few winter coats.

"She's planning to get the rest of her stuff later."

I forgot Gwen was standing there. Her eyes drift around the room in a sad way.

"Fuck that," I say, startling her. "She's coming back here. Now. There's no way I'm letting her give up a fortune for no reason."

"She won't come back." Gwen pries at the strings on her apron. "Trust me, we've been friends most of our lives, and I know Doll very well. This whole situation sucks, but she won't change her mind."

"Why?" I demand, stepping closer to her. "Tell me why she left. Is it because of me?"

Gwen looks up at me, her brows dipping together. "Why would it be because of you?"

"It's not?"

"No." She shakes her head. "But I'd like to know why you automatically jumped to that conclusion. What happened yesterday?"

I rub the back of my neck, more confused than ever. If Dahlia leaving had nothing to do with me, than why did she go? "Look, just tell me where she is."

"I can't," Gwen says, hugging her arms to her chest. "I don't know."

"You're a shitty liar."

"Well I can't tell you!"

I blink, shocked to hear someone yell at me. I'm not used to it. My defenses immediately go up, and my first instinct is to yell back at Gwen, but I stop myself. Arguing won't accomplish anything. It won't help me find Dahlia any sooner.

"Listen," I say in a softer voice. "Your employer is gone now, which leaves you potentially jobless."

She narrows her eyes at me. "Thanks for pointing that out, Captain Obvious. Is this what getting the axe feels like?"

"No, that's not what I'm—just tell me where she is, Gwen. I'll let you keep your job, I swear."

Her chests drops, and she stares at the floor. She stays like that for a moment, thinking, and I worry she still won't tell me. I've never been so on edge in my life, waiting for her to speak.

"I can't give you her new address," she finally says. "But I can tell you where she'll be at four o' clock today."

It's better than nothing. "Fine."

"Every Tuesday and Thursday she goes to Professor Barakat's class."

Barakat?

Why does that name seem familiar? "Wait a second, he teaches one of the capsule classes. If she's an anthropology major, she would've taken his class in one of her first semesters."

Gwen shrugs one shoulder. "From what she told me, his class had a huge impact on her. She sits in the back of the classroom where no one notices her and listens to him lecture."

I look down at my watch. Four o'clock is still six hours away. It's going to be the longest six hours of my life. "Thanks, Gwen."

She nods, reaching for a picture frame sitting on Dahlia's dresser. "Hopefully you can talk some sense into her. I couldn't."

There's a book that was sitting behind it, *The Count of Monte Cristo*, by Alexandre Dumas. I pick it up, noticing the worn pages and binding.

Gwen sets down the picture frame, a soft smile on her face. "It's her favorite. Don't ask me why; I couldn't get past the first chapter. The movie is way better."

"What's it about?"

"Treasure," she answers simply. "And revenge. You'd probably like it."

"What makes you say that?"

"I pay attention." She walks to the door, pausing outside of it. "You know, the two of you are more alike than you'd think."

"In what way?"

"In a lot of ways." She looks at the book in my hands and says, "Take it with you. I'm sure she won't mind you borrowing it."

I look at the book, and then around the room again. People who move away don't leave behind their favorite books or pictures of their best friends. Dahlia must've been in a hurry. It makes me wonder what caused her to leave like that, so spontaneously.

Gwen starts to leave, then stops again. "Oh, and don't tell her I told you about Barakat's class. She'll kill me."

"I won't."

"Good." She stares at me for a second, shaking her head. "What *happened* last night?"

She doesn't expect an answer, walking away right after she asks the question. It seems more like she's asking what happened to me—or maybe I'm just imagining it. Either way, I don't have a fucking clue how to answer.

CHAPTER ELEVEN

DOLL

Styler's condo is exactly how I imagined it would be. Scents of stale beer and pizza hit me as I walk inside, keeping me hovering by the entrance, afraid to see where I'll be living. So far I feel like running out the door and never coming back.

Styler carries my bag inside, tugging at my arm. "Don't be shy."

I look around at what I've given up my life for: Lawn chairs in place of furniture, beer cans scattered along every table surface, and desolate white walls. At least there's a flat screen in the living room, which is the only thing that makes this place feel like a condo instead of a garage.

"It's kind of messy," Styler says, shoving garbage off one of the tables.

Two half naked girls with olive complexions emerge from the hallway, both appearing comfortable walking around in their underwear. He didn't mention I'd be living with anyone else. "Is this her, Sty?" one of them asks.

He nods, looking at me. "This is Paola and Paulina," he explains. "They're sisters, and they share the third bedroom. Girls, this is my Dolly."

"I asked you not to call me that," I say under my breath.

Another girl with curly blonde hair walks into the room, this one slightly more dressed than the other two. She smiles at me, dimples imprinted in the sides of her cheeks. "Hey, I'm Jordan. Styler said you'll be rooming with me until you change your mind and move into his bedroom."

"That's never gonna happen." I slice into Styler with a hard look. "Funny, you didn't mention I'd be living in a harem."

"You know what you have to do to change that. Just say the word, and it's me and you in a life of sweet monogamy."

"You're disgusting."

He shrugs. "You didn't always think so."

"Everyone is allowed to make a few stupid decisions in high school."

I study Styler closely. I don't know what I ever saw in him. He's the tall, dark, and handsome type, with big brown innocent looking eyes. Every once in a while he displays hints of intelligence too. But as far as appeal goes, that's it for him.

"Look, Doll, this is what you're signing up for," Styler tells me point-blank. "Do you want the map or not?"

My eyes drift around the condo again, and then at Jordan, who is smiling at me as if she's met her new best friend. Paola and Paulina walk into the kitchen, whispering in Spanish and looking over their shoulder at me like I'm an alien species. I let out a sigh, my shoulders drooping.

This is going to be the semester from hell.

"Where's my room?"

Styler's whole face lights up. Lugging my bag over his shoulder, he heads down the hall, gesturing for me to follow. "This way."

An invisible chain and shackle drags me with him. He stops at the first bedroom and swings the door open. Half the size of my former bedroom, there's not much to offer inside. Twin beds sit opposite each other against the walls, separated by a dresser covered with clothes, makeup, and hair products. There's a hairdryer lying on the floor, surrounded by towels and more clothes, a bra hanging on the closet door handle and several pairs of high heels scattered in front of it.

Hayes would have a panic attack if he were here.

"The bed on the far side is yours," Styler says, dropping my bag beside it.

Jordan peeks inside the room from the doorway. "Hope you don't mind, but I took the bed by the window. I smoke a blunt every morning. It wakes me up."

"Oh…" I smile as sweetly as I can. "Um, the other bed is fine."

This is a perfect example of being careful what you wish for. I was bitter at not getting the chance to live like a real student, and now it's being thrown back in my face. Springs creak as I lower myself onto the bed. This is what I chose. I just have to remind myself it will all be over by Christmas.

Styler stares at me, his face still animated with excitement. "You can cook, right? I remember you used to talk about cooking with your mom all the time."

I feel a sharp pang at the mention of my mom. She would be ashamed of me for doing this. "Yes, I know how to cook."

"Awesome." He rocks back on his heels. "I haven't used the kitchen since moving in. Pizza and wings are all we eat around here."

"Okay," I say, nodding slowly. "I'll cook something later. For now could you um, give me some space, Styler? I need to unpack."

"Sure." He watches me curiously for a second. It looks like he's about to say something but changes his mind.

As soon as he's gone, I lie back on the squeaky bed and let out a long breath. The overhead fan is spinning rapidly, the pull chain to clinking against the side of the bulb. Every second there's another *clink*. That fan is right on track with my life. We're both becoming unhinged.

I can do this. If I keep repeating that over and over inside my head, I'll get through it.

I can do this.

I can do this.

Hopefully.

CHAPTER TWELVE

WESLEY

Four o'clock finally arrives, and I make my way into Professor Barakat's lecture hall, walking in with the other students like I belong there. Dahlia's already sitting in the back where no one is paying her any attention. Her strange makeup is missing, revealing the girl I remember from the library, but she's dressed in one of her oversized hoodies again.

I scoot into the next seat without her noticing. She's staring ahead at the podium, lost in thought. Whatever she's thinking about, it's troubling her.

"Come here often?" I ask, catching her attention.

She freezes into place, her eyes slightly widening. "Let me guess. Gwen told you I'd be here?"

Answering that question doesn't seem like it will help anyone, so I keep my mouth shut. Dahlia leans back in her seat, lifting her hood over her head. I think it's her way of withdrawing—a defense mechanism taking over.

"What are you doing here anyway?" she asks me.

"Seeing as how you've already taken this class, I could ask you the same question."

"I enjoy the lectures," she says matter-of-factly. "It reminds me why I chose this field."

She's really passionate about this stuff. That's most likely my Dad's doing. His love for archeology rubbed off on everyone that was close to him.

"Your turn."

"You know why I'm here."

"No, I don't." She stuffs her hands into the front pockets of her hoodie, studying me. "Actually, I don't get it at all."

Seeing her face makeup-free does something strange to me. I feel like I've known this side of her all along, like she's an old friend I'd forgotten, missing her without even being aware of it. I shift in my seat, but I don't break away from Dahlia's gaze. Reacting this way over a girl, especially *this* girl, isn't something I'm used to.

Professor Barakat shuts the door, indicating the class is about to begin. It shatters our stare down and bursts our short-lived bubble.

There's someone up front—the professor's assistant most likely—preparing the slide projector. When I look closer, I realize it's Christine. What's she doing here?

"That's his daughter," Dahlia tells me, noticing the direction I'm looking. "Every once and a while she stops by to help him with his lectures."

"I recognize her," I say. "But I didn't know they were related."

The lights dim, and the projector brightens the front wall. Dahlia pulls her legs up into her chair, tucking them beneath her. "Today is the analysis of language and phonology," she whispers, leaning her head toward me.

"Do you remember all of his lectures?"

She nods. "He never deviates from the curriculum." The professor begins to speak, and she stays quiet for a moment, her eyes sharpening in on him. "I don't think he's very adventurous."

"Why do you care if he's adventurous or not?"

She shrugs. "He focuses a lot on archeology, but I bet he's never been on an expedition in his life. He only admires the people who have enough courage to do what he teaches."

I don't know why it matters, but I don't say so out loud. She's been coming to the same class for a while, so I suppose Professor Barakat's personality nuances have become noticeable to her over the years.

For a while, I just sit there and listen quietly. Every so often, I'll glance over to check out Dahlia's face. She looks as if she's in a trance, and I wonder what it is about this class that's so interesting. It doesn't resonate with me the same way it does for her. I liked it, but there's a shit-ton of other classes more impressive than this one.

"He mispronounces the word *especially*," she says, a smile in her eyes. "It's kind of funny."

We wait for Barakat to say it again. A few minutes pass, and then he says, "And this part of the tomb was *expecially* unique."

Dahlia and I both crack up, trying to keep our laughter down. She hides her smile behind her hand, and I wish she wouldn't. She's got one of those smiles I could stare at for hours.

"I won't let you give up your share of the money." I didn't mean to get so serious so soon, but the words just sorta fell out of my mouth.

Dahlia pretends to be unaffected, but I catch the way she sucks in her breath. Avoiding this situation much longer won't do any good. If Francisco finds out she left, he'll remove her from the will. She has to come back before that happens.

"You should be happy about this." She clenches the arms of her chair, her knuckles turning white. "Everything goes to you now."

"Do I look fucking happy?" I turn to face her. "Look at me, Dahlia, and tell me if I look happy to you."

"There's a lecture going on," she says, gesturing ahead.

"I don't care. Look at me."

After a few moments, she faces me. She's stoic, but her eyes say it all. She's battling something.

"Why do you even care?"

Question of the century. Why do I care?

I look around at the classroom, taking in everything—the walls, the students, and the professor standing in front, wearing a dull gray suit, speaking in his monotone voice, still leaving me clueless as to what is so great about being here.

"For whatever insane reason, my dad wanted us to live together inside of Kent House until we graduate. If you leave now, you're dishonoring his last wishes."

"I can't go back, Wesley."

"Why not?"

"I want to…" She shakes her head. "But I can't."

"Are you in some kind of trouble?" For the first time, I start to think something might be wrong. "Tell me what's going on. I can help you."

"I'm not in trouble, I swear. This was my choice." Lowering her eyes, she adjusts the strings on her hoodie. "I appreciate your concern, I really do, but I moved out for a reason, and honestly we don't know each other well enough for me to owe you an explanation."

"You're throwing that in my face again?" My voice rises, and a few nearby students turn their heads. Whispering heatedly, I say, "I'm *trying* to get to know you, but you're making it almost impossible."

"You had three years for that." She stands up, throwing the strap of her tote over her shoulder stiffly. "There's no point now."

With that said, she walks away, garnering curious stares from several students as she exits the room. I get the feeling she doesn't cause scenes too often. Even small ones.

As much as I want to, I don't follow her. Maybe she's right about me being too late. It could be a lost cause. Even if it is, I guess I don't care.

~ ~

When I get back home, I regret not following Dahlia. All of the pointless junk in this house reminds me half of it should be hers. Hell, all of it. I used to think I cared about what happened to everything. Generations of the Kent legacy was built inside this house, not just my dad's legacy. I have a responsibility to ensure its survival.

But at the end of the day, they're just things. After college, I had planned to take the money and run. Go exploring. Fund a new expedition. Anything to make life more exciting without Sam.

Telling myself this is about my dad's will makes it easier to deal with the fact that Dahlia is gone, but deep down I know it's not what's tearing me apart. It's the not knowing. Not knowing where she is and what sent her running. Why hold out for three years, and then give everything up overnight? There's something wrong with that picture.

Without thinking about what I'm doing, I flip open my laptop and search for Dahlia online. I'm not sure what I'm looking for. Clues, I guess.

Most of her Facebook page is set to private, which doesn't surprise me. I scan the list of our mutual friends. There's only three, Charlotte, Miles, and Hayes.

Calling Charlotte is pointless. Even if she knew anything, I doubt she'd tell me.

Hayes, on the other hand, lives right down the street from us and has been friends with Dahlia for years. He might know something, and more importantly, he owes me one. I pull out my cell phone and dial his number.

"Hello. Wesley?"

He sounds surprised to hear from me. I don't call him on a regular basis.

"Hayes, I need to ask you something."

"Okay."

"You're still good friends with Dahlia, right?"

He pauses before answering. "Yes."

"Do you know where she is?"

"I um…I'm not real sure…"

"Don't lie to me, Hayes."

He clears his throat, and I can tell he knows where she is. After what went down at the bar the other night, he can't say no to me. He owes me this. "I don't think she wants anyone knowing where she went. She'll murder me if I tell you."

"She'll get over it."

"Why do you care anyway?"

There's that question again. I want to growl out that what motivates me is none of his or anyone's damn business. But I don't. I get why he's asking. I've never paid attention to Dahlia before now, and I shouldn't care.

"That's between me and her."

Hayes sighs heavily. Whatever he knows, he's having trouble saying it. "She moved in with her ex."

"She…what?"

I wasn't prepared for that. I'm so stunned, I'm not sure I heard him correctly.

"She's living off campus with an old boyfriend," he explains. "From high school"

"Uh. Okay." I have no fucking words right now.

Giving up everything for a guy doesn't seem like Dahlia. I know I never knew that much about her, but based on what I do know, this seems extreme.

"It's not what you think. They're not back together or anything."

"Then what is she doing there?"

"Maybe you should to talk to her about that. I'll tell you where his condo is, but the rest is her story to tell."

Images of Dahlia with some other guy take over my imagination. Of them sharing a condo. Of them sharing a bed…I'm not okay with this.

"Wes? Do you still want the address?"

"Yes," I snap without meaning to.

Hayes notices. "Hey are you okay, man?"

"I'm fine," I say, grabbing a pen. "Just give me the address."

My blood is boiling beneath my skin. I feel like beating the shit out of whoever this guy is that took Dahlia away.

Whatever happened last night, it was enough to change my mind about Dahlia Reynolds. Whoever she is, she's someone I never knew I wanted to know.

CHAPTER THIRTEEN

DOLL

"You should wear less clothes."

I look away from the article I'm reading on my laptop and over at Jordan. She's sitting on her bed, concentrating on painting her nails a bright shade of glittery pink.

"I'm wearing shorts and a tank top," I say, almost dumbfounded. These are the smallest pair of shorts I own, and I haven't worn anything like this since my junior year of high school.

"Yeah, but you should wear less. Styler likes it when we wear less."

Jordan curls up her hand and blows on her nails. Part of me thinks she's about to crack a smile, but she doesn't even blink. She's dead serious.

I shut my laptop, trying not to gape. "Did Styler ask you and the Fanta twins to walk around in your underwear all the time?"

Styler is sleazy, but it's hard to believe he's *that* sleazy.

"He didn't ask us to, but he said he likes it when we do. And we like to keep him happy so…" She shrugs. "We do what he likes."

"Why?"

Disgust is probably written all over my face, but I can't help it.

"It's not easy finding housing this close to campus, rent-free," she explains. "A girl's gotta do what a girl's gotta do, right? Tuition isn't cheap these days."

"No!" I say, shaking my head in horror. "No, no, *no!*"

Jordan glances up at me, surprised by my outburst.

Standing up, I say, "We're long past the days of women's lib, hun. You get a job, apply for scholarships, live on Ramen noodles if you have to." I start pacing because I'm so worked up, keeping my eyes trained on Jordan. "But you never *ever* degrade your integrity for some guy because he pays your bills. Nothing is worth more than who you are. If you sacrifice your character, you have nothing left."

"You mean he's not paying your rent too?"

Actually, Styler and I hadn't discussed that yet. But now that I'm thinking about it, I decide I'll be paying my own way while I'm here. I never needed a job while I was living in Kent House. But that doesn't mean I can't find one now. I've waited tables before. I can do it again.

"No, he's not paying my bills. I plan to work and make my own money. "

Looking unimpressed, Jordan begins working on her right hand. Apparently she's not big on girl power.

"So why are you here then?" she asks me. "You obviously don't care much for Styler. Why not go live somewhere else?"

"It's a temporary arrangement," I say, trying to stay vague. Telling her about the map is out of the question. "I want something he has. He's agreed to give it to me if I live with him this semester."

"So you're saying you wouldn't live with him under normal circumstances?"

"No, but—"

"So technically, you're sacrificing yourself for what you want too."

"It's not the same thing. I'm—"

"It's *exactly* the same thing." Jordan sets down her nail polish and looks up at me. "We're both here for something we want. Who are you to go all judgmental on me?"

I open my mouth, then shut it again.

Damn.

She's got me there.

"You're right." I sink back onto my bed, speechless. "You're so incredibly right."

We're no different. I hate myself for what I've sacrificed in order to be here, and yet here I am. Swallowing it all and living with Styler all because of something I want.

Looking at Jordan is like staring at a reflection of myself, only she isn't as bad as me. She actually enjoys walking around in her underwear.

My phone rings from the nightstand. Gwen found it nestled in the back of her purse after the party and brought it by earlier today.

Charlotte's smiling face lights up the screen. I take a breath, collecting myself, then answer her call. "Hey, Char."

"Doll, my love, do you know what tomorrow is?"

My eyes drift to the gift-wrapped box sitting on the floor next to my bed. "Um, it's Sunday."

"Yes, but what's special about it?"

"I don't know, is it a holiday?"

"Stop messing with me," she giggles.

"Oh, I remember now. It's your twenty-first."

"That's right!" she squeals happily.

Her enthusiasm is contagious enough to make me grin. "So what are the plans? Is Miles taking you out to get hammered?"

"No, we're going to dinner together tomorrow night. But the clubs on Sunday are lame."

"You should go out tonight," I suggest. "They'll serve you at midnight."

"My thoughts exactly—and you're coming with me!"

"What?" I fumble with the phone, almost dropping the thing. "What did you say?"

"Do you realize that neither of us has celebrated a birthday together since high school? Last time was my sweet sixteen luau. I remember because that was right before my boobs filled out."

"And Jason Miller pulled off your coconuts."

"God, I don't know what I was thinking," she groans. "I'm still traumatized."

"No one saw anything."

"Except for Jason, and trust me, his expression is forever burned into my memory. I'll never forget it."

I bite my lip to keep from laughing.

"Anyway, back to my birthday plans. Are you coming or what?"

Let me see, how do I tell her no in the nicest way possible? This is Charlotte Hart we're talking about. People don't say no to her, not even nicely.

"I don't know, Charlotte. I um, I'm not really the going out type. I'd rather celebrate with you later on in the week."

"Doll, don't start this crap."

"I'd just be in the way. I'm sure all your sorority sisters will be there, and I don't want to be the one hundredth wheel."

"No, it won't be like that, I swear. They have a pool party planned for me during the day tomorrow. Just me, you, and two of my closest friends. That's it."

"You should go," Jordan mentions casually. I hold my phone against my chest, prepared to give her my most menacing stay-out-of-it look, but then she adds, "Styler is staying home all night. He's planning to work his magic on you, whatever that means."

Nausea swiftly grips my stomach. I place the phone next to my ear. "Where and when should I meet you?"

~ ~

Hypnotizing melodies fill the small pub, too many people crammed inside because the band is a local favorite. Sitting at a bar around so many people without my makeup makes me anxious and uncomfortable. Since Gwen isn't around to do it for me anymore, and I haven't learned to perfect it myself, I don't have another option. Without it on, I feel like I'm standing in open gunfire, no bulletproof vest to protect me.

"I'm so glad you came!" Charlotte shouts over the music. Her pink lips curve into a smile as she sways to the slow song playing.

"Yeah, me too."

I sip from my cranberry juice, happy to find the bartender paid attention when I discreetly asked him to give me a virgin. Drinking so soon after the last time seems like a bad idea, and one of us needs to be sober enough to drive. Charlotte and her friends are already too far gone to fill that position.

"You look different," Vanessa tells me, slurring her words. "But in a good way."

Vanessa and Bryn are my favorite of Charlotte's friends. They're both the typical, cute sorority girls, and they're also genuinely nice. I'd been worried the catty girls from her party would be here tonight, but thank God she didn't invite them.

"You'd look better without these." Charlotte snatches the glasses off of my face before I can stop her, holding them up high above my head.

"Give them back, Char." Those are my last pair; the first I lost in the cab with Wesley the night he brought me home from Graffiti Bash. I can't afford to lose those too.

"Oh, my," Vanessa breathes. "You should look into contacts, hun. Those things aren't doing you any favors."

"Holy shit, you're a knockout!" Bryn adds, gaping at me. "Char's right. You need to ditch the librarian look. I know it works for some girls, but your face is so much prettier like this."

"Thanks," I say, not wanting to come off as rude. I do like hearing their compliments—what girl doesn't—but it's harder to appreciate when I'm out in the open like this. It reminds me of how much I'm revealing.

Reaching over Charlotte's head, I finally catch hold of my glasses. Charlotte and I play tug of war for a second, both of us yanking too hard. The glasses fall to the floor. Charlotte stumbles forward, her foot landing directly on top of the lenses, shattering them into tiny shards of glass.

She holds a hand over her mouth, her eyes rounding innocently. "Sorry, Doll. It was an accident."

I scowl at her, knowing damn well that step forward was too contrived to be accidental.

Vanessa pats my shoulder. "Don't worry, hun. She'll buy you new ones, won't you Char?"

"Course I will." Charlotte adjusts the sparkly tiara she's wearing, smiling wickedly. "Better ones."

Replacing my glasses will be next to impossible though. It took me weeks of searching to find the right style big enough and thick enough to change the shape of my eyes, and when I finally did, I purchased two, never thinking I'd lose them both.

"Twenty-one!" shouts some random guy carrying a tray full of shots. People have been buying Charlotte drinks all night, especially after they see her tiara. I feel bad for Miles; he's going to get the crappy end of this night. Literally. Because at this rate, she'll be waking up next to the toilet bowl, with Miles holding her hair. At least he's the type of boyfriend that does things like that.

Sort of like the way Wesley carried me through Kent House and cooked for me.

I wince, cursing at myself. As hard as I try, I can't keep my mind from wandering back to the perfection of his chiseled face and pretty blue eyes. I need to stop thinking about him, stat.

Forgetting him would be much easier if he hadn't come to Professor Barakat's class. I can't stop replaying the things he said and the way he looked at me over in my mind.

None of it makes sense. I forfeited everything, allowing him to inherit Harland's entire fortune. He should've been dancing on rooftops, not sitting beside me in the lecture hall, staring at me with those sad eyes, wanting so badly to understand my motives. I can't wrap my head around why. We're nothing to each other. The two of us amount to one kiss and a whole lot of confusion.

Granted, it was one really amazing, unforgettable kiss...

I groan, shaking my head. The not thinking about Wesley thing isn't working out very well.

"Hey, pretty girl. You want a shot?" The guy holds out his tray of shots, offering me one.

Looking around, I see everyone holding up theirs. Charlotte clinks hers against the glass of some guy I don't recognize, then looks over at me, giving me a little nod to get me to take one.

"Sure, thanks."

I wait until everyone is busy downing theirs before dumping the contents of mine on the ground.

"So what's your name?" the guy with the tray asks me.

It's just a simple question, one that shouldn't bother me. But it does. I've become so used to staying unnoticed. This guy is trying to strike up a conversation with me, which wouldn't happen if I were wearing my normal disguise, and it makes it clear just how exposed I really am.

My stomach lurches unexpectedly. "Excuse me. I don't feel so well."

I hop off my barstool and weave through the crowd, looking for the restroom. I find it near the back door. There's a huge line though, and I don't really need to go. I just need to get away for a moment. I need some air.

I push through back door, apologizing to the people I'm bumping into along the way. The outside air is humid, but it makes me feel a little better. I walk down a back alley to get away from all the smokers and the noise of the bar. Once I'm alone, I lean back against the building's brick wall and take a few deep breaths.

Staring up into the night sky, I wonder what the hell is wrong with me. When moments like these come along, I worry I've let my disguise run my life. It shouldn't be this hard. I should be able to go out and have fun with Charlotte, the way we used to in high school. I should be able to dance and laugh, and flirt with cute guys without feeling exposed.

Whoever this person is I've turned into, I'm not sure I like her.

"Dahlia!"

Around the corner, I catch sight of Charlotte stumbling out of the building. She's shrieking my name, waving her cellphone around frantically.

"What's the matter?" I ask, jogging over to where she's standing.

"A fight just broke out at the Estates between Wesley and that asshole you dated in high school. Everyone's gathered around outside watching. Do you know anything about this?"

My heart begins beating through my ears, the blood rushing from my face. Styler's condo is at the Estates. How the hell did Wesley find it?

"I need to get out of here."

"What's going on?" Charlotte asks me. "And what is Styler doing in Gainesville?"

"It's a long story."

"Don't care. You're telling me on the ride over because I'm not missing this."

"I don't want to ruin your birthday, Char. Stay and have fun. I'll be back later to drive you guys home."

"Oh, no you don't." She sticks her arm up to hail a cab. "I'm going so don't try and stop me."

"What about Vanessa and Bryn?"

Charlotte waves her hand in the air as if leaving them is no big deal. "They're busy making out with those guys that bought us the shots. They're not going anywhere anytime soon."

A taxi stops along the side of the street. Charlotte opens the door, holding it open for me. I hop inside and give the driver the address.

"Start talking," Charlotte says once the car takes off. "Don't leave anything out."

Grudgingly, I tell her how I left Kent House to live with Styler, how he's holding the map over my head in order to keep me with him, and that Wesley isn't taking any of it the way I expected.

"Styler always was a grimy blackmailer," she seethes. "What he's doing doesn't surprise me. But Wes? Since when does he give two shits about anything involving you?"

Heat rushes to my cheeks, giving me away.

"Oh my God—did you sleep with him?"

"What? No!" I say right away. "There was one kiss though, and well, I've been able to see a different side to him—"

"Dahlia Reynolds! You *like* him."

My whole face feels like it's on fire now, especially from the way she's grinning. "No, Char. I mean…God I don't know."

"You do. It's written all over your face."

"He's ignored me for three years. I don't want to like him. I don't want to have anything to do with him."

She leans back against her seat. "Wes isn't perfect, I'll give you that. But he's not one of the bad ones either. Maybe there's a reason the two of you are finally coming together. Maybe this is like fate or something."

I laugh, unable to help myself. "I doubt it goes that deep."

"How do you know? His father could be working some ghostly magic on the two of you from the other side." She shakes her head. "Man, this is enough to sober me up."

"Told you to stay at the bar."

"Please," she snorts. "Watching Styler get the shit beat out of him will be worth it. Don't think I don't remember how he cheated on you with that slut in the girl's locker room. What was her name?"

"Frankie, I think."

"That's right. Skanky Frankie."

The taxi pulls into the Estates a few minutes later, and sure enough, there's a crowd hovering outside by the gazebo. Charlotte and I push and shove our way through.

"It's all over," someone shouts, sounding disappointed. "Nothing more to see."

The crowd begins to break apart, allowing us to reach the center of it. Styler is sitting on a curb, wearing only a pair of jeans. He's using his shirt to stop his nose from bleeding, the white fabric soaked in red.

Wesley is standing on the other side of the gazebo, looking much better off. There's a small cut above his brow, and he's sweaty, but other than that, he looks fine.

"Wes?"

When he sees me, he freezes. "Fuck," he groans, his face dropping. He runs a hand through his hair and lets out a long breath. "I didn't mean for you to see any of this."

"I just got here," I admit. "So I didn't actually see anything."

He leans against the side rail, sighing.

"Are you okay?" It seems like a stupid question. Compared to Styler, he is much more composed and a lot less beat up. But I remember how adept he is at hiding his pain. If he's hurting, he won't show it.

"I'm fine."

My eyes drift over his stomach, looking for signs of his cut opening. There aren't any detectable bloodstains.

"So why were you fighting with Styler?" I ask, surprised at how calm my voice sounds. On the way here, I was angry enough to start a fight of my own.

Wesley looks directly at me. "He told me about the map."

My heart picks up it's pace. I don't want him knowing about that. I don't want him equating this all to a simple treasure hunt.

"There's more to it than what you're thinking—"

"Doesn't matter what I'm thinking. You left because of it, and now it's yours. Get your things. You're going home."

"Home? Wait a second, what do you mean it's mine?"

Wesley doesn't answer me. Instead, he leans forward and looks at Styler. "A deal's a deal, man. Give her the map."

Styler nods and gingerly picks himself up off the ground. Paola is there trying to help him, but he brushes her away. He limps over to where I'm standing, lowering the shirt from his blood-smeared nose. Sweat drips from his face and chest, and he breathes heavily, exhausted. Wesley walks ahead a few paces, giving us privacy.

"He fought me for the map," Styler says quietly. "My testosterone got the better of me, and I went along with it like a fucking idiot."

Wesley went to those lengths—for me?

My brain is having trouble processing this. Across from where we're standing, I see him lean against his motorcycle. He's talking to Charlotte, but I can't make out what they're saying.

"I'm sorry, Sty."

I don't know what to say. His pride looks wounded, and strangely, I feel bad for him.

"There's nothing for you to be sorry for."

I touch his arm. "Come on, let's get you cleaned up."

He shakes his head, brushing me away. "No. It's bad enough that I lost. I don't think I could handle you patching me up on top of that."

I nod, backing off. "Okay then."

"Just tell me one thing, Doll. Did I ever stand a chance?"

I fidget with the bracelet I'm wearing. "Styler—"

"Tell me the truth."

I look up, meeting his miserable gaze. "No," I whisper honestly. "You cheated on me, Sty. There are no second chances for that."

"I was a sixteen-year-old dumbass."

"Monogamy isn't your thing. Look around you, Sty. You surround yourself with women. I'm not saying there's anything wrong with that. It's who you are."

"I would've ditched them all for you."

"Maybe for a little while, but you wouldn't have been happy. We were never on the same page."

He knows it's the truth. I want the necklace. I want the guy who will choose just one woman to give his love. Styler was never that guy.

"I'm sorry," I say again. "I really am."

His eyes tighten around the corners. He looks sad, the pitiful kind of sad. But I know he'll get over this. Styler has never been one to let himself be depressed over a girl. He'll rebound quickly.

"So what's with this guy?" he asks me, nodding toward Wesley. "Is he the one for you?"

I snort, surprised by the question. "Why would you say that?"

"Because his eyes haven't left you once since we started talking. Because he fought me for you. And I'm guessing he would've stopped at nothing."

I quickly peek over my shoulder at Wesley. He's still standing there talking to Charlotte, but he keeps his eyes on me.

"He's Harland's son," I explain, shrugging. "We live together, but we're not close or anything."

Styler wipes his forehead with the back of his hand, then looks back at me. "I don't know if I buy that. He fought me like his life depended on it."

"Apparently he gets in a lot of fights. Trust me, this isn't anything new for him."

"No, Doll, you don't understand. That guy wasn't leaving here without you."

I rub the sides of my arms, uncomfortable with where this conversation is headed. "Are you really planning to give me the map?" I ask, hoping to change the subject.

"I always intended to give it you. Whether I convinced you to live with me or not, it was meant for you. My way of saying sorry. For high school. For everything."

My eyes begin to water. I can't speak for a moment, and when I finally do, my voice comes out squeaky. "You found it for me?"

"Yeah, of course." He sniffs and wipes at his nose again. "I remember how hard you and the old man searched for it. When I heard he passed, I knew I needed to get it for you."

"Wow, Sty...I don't know what to say."

"You deserve it, Doll. You don't need to say anything."

"Does this mean we're friends?"

"No." He shakes his head. "We'd make terrible friends."

"Oh. Okay."

"But it does mean I'll never forget you."

I smile. That's enough for me.

~ ~

WESLEY

"What game are you playing at, Wes?" Charlotte asks as she studies me.

"What do you mean?" I lean against my motorcycle, not taking my eyes off Dahlia and her ex. "I'm not playing any games."

"Yeah. Okay. Like I'll believe that." She snorts. "So what is this about? You're practicing to become the next world-fighting champ?"

I don't bother answering that question.

"Or do you have something to prove, huh? You gotta show everyone you're bigger and badder than the rest of them?" She steps closer, forcing me to give her my attention. "Everyone at Thrill-Seekers Anonymous will be so disappointed to know you've relapsed again."

"What do you want from me, Charlotte?" I growl out.

She points toward Dahlia. "That's my best friend right there."

"So you've told me."

"Where's your sudden interest in her coming from? I've known you since freshman year, Wes, and the only interest you've ever expressed was in getting the hell away from her."

"I know." I swallow, hoping Dahlia isn't aware of that. "I was wrong. She's not...she's not what I thought she was."

"And you're just now figuring that out?"

Yeah, I am. It didn't matter before. I didn't want to know her. One night can change your life, I guess. But since I'm not ready to deal with those feelings, I'm definitely not shedding any light for Charlotte.

"I don't want to talk about it, Hart. What are you doing here anyway? Isn't it your birthday?"

"Aw, you remembered. How sweet."

"Saw it on Facebook. Congratulations. Now you can legally do what you've been doing for years."

"Thanks for the well wishes. Truly heart-warming."

"You know what I don't understand?" I say, glancing at her. "How are the two of you friends?"

"What doesn't make sense about it?"

"Well for one, your personalities are like night and day."

She rolls her eyes. "We're not as different as you'd like to think. And you don't know her personality well enough to judge it."

"Okay, point taken. But I've never seen the two of you hang out before tonight."

Charlotte swallows, and I know I've hit a sore spot. "We've both been busy, and we have different things going on. I'm a Journalism major and she's Anthropology. It's not as easy as it was in high school."

"And yet I've seen you make time for less important people."

Like every member of her sorority. She's one of the most social people at the university, which is why it's hard to buy her story about being Dahlia's so-called best friend.

"You don't know what you're talking about. Doll and I get together when we can. Just because *you've* never seen it, doesn't mean it doesn't happen." Charlotte looks away, inspecting her perfectly manicured nails. Something changes in her face, quieting her attempts to draw information out of me. That's when I see it. Guilt.

Now it's all starting to make sense. They probably were good friends at one time, but not anymore. That's where the guilt steps in.

"I'm glad you're getting her away from Styler," Charlotte says in a softer tone. "I still don't know what you're up to, and I don't like not knowing what you're up to, but I am grateful to you for getting her away from him."

"What's the deal with those two anyway?"

I shouldn't have asked. Dahlia's love life is none of my business, and Charlotte will probably say as much.

Then she surprises me by actually answering. "They just grew out of each other." She glances over at me. "And Styler is a scumbag, but that's beside the point. Thanks for giving him the bloody nose, by the way. Made my night."

I want to ask Charlotte why she thinks he deserves it, but I keep my mouth closed, feeling like my limit of questions has been reached—especially since I haven't been as forthcoming as her.

"Glad I could entertain you." Tearing my eyes away from Dahlia, I turn to face Charlotte. "You should stop by the house this weekend. We're having a party. I'm sure Dahlia would like to see a friend there."

"But she never goes to your parties."

"Yeah, well…she's never been invited before."

That's an understatement. We've never been invited into each other's lives, period. Looking back, I can see it now. Every word, every glance, every movement that passed between us was carefully played out with the bare minimum of interaction. I don't know how we ignored each other for so long, but I'm done. There's something about Dahlia I need to understand, and I think my dad knew that too. As much as I resented him, he never forced me to do anything I didn't want to, with the exception of my inheritance stipulations. There's got to be a reason for that.

"Will the two of you be able to get home okay?" I ask Charlotte, sliding a leg over my motorcycle.

Dahlia and her ex walk toward the apartment building, I assume for her treasure map and the rest of her things. Red and blue lights flash from down the street. The fight is over, but I don't want anyone pointing me out once the cops get here.

"Yeah, of course," she says.

I pull the clutch and start the engine. "Happy Birthday, Charlotte."

"Thanks." A small smile pulls at her lips. "See you later, Wes."

CHAPTER FOURTEEN

DOLL

"Check it again. Please make sure."

My stomach sinks as Hayes places the worn map Styler gave me back on my desk. "I'm sorry, Doll. It's only a partial."

I place my head in my hands, feeling like it weighs a thousand pounds. My whole body is anchoring me down, and I just want to melt into the floor. This must be what it feels like to watch your dreams disappear before your eyes.

When I was seven my mom brought home a crystal music box; it was a birthday present from my dad. I played that music box night and day, holding it for hours on end, staring at each intricate detail, watching the little dancing bears and ballerinas twirl, in a trance. One day it slipped from my hands. An accident. The crystal shattered, thousands of pieces laying broken across the tiled floor. The only gift I'd ever received from my dad was destroyed. I can't explain it, but I swore he knew I'd broken it, because I never heard from him again. The music box was gone, my dad was gone, and so were my hopes and dreams.

That's exactly how I feel now. Hopeless.

"Styler probably didn't know any better," Hayes says softly, a sympathetic look on his face. He lifts his hand as if he wants to pat me on the shoulder, then changes his mind and tucks it safely against his side.

"I'm sure he didn't, but still…I put my inheritance on the line for this thing, and it's only a partial."

"Better you found out now, rather than at the end of the semester."

I squeeze my eyes together. This hurts way too damn much. Way more than it should. It's only a treasure map, I try to tell myself. Short-lived fame and museum mentions are the only things waiting at the end of that road.

Deep down I know I'm lying. It means so much more than that. It was supposed to be my freedom. My chance to prove myself.

Would I have really gone through with it though? The Kents come from a long line of explorers, but I'm not sure I ever had the chops to go on a real hunt. Maybe it was a pipedream all along.

A knock at the door pulls me out of my lapse into self-pity. I assume it's Gwen, so I yell, "Come on in."

The door opens slightly, and I see Wesley's head peek around. I jump up from my desk chair and smooth out my shirt. His gaze locks with mine, and I hope I don't look as depressed as I feel.

"What's wrong?"

Guess I didn't do such a great job. "Nothing, I'm fine."

The door opens wider, and Wesley's eyes drift around the room. He nods hello to Hayes, then looks back at me. "You don't look fine."

"I um…it's nothing," I sigh. "Just a disappointing morning. Apparently the map Styler gave me was only a partial—and not the part I need."

Wesley winces, as if he understands that kind of disappointment. I'm sure he does, considering all the treasure hunting he has under his belt. "I'm sorry," he says softly. "I know it meant a lot to you."

I shrug as if it's no big deal. "There's still a chance I could track down the rest of it."

"Let me know if there's anything I can do to help."

With his skillset, he's probably one of the best people out there to ask for help, but I know I won't. I already feel indebted to him as it is. For last night. For the map. For giving back half the inheritance he could've easily claimed for himself.

I move closer to where Wesley's standing. There's something I need to say to him, but I'm not sure how to say it.

I glance at Hayes. He walks to the far side of the room and stares out the window.

"Listen," I say to Wesley. "I never got the chance to thank you for what you did last night."

"It's nothing."

"It was something to me. At first I wasn't happy with the way you and Styler handled it. It was stupid, on both your parts. Not to mention reckless, especially since you're still recovering—how's your stomach by the way?"

"Fine." One corner of his mouth pulls up into a grin. "Don't worry, he didn't hurt me."

"I-I wasn't worried," I stammer. He makes it sound like my concern goes deeper than it should. "Look, when everything is said and done...I appreciate it. So thank you."

"You're welcome." He rubs the back of his neck, looking like he has something else to say. "I ah, know of a way you can repay me."

"Of course. Anything."

"Let me take you out to dinner."

"What?" *Did I hear him correctly?* My brows raise, and I'm almost positive I look as shocked as I feel. "You want to take me to dinner?"

"Yeah."

"But...why?"

In the background, I hear Hayes clear his throat uncomfortably.

Wesley's voice lowers. "I want to get to know you, Dahlia. We're here for a reason, you and I, and we've never put much effort into figuring out what that reason is. And apart from that, I like you."

I bite the inside of my cheek, not knowing how to react.

I like you.

Those three little words reverberate inside my head over and over.

This is not how things work around here. Wesley and I are supposed to be strangers, living here until we can safely extract ourselves from each other's lives. We're not supposed to care about each other. We're not even supposed to acknowledge each other. When did that change?

What he did last night was amazing and selfless, and I'll never be able to express my gratitude enough. But it's like my mind can't fully trust him, like he's the pet snake I've felt comfortable around while it was tucked away inside of its cage. Except now he's been let loose with no glass barrier between us, leaving me under the constant fear of being bitten.

I don't want to get bitten.

Wesley Kent has fascinated me for years, but now that he wants to know me too, I can't understand why—or why *now*.

"So what do you say? Go out with me?"

His blue eyes watch me expectantly, glimmering with hope. Part of me wants to say yes, but the other more sound part of me knows if I do, there's no going back. He's the type that could make me do something crazy, like fall in love. And that poses a problem. I've watched girls fall for Wesley over the years. Stupid girls. Intelligent girls. Beautiful girls. Creative girls. It doesn't matter what type of girl he's into, because there's none I can remember him being attached to, no one he let stick around for more than a few weeks.

"I can't," I finally say.

Although I'm pretty sure I was never in love with Styler, what he did was enough to make me learn my lesson. There's no reason to repeat that mistake.

"You can't?" The way he says that gives me the impression he doesn't get told no very often. "Why not?"

"Because…because…" My eyes drift around the room as I scramble to come up with a good enough answer. I see Hayes in the corner, and I blurt out the first thing that comes to mind. "I have a boyfriend. Hayes and I are dating."

Hayes spins around and chokes out, "We're what?"

I glare at him, daring him to contradict me. He closes his mouth, his lips thinning into an annoyed scowl.

Wesley looks at us both, absorbing the news. "You…and Hayes," he repeats as if he's trying to work it out in his head, "are together?"

"Uh huh." I sidestep my way over to Hayes and wrap an arm around him, plastering a proud smile on my face. "Hayes and I are together."

Hayes tries to shrug away from me, looking extremely grossed out by my display of affection. I shoot him a desperate look, begging him to play along.

After about five seconds of us battling each other with our eyes, Hayes gives in, and then cringes before wrapping his arm around me too. "What can I say?" he says in the most blasé, monotone voice I've ever heard. "Our love is sweeter than apple pie. I can't get enough of this girl. She's the sun to my moon. My everything."

Oh God. I'd like to bury myself beneath a rock right here and now. Wesley slowly, making me wonder if he fully believes us.

"Okay, I get it," he says.

I'd like to know what exactly he gets. Does he think I'm trying to avoid going out with him, does he believes Hayes and I are dating? Although I doubt he's that stupid, I'm hoping it's the latter.

"By the way, Hurricane Hector steered off its course," Wesley tells us, pausing by the door. "The weather forecast predicts it'll hit north Florida around midnight. I'm going to board up the windows. The last thing this old house needs is storm damage."

Panic erupts inside of me, seizing my breath. The reaction catches me off guard. Storms have never frightened me before. Violent thunderstorms have been passing through all summer, and the most I do is flinch.

Hurricanes are different though. I've never gone through one without Harland or my mom. I'm an adult now though, and I need to get it together.

"You okay?" Wesley asks me. "You look pale."

"I'm fine," I say, waving a hand in the air. "Is there anything I can do to help?"

"Yeah, actually I noticed we're out of batteries."

"Okay. I'll pick some up at the store. What about candles?"

"I don't think we have any of those either."

"All right then. I'll get candles and batteries. Anything else?"

"That should be good. Thanks." He glances at me one last time and then disappears out the door.

The moment he's gone, Hayes pushes away from me, making *ick* noises as he holds his arms away from the rest of his body. "I need a shower."

"Oh stop it. You endured two whole minutes of human contact."

"I want to douse myself with bleach."

I roll my eyes. "Your repulsion is doing wonders for my self-esteem."

"Why, Doll? *Why* would you make something like that up?"

"Trust me, it wasn't to torture you."

"Then what in God's name possessed you to tell Wes the two of us are," Hayes pauses to shiver, "a couple?"

"I don't know, I panicked," I say, my voice sounding semi-whiny. "Going out with him is a bad idea, and I don't want to hurt his feelings, especially considering how nice he's been to me lately."

"Why is going out with him a bad idea?"

I grab my purse hanging on the wall hook. "It just is, Hayes. Now please drop it and come to the store with me."

"I'll come." He pushes his glasses up the bridge of his nose. "But this conversation is not over."

When we get outside, Wesley is already out there stacking boards in a pile on the front lawn. "Quick, hold my hand," I whisper to Hayes.

"No, thanks."

I reach for his hand, but he dodges me. "Hayes," I say through ground teeth. Glancing over my shoulder, I look to see if Wesley caught that, but he's busy setting up a ladder. "Will you cut it out?"

He scowls, letting out a frustrated breath. "Fine. But you owe me for this, Doll. Big time."

"It's a deal. Whatever you want."

He links his fingers through mine. "Just so you know, I never got the point of this hand-holding business. It seems like such an archaic, insignificant gesture. I mean what is our physical contact really doing for you? Other than giving you a sweaty palm?"

"We're trying to convince Wesley we're a real couple, Hayes."

"Well I doubt he's buying it, but that's not what I meant."

He's probably right, but I've already dug myself this deep in the hole. Might as well keep going with it.

We stop in front of my Nissan, and I wait for Hayes to open the door for me. When he doesn't, I let out a frustrated sigh and open the driver's door for myself. Hayes gets in on the other side, buckles up, and then takes out a bottle of hand-sanitizer from his pocket. The smell of alcohol fills the car as he slathers it between his fingers.

"Holding hands is comforting," I say, turning the key in the ignition. "And romantic."

"Exactly how is it romantic?"

"I don't know." I shift the car into drive, then press my foot against the gas pedal. "I guess it's like saying I am yours and you are mine."

"Why not just say it? Wouldn't it be easier?"

"I suppose so, but don't you think it means more when someone shows you how much they care, rather than using their words?"

"Personally, no."

"Well most people aren't like you, Hayes. Most people appreciate affection. Most people crave it." I adjust the rearview mirror, catching a glimpse of Wesley as I drive away. "How do you ever expect to have sex with someone if you can't bear to touch them?"

"Not all physical contact is repulsive to me, Doll."

"So you're saying sex isn't off limits?"

Hayes shifts in his seat. "I'm sure it will happen one day—with the right, hygienic girl."

Of course he would have to describe his ideal girl as hygienic. "Good to know," I say, smiling. "There's hope for you yet."

The nearest drug store is only five minutes down the road. When I pull in, the parking lot is packed. Looks like everyone in town is stocking up on their supplies. "Geez, do you think there will be anything left?"

"This is what happens when you're not prepared. My mom and I keep an entire closet stocked with supplies and canned goods for emergencies like this."

"Harland was never big on preparation. Most of the time he was the absent-minded professor."

"You're like that too, Doll. I've seen you stay up all night in research mode."

Hearing him say that makes me pause. He's right; I have done that. Sometimes I'll be so engrossed by a book, I'll forget to go to class or miss an appointment. It's amazing how someone can rub off on you in such a short time. I used to think I was just like my mom. Turns out I'm more like Harland than I realized.

Customers shuffle past us, carrying their bundles of plastic bags. Hayes and I duck into the store, squeezing through the tight crowd. I spot a uniformed employee near the entrance. "Excuse me, where are your batteries?"

"Up front, but all we have left are triple A's."

Dammit. "Okay, thanks."

Hayes and I throw a few packs into our basket, and then we look around the store for candles. We find them a few minutes later in a back isle.

"There aren't any plain-scented ones left," Hayes says while scanning the racks. "Looks like your only options are tropical hibiscus and fresh rain."

"Might as well go with the theme of the night," I say, throwing a handful of the fresh rain into my basket.

We head toward the register to checkout, stopping short when we see the line. "Holy Mother of God," Hayes mutters.

I crane my head around to see what he's talking about. The line is so long, it snakes along the side of the store. Grumbling, we weave around the people and take our places at the back of it.

Hayes shifts his weight to one leg. "Since this is bound to take a while, it's the perfect opportunity for you to tell me what happened back there with Wes."

Wesley's voice flows through my head, causing me to shiver. *I like you.* My stomach does a little flip at the memory. "Do I have to?"

"Yes, you have to," Hayes snaps, almost indignantly. "I'm parading around acting as your personal man candy; I think I deserve an explanation."

I squeeze the handle on the basket I'm carrying, unsure where to begin. Hayes has known us for years. He's watched Wesley and me keep our distance from one another without asking a bazillion questions. He's always been the don't ask, don't tell type, and I appreciate that about him. Charlotte and Gwen mean the world to me, but sometimes it's a relief to hang out with someone who doesn't press to know all your baggage. Moving here right after my mom died, that was incredible to find in a friend. He just accepted me, no questions asked. But I guess I couldn't expect him to stay that way forever.

I let out a small sigh. "The other night Wesley and I spent some time together. It's hard to explain, but something happened. It's like we finally saw each other."

"That's…interesting." Hayes scratches the side of his head, blonde pieces of hair falling across his forehead. "So your weird estrangement is ending. Doesn't seem like such a bad thing."

"Not at all," I say, stressing that point. "Getting to know him has been a great experience. He's actually sort of likable, and since I've always thought otherwise, I'm happy to be proven wrong."

"So why are you opposed to going out with him?"

There's the loaded question. I stare at scuffmarks on the floor, thinking. There's no right way to answer that. "He and I simply aren't a good idea."

Hayes's eyes drift over the line of people. "Still quite a few people in line."

I rest the weight of my shopping basket to one hip. Enlisting Hayes as my pretend boyfriend may have been more trouble than it's worth. I prefer the don't ask, don't tell version of him.

"I've lived with Wesley a long time," I say, thinking back to when he first moved in. "I may not know him that well, but I've seen enough of his history with girls. And before you say anything, I know I shouldn't judge people based on their past. It's just…he's Harland's son. Whatever relationship I have the ability to form with him, I want it to be a positive one."

I look up, seeing that Hayes is listening to me thoughtfully. The line moves and we take a few steps.

"And you think if there's romance involved, it won't be positive?"

"Pretty much."

He considers that for a moment. "Do you remember how we met, Doll?"

I smile, picturing that day in my mind. "Yeah, I remember."

It rained most of the morning, and when it finally stopped, Harland sent me to pick up take-out for dinner. Along the way, I noticed Hayes trying to push his car out of a muddy ditch. Being the compulsive freak he is about dirt, he wasn't getting very far on his own. I stopped to help him push his car back on the road, and he looked at me like I was an angel sent from heaven. We've been friends ever since.

"I've never told you this," he begins, his tone intriguing me. "But when you and Harland first moved in, my mom told me go over to your house and make you feel welcome."

"I don't remember that happening."

"Because I never did."

I lift a brow. "Why not?"

"I don't know. You were this beautiful girl, a few years older than me." He pauses, and I see his mind working to explain himself. "I figured we'd have nothing in common, and worse, that you'd want nothing to do with me. And Harland—well Harland was intimidating. I'd heard the stories about him. He was known as the famous archeologist around town…do you get where I'm going with this?"

"I think so."

"My point is, we'd have never become friends if I didn't give you a chance."

"Lesson learned. Never be nice to the weird kid. You'll get stalked for life."

Hayes grins. "In all seriousness, I'm glad you pulled over for me that day."

I set the basket down on the floor and stretch out my arms. "Aw, Hayes. That deserves a hug."

He backs up, holding his hands up to ward me off. "We've touched enough today to last me a lifetime."

I start to laugh when the woman behind me taps my shoulder. "You're next," she remarks brusquely, waving me on to the checkout counter.

"Sorry." I quickly pick up my basket. Hayes and I exchange a small smile as we scamper toward the register like children who've just been scolded.

"Hey, I've been meaning to ask you something," I say to Hayes on the way back to the car. "Did you have anything to do with the bar fight Wesley got into?"

"How did you find out about that?"

"I heard his friends mention your name." I unlock the car doors, and we both slide into our seats. "It was the night he came back."

Hayes fastens his seatbelt. "Last year I helped him map out a side project for his Egypt expedition."

"A side project?"

"Yeah, but don't ask me anything about it. Wes was extremely secretive about what he was looking for."

"What did he want from you?"

"He asked me to decipher a few hieroglyphics he couldn't figure out."

"Were you able to?"

Hayes cocks his head to the side. "Seriously? Have we met?"

"All right, all right. Enough with the ego. So are you saying Wesley used the school's expedition as a cover for his own personal treasure hunt?"

Hayes nods. "I think so."

I shake my head, wondering why I'm surprised. Harland used to do the same thing, using his role as a professor to buy him access to whatever locale he had in his sights. Wesley is definitely his father's son, even if he doesn't want to admit it.

"So what does all this have to do with him getting in a fight?"

Hayes stares at the dash. "The night Wes got back, he asked me to meet him at bar near campus. He wanted to celebrate and thank me for helping him. I think he found whatever he was looking for."

"You? A bar?" I ask, smiling. "I'm shocked."

"Despite being closely confined with a ton of strangers, it was fun. That is, up until these guys cornered me outside. They caught wind of the research I did for Wes, and they thought I knew more about it than I did."

"So they tried to *beat* the information out of you?"

"Well, not exactly." Hayes tugs at his shirt collar. "First they tried to scare me, but apparently I'm an aggressive drunk. The liquor gave me a feeling of invincibility, making me believe I could take on three guys by myself."

I clamp a hand over my mouth, picturing Hayes trying to be a badass. He probably looked like a feisty Chihuahua trying to take on three Rottweilers.

"I'm glad you find this amusing, by the way."

Beneath my hand, my grin spreads wider. I try to remind myself it's not funny, and that Wesley was seriously hurt as a result of this, which finally gives me the ability to put on a straight face.

"Sorry. Please continue."

"After that, Wes found out what was going on, then came outside and stepped in. If he hadn't been drinking, I honestly think he could've held his own."

I don't tell Hayes about the stomach wound Wesley had at the time of the fight, and how that probably limited his capabilities as well. "Good thing he stepped in when he did."

"Yeah. Guess I'm pretty lucky." Hayes shifts in his seat, and I know he's thinking about what might have happened if Wesley never came to his aid. "You should give him a chance, Doll. He's not so bad."

Now that I think about it, Charlotte said something similar. It's ironic to me how everyone says Wesley isn't so bad, but no one talks about how great he is either.

"You should go to dinner with him."

"Maybe."

I start the car and twist the knob on the stereo. I'm silent on the drive back to the house, thinking about my conversation with Hayes. The logical part of me knows he's right. Fearless people intimidate me, and Wesley is one of the most fearless people I've ever met. He carries himself as if he can belong anywhere, whether it's in a wholesome American college campus or deep in the deserts of Egypt, radiating an unwavering comfort within his own skin. It's the type of confidence fear deprives me of having for myself.

My fear of Wesley gets in the way, but that only scratches the surface. I'm still bitter, I think. For years I've wondered why we avoid each other, but I've never brought it up. I'd rather pretend he's an empty shell like his bedroom, allowing myself to feel justified in not trying, than to simply ask him why we never speak. God, and it's such a simple question. Why didn't I ever walk up to him and say, "Wesley, why are you ignoring me?"

I've been too afraid to ask questions. Too afraid to find out why he couldn't stand be in the same house as me.

If I tried and failed, it would be like failing Harland. After everything he gave me, the thought of failing Harland is just…unbearable.

"Isn't it strange how blue and cloudless the sky is?" Hayes murmurs, staring out the window. "The sun is shining bright, no detectable wind or sign of a storm coming. It's like Mother Nature wants you to let down your guard, and then she goes in for the kill."

I glance across the seat at Hayes, giving him a look that lets him know he's freaking me out. "Good thing Doppler radar does what it's supposed to."

When we pull into the driveway, a few of the windows have already been boarded up. I look for Wesley and spot him on top of the ladder, hammering away. I sit there in my car for a few seconds, unable to look away from the muscles straining through his white T-shirt.

Hayes shuts the passenger door, and I flinch. I get out of the car, start walking up the long driveway, and the next thing I know, I'm being screamed at. Loudly.

"I've never been so disgusted in all my life!"

My eyes round on Hayes incredulously. His normal, eloquent speech reverses to a deep southern twang within a matter of seconds, and he's furiously pacing the pavement.

"Um, why are you yelling at me?"

"Drop the act, sweetheart. My momma warned me you weren't nothing but a two-timing hussy!"

My gaze flicks to Wesley. He pauses his hammering to listen to us, and I suddenly get it. Hayes is creating a scene on purpose.

"This isn't necessary," I whisper. "I can just tell him we're not really dating."

"Don't try to sell me your sob story, sweetheart. It won't work!"

I roll my eyes, groaning. "Hayes."

He spins around, pointing at me. "You and I are over. You got that? O-V-E-R, over!" With a dramatic huff, he stomps off to the side of the house where he keeps his bicycle, leaving me standing there, speechless.

I look up and catch Wesley doing a bad job of hiding his grin. Heat rushes to my face, and I hurry inside the house before I die right here of humiliation. I can't believe Hayes did that to me—and in the way that he did it—God I'm never going to forget that. If Wesley didn't suspect we were lying before, he certainly knows now.

I shut the door behind me and drop my bags. I dig through my purse for my cellphone. When I find it, I send Hayes a text.

Hope u burn in hell!

Only a few seconds pass before it dings again.

:D

Nothing else, just the stupid little smiley face. I throw my phone back into my purse, wishing I could punch something.

CHAPTER FIFTEEN

WESLEY

I want to laugh my ass off, but I wait until Dahlia's inside before I do. From the look on her face and the way her cheeks turned bright red, she didn't know Hayes planned to dump her so dramatically on our front lawn. She looked like she was dying, and I couldn't help but enjoy every moment of it—serves her right for trying to feed me that shit about Hayes being her boyfriend.

I'm boarding up the last window and still chuckling when Francisco pulls up in his black Audi. He steps onto the circular driveway, takes a look around, and lets out a low whistle. "Look at you, stepping up to be a real man of the house. Here I am, thinking I need to come over and help you out with this stuff, but you've already got it taken care of."

I wipe the sweat from my brow, squinting at him through the sunlight. "I'm not an idiot, Francisco."

"No, you're not." He takes a few steps toward me, carrying a brown paper bag. "But you've never seemed to care much about this place."

"I don't want to see it destroyed, especially while I'm living in it."

"Point taken. But why didn't you get one of the staff to see to it?"

"I gave them all time off." I shrug one shoulder. "Figured a hurricane was a good enough reason for them to spend time with their families."

"Is that so?" He looks over me as if he's sizing me up. "You look different today. Happier."

"Classes were delayed. Everyone's happy." I can't tell him Dahlia is the reason I'm grinning like an idiot. More questions would follow, and I don't have the answers to those questions. "What's in the bag?"

"A lock for the library door." He holds it out for me to take. "In case the electric goes out."

"You really think someone would try to rob us in the middle of a hurricane?"

"You never know. There are a lot of valuables in there. Better to be prepared."

I take the bag and tell him thank you, even though I doubt anyone would be that stupid.

"So how is everything?" he asks casually.

"Fine. The same."

"Have you applied to any schools yet?"

"Getting my master's isn't the right path for me, Francisco. You know that."

He manages to both smile and look sad at the same time. "Shame you don't think so. Archeology is in your bones."

"Doesn't mean I have to give it up."

"True." He looks over his shoulder at the white Nissan parked in the driveway. "Dahlia here?"

"Yeah, she's inside."

"I noticed her car wasn't here yesterday."

My muscles stiffen. Although I've been close to Francisco for years, I feel the need to protect Dahlia from him. I'm not sure if her moving out for two days gives him the power to remove her from the will, but either way, I'd prefer he didn't find out. "It was her friend's twenty-first birthday."

"So she stayed out all night?"

"Last time I checked, we didn't have curfews."

"Take it easy, man. I was only asking because that's odd behavior for Dahlia. I'm happy she went out to have some fun; she needs to do it more often." He looks up at me, studying me closely. "Is everything okay with you two?"

"Why do you ask?"

"I don't know. You don't usually involve yourself in Dahlia's business."

"I'm not involved now." My hand tightens around the bag, crinkling the paper. "Just wanted to make sure the rules hadn't changed."

I can tell he's doing his thing again—trying to read between the lines. "Well I better get going," he finally says. "I have my own fort to hold down."

"Thanks again for the lock."

He stares at me a few seconds longer before heading for his car. "Call me if you need anything."

I wave goodbye, feeling strangely relieved. Without thinking about what I'm doing, I run into the house, and keep running until I'm upstairs inside my dad's old bedroom. Standing there in the middle of the room, I look around, wondering what the hell I'm doing. I haven't been in here since his funeral, and I really had no intention of ever coming back in here.

Everything looks and smells the same. Mahogany furniture, desk in the corner, and the scent of the cologne my dad wore in the air. It's almost like he isn't gone.

Almost.

I do my best not to think about why his presence is still so strong. When people die, everything they leave behind should die with them. This room shouldn't still smell like his cologne. The furniture should be just that, furniture. I shouldn't see a desk my dad imported from Morocco. I shouldn't see the chair he shipped from India because the craftsman told him it would bring him luck. Or the bed he and my mom bought right before he disappeared.

My dad is everywhere in this room, and it fills me with anger all over again. I'm angry because when I look around, I see only the good parts of my dad. I'm angry because I never got the chance to tell him how much I hated him for leaving without an explanation. How much I hated him for throwing away the perfectly good life he had with Sam, my mom, and me—and it was fucking perfect too. If my dad was unhappy, he did a damn good job of hiding it. That's what pisses me off more than anything. He walked out on us without leaving me any bad memories to hate him for. I sort of wish he had. Would've made things easier.

I walk to the desk drawer and open it. Inside there's an unopened envelope with my name on it. I never saw any point in reading it. Whatever my dad needed to tell me, he should've said while he was alive. I didn't want to give him the satisfaction of thinking he righted his wrongs.

Carefully, I pick up the envelope, feeling like it weighs a thousand pounds. Something has changed between now and my dad's funeral. I'm not sure if it has to do with Dahlia, or if it has to do with this being my last year in Kent House, but for the first time since I moved in, I want answers. I want to understand.

Everyone in the room is quiet as Francisco explains the details of my dad's will. I'm listening, but I don't hear him. The things he's saying, what my dad wants me to do—it's too much for me to swallow.

My mom tenses in the chair beside me. No one else apart from me knows her well enough to know she's barely suppressing her anger. I send her a look to tell her to stay calm. Her face tightens, but she doesn't say anything.

"So you're saying he wants me to enroll at the university?" I ask Francisco. My voice sounds as confused as I feel. He's already explained it once, but I can't seem to let the information sink in.

"That's right." He shuffles a pile of papers together, then pushes them toward me and my mom. "It's all there in his will. You and Dahlia must remain in Kent House for the term of four years, obtain any bachelor's degree of your choosing, and then you'll both stand to inherit the house, Harland's belongings, and all of the monies in his accounts, which total to approximately four and a half million dollars."

"Why does he want us to live together?"

I glance across the table at her, *examining the girl my dad decided to stick me with. Dressed in all black, she's sitting there staring out the window, a lifeless look on her face. I don't think she's heard a word that's been said, but then again I haven't paid attention too much either. I wonder what's going on in her head. They say my dad's death didn't come as a shock. Apparently he'd been sick for months, but the girl looks like she's in shock. I'm not sure if I buy it—the tear-streaks on her pale face, the sadness in her eyes—who the hell cares that fucking much about my dad? I sure as hell don't, and I'm the only family he had left.*

"Wes? Wesley? Are you listening?"

I look up at Francisco. How long has he been trying to get my attention?

He points to the envelope with my name on it. "I don't know his reasons, Wes, but I imagine they're in that letter. Maybe when you read it, you'll get a better understanding."

I fling the letter across the room, missing the trashcan by a few inches. "I don't give a shit about understanding Harland Kent."

Francisco's face drops into a pained frown. I immediately feel like an asshole, because Francisco isn't a bad guy. He's just doing the job my dad left him to do.

When I look up, I notice I've caught the girl's attention. Her eyes are glued to the envelope I've thrown. I hold my breath, wondering if she's one of those hysterical girls, the kind that burst into tears. God, I don't think I could fucking handle hearing someone cry right now. All I want to do is bring my dad back to life so I can strangle him for what he's put my mom through—what he's continuing to put her through even in death.

But the girl doesn't cry. She slowly gets up from her chair, crosses the room, and picks up the envelope from the floor. Almost robotically, she sets it on the table next to Francisco and then walks out the door without saying a word.

As soon as she's gone, my mom slams her fist against the table. "This is ridiculous!"

"Mom, stop—"

She pushes up from her chair, the legs screeching against the floor. "Explain to me why Harland expected my son to share half of his inheritance with that girl—that nobody! We're talking about generations of Kent heirlooms passed down to the daughter of one of his sluts—"

"Mom!" I pierce her with a hard look. "This isn't about you."

She stands there for a few seconds looking startled. I've never yelled at her before. I'm sure she wasn't expecting it. After a moment, she grudgingly takes her seat again. I know there's a lot more she'd like to say about my dad and his girlfriend, but I've heard it all before. Screaming and complaining about how much of a dirtbag my dad was isn't going to change anything.

Francisco places his hand across my mom's, squeezing gently. "I understand that you're angry, but you should know that Harland loved Dahlia like a daughter, and well, he's the closest thing to a dad she's ever had."

My mom purses her lips. She doesn't care. She can't see anything pass my dad leaving her for another woman, and I don't blame her.

"It's fine," I tell Francisco. "Draw up the papers. I'll stay here the four years."

"You don't have to do it, Wes," my mom says, her voice sounding depleted. "You can make your own money. There's no need to be his puppet."

"And watch years of my ancestor's treasures go to someone outside the family? I don't think so." I nod to Francisco. "Draw up the papers."

She's not happy about my decision, but she doesn't say anything else. There's no changing my mind. I'm not doing this for my dad; I'm doing it for my grandfather and his grandfather before him. I'm doing it for myself.

Hours or seconds may have gone by, I'm not sure which. Time and space absolve within the walls of this room. I'm still holding the envelope, debating whether or not I'm ready to read his last words. There's something in me that wants to know, but whatever it is, it's not strong enough to get me to open the envelope right now. Even written down on paper, I still can't bear to hear his voice, so I stuff it inside my pocket and leave the room.

CHAPTER SIXTEEN

DOLL

Apparently hurricanes come with perks. All classes are postponed until next week, giving me plenty of free time. Unsure of what to do with myself, I sit in bed eating popcorn and watching TV. Summer classes are officially over. There are no more exams to worry about. No more papers to turn in. Normally, I spend any extra time I get researching, but I'm still too disappointed over the map. I need some distance from it for at least a day or two until I can get my head straight. Besides, I'm content to do nothing for now. It's nice to be in my own bed again. Sometimes I hate Kent House, but then there are times like these when I feel completely at home.

When Gwen breezes in through my door wearing a miniskirt and bright red lipstick, my mouth pulls into a frown. Miniskirts and red lipstick are her favorite date night combination.

"Are you going out?" I ask.

"Yes, ma'am! Your advice worked. I told Luke I was dating someone and *bam*! He invites me to his friend's hurricane party."

"What?" I sit up straighter, kicking my legs off the bed. "But you said he lives in Tallahassee."

Gwen shrugs. "Apparently he's down here for the weekend." She checks herself out in my vanity, running a hand through her long dark hair. "Isn't it great, Doll? I finally get to meet Mr. Sexy Voice."

"Can't he wait until tomorrow night?" There's a slight pleading in my tone. "I brought up two bottles of wine from the cellar. Oh and look." I dig beneath my bed, pushing boxes aside until I find the right one. "We can do girl stuff, like mani-pedis."

"Since when do you like doing mani-pedis?"

Ignoring her question, I hold up the nail kit I ordered a few weeks ago and show it off like I'm a spokesperson for QVC. "It comes with all these little stickers and gems. Cool, huh?" Biting my bottom lip, I wait for her to answer, praying she'll be impressed enough to stay. Being stuck by myself in a torrential storm sounds like a nightmare. I don't want to go through it alone.

"No way. I've waited years for Luke to come around. I'm not missing out on an opportunity like tonight."

My mouth forms a pout, and I narrow my eyes on Gwen, the traitor. "Where's your loyalty? Oh never mind," I grumble. "The penis has been winning that battle for centuries."

"What's with you today?" she asks, laughing.

"You're challenging my codependency issues."

"You are not codependent." She taps her chin as she looks at me. "Are you afraid of the storm?"

"Oh please." I sit back against my pillows, refocusing my attention to the TV. "That's ridiculous."

"You *are* afraid of the storm."

"No, I'm not."

"It's only a category two, Doll; it won't be that bad."

I don't care what category it is. Hurricanes come with tornadoes, strong winds, a lot of rain, and a high probability of the electric going out, but I don't voice those thoughts aloud.

Gwen plops down on my bed, leaning back on her arms. Her lips expand into a devious smile. "Here's an idea. Why don't you call your hot roommate into your bedroom for a slumber party?"

I change the channel, trying to act as if that idea doesn't appeal to me in any way whatsoever. Even though it does. A lot.

"You know I'm not going to do that."

"I know." She sighs as if I'm a lost cause. "You'll probably sit in your room all night watching *Ancient Aliens* or some other dumbass show on the History Channel."

"First of all, that show is entertaining," I say in my most serious voice. "Second of all, I was excited to watch chick flicks and do nails until you came in here and ruined my plans." I grab my bowl of popcorn and start crunching on a handful dismissively.

"He likes you, you know."

Fidgeting with the remote, I stare at the TV guide and pretend to tune Gwen out. "Oh look. *Ancient Aliens* is on."

"When he found out you were gone, he had this look of devastation on his face. He came in here looking around your room, all lost and sad. It was really cute."

I glance at her sideways. "You could be describing a puppy."

"That's how he looked. I swear."

"Yeah right."

"It's the truth. You can't deny it, especially after telling me what he did to get you back here."

I like you.

Those words haunt me all over again. I think about telling Gwen how Wesley asked me to go out on a date with him, but then I realize I would have to explain why I said no, and by the time she got done lecturing me, the storm would be here. And as much as I wish she weren't leaving me to fend for myself, I'm kind of glad she's finally meeting Mr. Sexy Voice. She seems really happy about it, and she deserves to be happy.

"You look nice. Luke will be head over heels."

"Is this your way of dodging all Wesley conversation?"

"Maybe." I shrug evasively. "But it's also the truth. Hope you have fun."

"Seriously?"

I nod. "Seriously."

"Okay." Her red lips pull into a hesitant smile. "Are you going to be all right?"

"Of course." I look around the room. "This place has held up for far too long to let a little hurricane destroy it."

"Very true." She pushes up off the bed. "Well I better get going. I need time before the storm gets here in case I decide to leave the party."

"Why would you need to leave?"

"You never know. What if there aren't any sparks?"

"There will be sparks, Gwen. There has to be."

"Hope you're right." She checks herself out in the mirror one last time before leaving. "Call me if you really start to freak out," she says, closing the door behind her. "I'll talk you through it."

"I won't freak out," I shout back. "Because I'm not afraid of a stupid hurricane."

Her heels click against the floor as she makes her way down the hall, growing fainter and fainter with each step. A strong gust of wind blows against the house, forceful enough for me to hear it. I look at the clock on my nightstand. Still a few hours to kill before it gets here. With any luck, I'll sleep through the whole thing.

I watch TV until dark. The winds begin to pick up their pace, growing louder and faster against the walls. Grabbing my headphones, I plug into my mp3 player, hoping to block everything out. It works for a while, and eventually, I fall asleep.

I'm not sure how long I'm out because when I wake up, it's still dark. I pull off my headphones, blinking into the darkness. It's raining now, but I can't see anything outside my boarded window. Spiraling winds rush against the house, shaking the walls. I flinch at the sound.

Was it too much to hope I'd stay asleep?

For a few delusional seconds, I lie there in my bed with my eyes shut. It doesn't take long to realize there's no going back to sleep. I look at the clock on the nightstand. The brightly red numbers are missing.

No, no, no.

Just to make sure, I try switching on the TV.

Nothing. The power is definitely off. Another howling wind rattles the window. I jump off my bed, hugging my arms to my chest.

I don't like this, any of it.

The havoc being wreaked outside is too noisy compared to the quiet of my electronic-free room. There's something unsettling about the contrasts. I need the humming of my fan, the buzz of my television—something to keep me calm.

Then I remember. The batteries. I left them on the kitchen counter along with the candles. I grab my flashlight and leave the room in a hurry to get them.

The hallway is dark, and I can barely see a thing. I turn on the flashlight, but it doesn't help much. I hold out my free hand, running my fingers along the wall for a sense of balance. Up ahead I see the outline of one of the staff members hovering outside the library door. Seeing someone else instantly helps me breathe easier.

"Hey," I call out. "If you're looking for a generator, we don't have one."

The person swings around as I close the distance between us. When I look up, I stop in my tracks, my body going rigid. Dark eyes dart to mine beneath a black ski mask.

Not the staff.

I tighten my hand around my flashlight, feeling my heart slam against my chest. My mind furiously tries to grasp what I'm seeing, my eyes working hard to recognize the cool brown ones staring back at me. By the time I realize I should run, it's too late. They move first, rushing me all in two short steps, shoving me against the wall.

"Where is it?" a scratchy male voice growls. One of his hands presses against my ribcage, and the other he uses to hold my throat.

"Where is what?" My voice sounds small and choked, nothing like me.

His fingers dig into the sides of my cheeks. "Tell me where Wesley's hiding it," he demands.

"I don't know what you're talking about," I whimper.

My assailant moves just enough to give me room to lift my leg. I take advantage of the moment, kneeing him in the gut. He moves his hand away from my throat, grunting, but keeps me pinned beneath him. I squirm to get away from him, but I can't move.

So I scream.

With every ounce of voice I can draw out of my body, I scream.

CHAPTER SEVENTEEN

WESLEY

Noises come from upstairs, distracting me from the game I'm playing on my phone. Strange noises aren't unusual for this house, but this kind is different. Tossing the phone aside, I leave the living room and make my way into the foyer. I stand there for a few moments, listening, not sure what I'm listening for.

Screaming.

At first I think I'm imagining it. It can't be staff; I told the few employees that live here to take the night off and go be with their families. It must be the storm playing tricks on me. Howling winds, squeaky gutters—any of those things could sound like screaming.

But I'm wrong.

The screaming gets louder and more terrified. It's definitely not the storm I'm hearing. I break out into a run, taking the stairs two steps at a time. I'm halfway up when I recognize the voice behind that scream. *Dahlia*.

Fear grips my stomach, and I run faster. When I get into the hall, everything goes black. The boarded up windows shut out every ounce of light, and I don't have a flashlight on me. *Dumbass move, Wes.* I should've thought to bring one with me.

But I'm too terrified to go back for one at this point, so I scramble through the darkened halls, shouting for Dahlia and praying she hears me. When she doesn't answer, I start to break out in a sweat. Her scream didn't sound like it was over something stupid, like the kind girls do when they see a mouse. It was the ear-splitting kind that chills your blood.

"Dahlia, are you up here?"

She doesn't answer.

I continue to call her name, stumbling through the hallways. Each time I shout, the panic in my voice increases. Why the hell isn't she answering? Frustrated, I pound my fist into the wall. This place is too fucking dark. The longer it takes, the more pissed off I get.

Where the hell is she?

As I round the next corner, I recognize the library doors. Looking down, I catch sight of a flashlight lying on the floor.

"Wesley?"

Behind the flashlight, Dahlia is sitting on the floor, pressed up against the wall. She's holding her knees to her chest, violently shaking. Dropping to the floor beside her, I take her face in my hands. "What happened?"

She lifts her arm, pointing at something across the hall. I pick up the flashlight and steer the light in the direction she's pointing. Broken glass litters the floor. Above the glass, there's a busted window. I swallow. That window isn't storm damage; someone broke in.

The outside winds push against me as I make my way toward the window, rain needling against my face and arms. I look for signs of movement, but it's no use. I can't see anything through the storm.

"How long ago did they leave?"

When Dahlia doesn't answer me, I turn back around, shining the light on her pale face. She's still in shock. I go back to where she's sitting, kneeling beside her. I have no fucking clue what to say right now. Where do I even begin? She's still shaking and staring at the window, and I'm not sure how to make her any less afraid.

"Dahlia," I whisper. "Did they hurt you?" I hold my breath, afraid to hear the answer.

"No. Well…he grabbed my throat."

"He?" I ask, confused. "Did you know him?"

"I'm not sure. He was wearing a mask."

"How long ago did he leave?"

She lifts her shoulders in a small shrug. "Maybe five minutes."

I tilt her chin up, using the flashlight to inspect her neck. Angry red marks outline the imprint of fingerprints.

I lose it.

I pull her into my arms, crushing her against me. "Fuck, Dahlia. I'm so sorry."

The girl who shied away from me disappears. She wraps her arms around my shoulders, clutching the collar of my shirt in both of her hands. For a few moments she stays like that, stiff and trembling at first, and then slowly relaxing against me. "What are you sorry for?" she finally asks, sniffling.

"This may have been my fault." Heaviness weighs my voice down. "I think I know what they were after."

"Treasure?" she guesses.

"Yeah."

"Does it have to do with Egypt?"

I pull back, meeting her gaze. "How do you know about that?"

"Hayes told me," she admits. "He said you asked him to help you with a personal project. He also told me about the bar fight."

"Hayes has a big mouth," I grumble. Matter of fact, I'm beginning to think that's how Black Templar found out about the sword in the first place. "But yeah, I think that's what this is about."

She stays silent for a long time. Probably realizing she should hate me for this. I wouldn't blame her if she did.

"We should install generators and get a really good security system," she says, surprising me. "Allowing the Kent legacy to be stolen by some petty thief would be a shame."

"Wait a second—you're not angry?"

"Why would I be?"

"Because chances are, this is all my fault."

"Occupational hazards aren't your fault. It's Harland's for not installing generators. He should've seen this coming sooner."

She shifts her weight, laying her cheek against my chest. My whole body constricts as I try to keep my hands off of her. I've never comforted a girl before, but I'm pretty sure you're not supposed to grope them in the process. I should pull away from her altogether, but I can't.

"Sorry I didn't get here in time," I say, trying to distract myself. I smooth back her hair, unable to keep from touching the silky strands. "Then again maybe it's a good thing I didn't. If I'd have seen him hurt you, I would've killed the guy."

"He didn't really hurt me," she says, her voice a lot calmer than before. "He just scared the shit out of me."

"He put his hands on you." I run my fingertips down the side of her neck, knowing some of those red marks will turn into bruises. "That's hurting you."

She swallows, her throat rising and lowering beneath my fingers. "Should we call the police? Will the call even go through?"

"Yeah, we need to report it. But I doubt anyone will come right now." I gesture to the window. "Not in the middle of this."

Dahlia breathes in, slowly beginning to collect herself. She slides off my lap and pulls herself up off the floor. "They'll never catch him."

She's probably right, but I don't tell her that.

I stand up and hand her the flashlight. She takes it from me and shines the light on the library door. "Looks like he didn't get what he wanted."

The lock Francisco gave me is still chained to the door. Hundreds of thousands of dollars worth of collectibles are in there, but if the Black Templar assumed that's where I'd put the sword, then they're bigger idiots than I thought.

The sword is worth more than everything in the library combined. I'd never hide it in this house, let alone the library.

"Wes?"

"Yes?"

Dahlia folds her arms across her chest, hugging herself. "This is going to sound ridiculous, but is it okay if I um…" She can't seem to finish her sentence. "Is it okay if I…"

"Whatever it is, the answer is yes."

I can't see her face very well in the dark, but I think that makes her smile. "I was going to ask if it's okay if I hang out with you for a little while."

"You kidding me? I wasn't planning on letting you out of my sight." I reach for her hand. "Come on. Help me find the way out of here."

She sighs, sounding relieved, and points the light toward the stairwell. "Thanks. I probably shouldn't admit this out loud, but the thief isn't the only thing that has me on edge."

Almost as if on cue, a strong gust of wind pushes against the house, shaking the walls. Dahlia shudders.

"You're afraid of storms?" I ask.

"Not usually, but it's my first time going through one alone. There's always been Harland or my mom. I thought Gwen would be here, but she ditched me for a guy."

"Ditched you for a guy, huh?"

"It's almost unforgivable."

I squeeze her hand, grinning. "Well you're not alone anymore. Speaking of your mom, where is she? Does she still live in Savannah?"

We walk down a few steps. When Dahlia doesn't answer me, I glance over my shoulder. Her shadowed face grows sober. "Um…your dad didn't tell you?"

"Why would he tell me where your mom is?"

We round the corner, heading down the next flight of stairs. "She, ah, died a few years ago. I figured Harland would've said something."

I stop in the middle of the stairwell, going still. Her mom is *dead*?

"When did she die?"

"A little over a year before Harland."

I turn around, grabbing the flashlight from her hands.

She squints as I shine the light in her face. "What are you doing?"

"Trying to find out if you're joking."

"Why would I joke about my mom dying?" Her voice sounds slightly annoyed. "Are you suggesting I think it's funny?"

Her mom is dead.

I can't fucking believe it. That's why my dad kept her with him. All this time—I never understood. "Dahlia, I feel like such an idiot."

She narrows her eyes on me. "He really never told you?"

"No." I rub the back of my neck, looking away. "Then again, I never gave him a chance to explain much."

I feel the weight of her eyes on me. A few seconds pass, and then she shrugs one shoulder. "It's not a big deal, Wesley. I don't know much about your mom either."

"No, you don't understand. It *is* a big deal."

I'm unsure of how to explain myself. Part of me has always suspected the only reason Dahlia stuck around was to get a piece of my dad's money. Now I'm beginning to see Harland was all she had. My mind drifts back to the day Francisco read us the will. She seemed so lost, so devastated, and I couldn't understand why. The possibility of her genuinely being lost and devastated never crossed my mind. "I misjudged you, Dahlia. Completely."

"It's okay."

"I'm telling you I thought the worst of you."

A slow smile pulls at her lips. "I understand—and it's okay."

"Amazing." I shake my head. "I tell you I'm a judgmental asshole, and you smile."

"That's because I did the same to you. Granted, you never really allowed me the chance to get to know you, but I filled in the blanks where you didn't. So you see, we're both judgmental assholes."

"I don't understand. What blanks did you fill in?"

"Well," she says, tucking a piece of hair behind her ear. "I'm not proud of this, but I summed up your personality to a box of condoms and a set of dumbbells."

"Okay, now I'm really confused," I say, laughing. "Why condoms and dumbbells?"

"Because those were the only things I found in your—" She slaps her hand over her mouth.

"In my room?" I finish the rest. "You went through my room?"

"No!" She hides her face in her hands, groaning. "Well, sort of."

"Why?" I can't help but grin. She's still hiding her face, assuming I'm pissed, but I'm shocked as hell she was curious enough about me to go to those lengths. These past few days, she's made me believe she wants nothing to do with me. Knowing she's as curious about me as I am about her unsettles everything I've stamped down because of that.

"I wanted to know who I was living with," she finally says, her voice coming out muffled.

I reach for her hands, peeling them away from her face. "That's an invasion of privacy. You should be ashamed." I'm having difficulty keeping a straight face, but she doesn't seem to notice.

"I know." She winces. "I am really sorry. Trust me, it only happened once, and I'll never go in there again."

As much fun as I could have with this, I figure it's easier to let her off the hook. The embarrassment is practically killing her. "I hope you don't mean that."

Her brows furrow together in confusion. "You *want* me to snoop through your room?"

"You can go in my room anytime you want, babe," I say with a wink. "I promise I won't mind."

Speechless, she stares at me for a moment, then punches me on the arm. "I thought you were angry."

"Let's just call it even." I tug her by the wrist, heading back down the stairs. But there's still one thing I want to know. "So tell me, what exactly were you hoping to find?"

"I don't know. Pictures on the wall. A collection of hidden treasures. Your room is boring, by the way."

I laugh to myself because I've always hated having too much stuff. This house is filled with pointless things. Simple is better. For a treasure hunter, I suppose that's a strange habit. But the treasure doesn't drive me. It's the hunt.

"So you thought I was boring too?" I ask her.

"Not boring, exactly. More like vacant."

"That's not much better."

"If it makes a difference, I don't think so anymore."

"And what do you think of me now?"

"Um…I'm not sure yet."

We step off the staircase, entering the foyer together. Candlelight glows from the living room, brightening the space. I turn the flashlight off.

"Guess I'll have to help you make up your mind," I say, glancing over my shoulder.

Somewhere in this moment, I realize I'm going to pursue Dahlia with everything I have in me. She may have turned me down earlier, but I'm beginning to think it's all a front.

Who knows.

Maybe she's the kind of girl Sam dreamed about finding. Maybe she really is worth the chase.

CHAPTER EIGHTEEN

DAHLIA

The police tell Wesley pretty much what I figured they would. Since there is no immediate threat, they'll send an officer out to the house as soon as it's safe.

Wesley hangs up, tossing his phone on the couch. He moves to a cabinet in the corner and opens it, removing a small decanter. "Welcome to Hurricane Survival 101," he tells me, setting out two glasses on the coffee table. He pours an amber liquid into each glass. "First off, you need whiskey. Strong whiskey."

"Never tried it," I admit. He raises his brows at me, and I shrug. "What? I'm a wine drinker."

"Wine is for girls," he snorts, handing me a glass.

"In case you haven't noticed, I fit into that category."

"Trust me, I noticed." He clinks his glass against mine. "Cheers."

I lift the glass to my lips. "Wow." I crinkle my nose as the liquid sears its way down the back of my throat. "That *really* burns."

He laughs. "Forgot to mention that it takes some getting used to. Now let's get the second thing you need for hurricane survival."

"And that would be?"

He leaves the room, coming back a moment later with a deck of cards. "Do you play Crazy Eights?"

I lower myself onto the floor and tuck my legs underneath the coffee table. "Correction. I *win* at Crazy Eights."

His eyes widen for a brief moment. "Those sound like fighting words, little girl."

I don't mention how Harland and I used to play this game all the time. I also don't mention my photographic memory or how I've yet to be defeated. "Let's make things more interesting," I suggest.

"You want to turn it into a drinking game?"

I shake my head. "I mean, we can do that too, but I wanna figure out a way we can make it last longer." I chew on my lower lip, thinking. "How about this. Each time one of us is forced to draw from the stack, we say something about ourselves. Something we don't already know about each other."

Considering how we're basically strangers, it shouldn't be too hard to come up with things to talk about. But I have an ulterior motive. I *want* to get to know Wesley. Badly. We've got three years of not speaking at all to make up for. This might be the sneaky way of doing it, but at least I'll learn a few things about him in the process. "So are you up for it?" I hold my breath waiting for him to answer.

He trails a finger across his jaw for a moment before nodding. "Okay. But only if we drink every time that happens."

"Deal."

I bite back a smile. Before he knows what hits him, he'll be drunk and telling me his life story. I'm going to enjoy kicking his ass.

Wesley shuffles the deck, then deals us both a set of cards, putting the remainder of the deck between us. "Ladies first," he says, gesturing for me to go ahead.

I reveal the seven of hearts. I place my nine of hearts on top of it.

He sets down a nine of spades.

This goes on for a few turns until Wesley is forced to pick up a card. He sips from his whiskey. "So what do you want to know?"

"Anything. You can tell me what day your birthday is or you can tell me your darkest secret. It's up to you."

"Hmm…birthday or darkest secret." He looks up at the ceiling as he decides. "Obviously I don't know you well enough to reveal my birthday, so that's out of the question."

"And here I was, looking for something to blackmail you with."

"I'm fluent in French. Does that count?"

I look up from my cards. "Really?"

He nods.

"Prove it."

He stares at me for a long moment, then says, "*Tes yeux, j'en reve jour et nuit.*"

I suck in a sharp breath. That was seriously hot. Coupled with Wesley's rugged good looks, the soft romantic French is a huge contrast to everything I know about him.

"What does it mean?" I ask.

"It means, 'Would you like fries with that?'"

I frown, feeling let down. "Well that's lame."

There's a ghost of a smile on his lips, which makes me wonder if he's telling the truth. "Sorry, babe. You can say anything in French, and it would sound pretty." He sets down a card—the king of clubs. "Your turn."

I set down the two of clubs. "How did you learn to speak it?"

"Sam and I spent a few summers with our uncle in Morocco. He wouldn't speak to us in English. Only Arabic or French. Guess the French was easier for us to pick up."

"Harland never mentioned a brother."

He sets down the ace of clubs. "Because he doesn't have one. He's my mom's brother. That's how my parents met, through my Uncle Rooney. He's a geologist in Morocco. He and my dad teamed up on one of his expeditions back in the eighties. My mom was there visiting, and she and my dad got to know one another pretty well. They hit it off, and the rest is history."

I want to ask Wesley what happened to his parents, why they didn't work out, but I feel like it isn't the right time.

There's still bitterness there, and I don't want to ruin the lighthearted mood with a heavy subject.

"What'll it be, babe?" he asks me. "You out?"

Tapping my fingers against the top of my cards, I look to see what I have. I don't have aces, or clubs for that matter, which leaves me kind of stuck. I do have an eight, but it's too soon to give up my wild card. Holding onto the eights until the perfect moment to strike is how I usually win.

I draw from the stack and take a swig of whiskey, coughing because the taste hasn't gotten any better. "I served as a waitress in a sport's bar for two years," I say, wiping my lips with the back of my hand. "The cook was Italian, and he taught me how to make the best lasagna in the world. My mom and I practiced his recipe for a month before we got it right. That was our thing, cooking."

"You do know you're going to have to make this legendary lasagna now, don't you?"

"Didn't you hire a professional to cook for you? Why don't you ask *her* to make you lasagna?" I'm teasing, but there's a hint of contempt in my voice. I did a bad job of hiding it.

"Not anymore, I don't."

"Oh?" I say casually, setting down the ten of clubs. "What happened to Hannah?"

"My underhanded roommate fired her."

"Thought you rehired her."

He sets the ten of spades down. "I planned to, but then I realized how awful her food is. Don't know why I kept her around as long as I did."

Shock ripples through me. I thought for sure he'd let Hannah come back. The thought of never having to deal with her again, of never having to listen to her and Gwen's fights—oh man Gwen is going to be so freaking happy. I can't wait to tell her.

"She's really gone?" I ask, just to make sure I heard him right.

"Yep. Try not to look so pleased with yourself."

Am I that easy to read? I'm doing a little happy dance in my mind, but I thought I was keeping it suppressed. Guess not. "Who says I'm pleased?" I set down another card. "I couldn't care less who you keep on your staff."

He watches me over the top of his hand. "You're definitely pleased. Because deep down you know I did it for you."

My cards become a blur of numbers and shapes. I can't see any of them. "What do you mean you did it for me?"

"You didn't want Hannah here. And for whatever reason, the things you want are beginning to matter to me." He shrugs noncommittally. "So I let her go."

I hide my smile behind my hand of cards, feeling a blush work it's way into my cheeks. "Well…thanks for thinking of me."

"Anytime."

We continue to play, and Wesley reveals more random facts about himself. He hates cats, but he found one injured on the side of the road when he was eight, so he took it in and nursed it back to health. He's a huge soccer fan. Football is just okay, but I'm not allowed to say anything, because we live in Gator Nation, and it smacks of treachery. Like most guys, he can stay up until dawn playing video games. His favorite is *Call of Duty*. His favorite city is London. Also, he ended up telling me his favorite color, which is blue. "But I'm beginning to like amber too," he says, and it takes me a moment to realize he's talking about my eyes. I'm smiling so much over this, my cheeks start to hurt.

"I'm a huge *Star Wars* fan," I say, drawing a card. "But mostly because of the old ones, not the new ones. I'm not an old movie aficionada or anything like that. I just think the old ones have more heart."

"You're sexy as hell right now, do you know that?"

I don't say anything. Flirting never used to get to me the way it does with Wesley. He's like one of those songs you can listen to all day and never get tired of. I'm so affected and fascinated by him, I almost think he has a chance of beating me.

There's just one card in his hands when he's forced to draw again. His eyes watch me as he takes a drink.

"Well?" I prompt him. "Tell me about yourself. You owe me another piece of info. Make it a good one."

"I could tell you a lot of things," he says. "My birthday is July twentieth. I eat too much Chinese food. Also, I can't stop thinking about your lips."

Wow. Okay. That was definitely a good one.

I hold my breath, suddenly all too aware of my lips. A second ago they were a body part attached to my face. Now they're the only part of me I can focus on. And now I'm remembering what it felt like when my mouth was pressed against his.

He sets down a card. I set down one after his, not entirely sure it's a legal one since I can't think straight. "I'm onto you, you know. I see that you're trying to distract me." It just now occurs to me that I set down my eight. "And I'm changing the suit to clubs."

He sets down his last card—the four of clubs. "If I was trying to distract you, it worked."

I'm so stunned, I stare at his card for a few seconds, dazed. By my count, there shouldn't have been any more clubs in the deck. Diamonds and spades should be the only ones left. He actually beat me.

Well, damn.

I narrow my eyes on him. "You fed me compliments to distract me."

"Maybe. But I still meant everything I said."

"I demand a rematch."

"Fine by me," he says, grinning. "If you want to lose twice."

We play several hands of Crazy Eights, followed by a few of Go Fish. As the night wears on, Wesley moves the coffee table out of the way and places a blanket and throw pillows across the wooden floor. We continue to play cards on the blanket until we're both buzzed and sleepy.

"Do you hear that?" I ask him.

"What?"

"Silence. I can't hear the rain."

"We're in the eye of the storm," he says. "It's not supposed to be over until five in the morning."

I lay down, resting my head against one of the pillows. Wesley lies beside me, passing me the bottle of whiskey. I take a sip, no longer feeling the burn it caused when I first started drinking it. Now it goes down smooth and easy.

Wesley scrolls through his phone, trying to view his Doppler radar app. "No use. There's still no signal," he says, turning it off.

I give him back his bottle. He tucks it into the crook of his arms, staring at the ceiling. I stare at the ceiling too, watching shadows dance back and forth as the candle flames flicker. Most of them have burnt out, darkening the room.

"Hey Wesley?"

"Yeah?"

"I want to ask you something."

"Okay."

"I know why you misjudged me, and I get it. I really do." I turn my head to face him. "But why didn't we speak to each other? For three years, we just went about our lives without getting to know each other. For the life of me, I can't understand why."

Although that question has been weighing on my mind, I never really intended to bring it up. I don't think I wanted to know the reasons why. But there it is. Out in the open. Not sure if that's a good thing or a bad thing, but it's too late to take it back now.

Wesley's eyes tighten at the corners. "I don't know if I have a good answer for you."

"There are no good answers. Only the truth."

He lets out a small sigh. "It wasn't so much that I was ignoring you as it was pretending you didn't exist."

In some ways, that's worse than being ignored. "Your dad?" I ask, swallowing.

He nods. "Guess I was still trying to punish him even while he lay in his grave."

As much as I hate how it played out, I understand where Wesley's coming from more than he'll ever know. Although my dad is technically alive, sometimes it feels like he's dead. If I could punish him for that, I would. "Whatever he did to make you hate him so much, I'm sorry," I say. And I mean it.

"You didn't know that version of Harland," he says. "You cared about him."

"True," I allow. "But I do know a thing or two about deadbeat dads. Those are more common than you think."

His eyes shift to mine, and we both stay silent, frozen in the moment. Several seconds tick by. He continues to stare at me with so much intensity I'm afraid to breathe. "So what's your reason?" he asks, breaking the almost supernatural hold. "Why did you ignore me?"

I look away, refocusing on the ceiling. "It's obvious Harland wanted us to be friends. I figured if I tried and failed, I'd be failing his last wish. So I blamed you instead. Pretending it was all your fault gave me an out."

He doesn't say anything right away, and I'm afraid to look at him. In the space between us, I feel his fingers thread through mine. What did I tell Hayes about holding hands? Oh yeah. That it's a way of saying I am yours, and you are mine. A really powerful way of saying it …

"Wesley, I—"

"I want to kiss you."

My eyes dart to his. I shake my head. "Bad idea."

"How could it possibly be a bad idea?"

I don't want to tell him the truth. I don't want to tell him I can't remember the last time I had so much fun doing nothing. Or that I'm afraid that, like all moments do, ours will eventually come to an end. But most importantly, I don't want to tell him how afraid I am of jeopardizing whatever is going on here by confusing it with sex.

I like Wesley. I feel like I just found him. But I've seen how he works. When sex is involved, he doesn't stick around for long. Friendship is another matter. His loyalty is admirable; I've seen him stay friends with the same people for years.

I turn on my side, propping my head up on my elbow. "Here's an idea. What if we became friends?"

"I don't believe in being friends with girls."

I blink a few times, absorbing that one. "Why not?"

"Because someone will eventually develop feelings. I don't care how much you try to convince me otherwise."

"That's seriously the most ridiculous thing I've ever heard. Not to mention sexist. Lots of guys can be friends with girls. It happens all the time. I'm friends with Hayes," I point out.

"Don't you mean your ex-boyfriend, Hayes?"

"Okay, I should probably admit something." I twist my bracelet around my wrist, fidgeting with the charms. "Hayes and I were never really a couple."

"Wait—are you telling me your epic romance was all a lie?" Wesley starts to laugh. "I can't believe it."

Angry now, I shake my hand out of his. My gut told me he knew the whole time, but he could've said something and saved me the embarrassment.

In one quick movement, Wesley flips over me, pinning me beneath him. He traces one of his fingers over my lips. "Just kiss. I swear that's all we'll do. Afterward, we can carry on and pretend that nothing happened if you want."

My body goes completely still. He's hovering above me, and I feel like the patient in the board game *Operation*. The moment he even brushes against me, a loud buzzer will sound off like a warning. I shake my head to tell him no.

He lowers his mouth to the side of my head, pressing his lips against my ear. "Tell me you want me to kiss you. Please. I need to hear you say it."

His warm breath makes me shiver. Maybe it's the candlelight, or maybe it's the whiskey, I'm not sure, but my thoughts begin to slow down. One by one, they fall out of my head until I'm no longer thinking about anything other than the feel of him slowly pressing against my body, conforming mine to his.

I stare at his lips. There are so many good, valid reasons to say no, but I don't want to. It's almost killing me how much I don't want to.

"Kiss me, Wesley."

That's all it takes. His mouth collides into mine. Just like before, there's a magnetic energy attached to him. His tongue slips into my mouth, and it feels like the blood is rushing from my head. My hands glide up his back and into his hair. I try to touch every part of him I can grasp, memorizing the way he feels.

Before I can think about it. Before I can regret it.

I'm not thinking at all anymore, just feeling, and it's incredible. Explosive. Tormenting. Beautiful. I writhe my hips against him, doing anything I can do to get closer. When I feel the hardness between my legs, it makes me want him that much more. I begin to kiss him with a fierceness I didn't realize was in me.

"Fuck, Dahlia." He breathes against my neck. "We need to stop, or I won't be able to keep my promise."

"Don't care about your promise," I murmur. And I don't.

My body is developing a mind of its own. All I can think about is how amazing the pleasure and excitement he's driving into me feels. Ending it would be tragic.

Wesley lifts up slightly. "Have you ever done this before?"

I have a feeling the answer to that question might change the outcome of what's happening. I don't want to tell him the truth, but I know I have to. I shake my head, and as soon as I do, he drops his head against the pillow beside me. A muffled groan escapes.

"Why does it matter?" I ask, touching his arm.

I hate that he's not touching me anymore. Or kissing me anymore.

Wesley pulls himself up and slides away from me. "Trust me, it matters."

I scoot toward him, inching closer. "Wesley, I—"

"Stay right there." He holds out an arm as if to keep me at bay. "I need you to stay right there."

"This is crazy." I laugh once. "First you want me, and as soon as you know I'm a virgin, you don't want to be anywhere near me."

"That's not true." He takes a few breaths, still holding his arm out to ward me off. "Make no mistake. I want to fuck you into oblivion right now. You have no idea."

I bite my lower lip. Hearing him say that makes me want to beg him to do it. "So what's the problem then?" I try not to sound as dejected as I feel. It doesn't work.

I lean back against the pillows behind me, grabbing one and hugging it against my chest. I hear Wesley sigh and make his way back to me. He pulls my chin up so that I face him. "Your first time shouldn't be clouded by whiskey. You should have every available sense so that you remember the entire experience. The excitement. The awkward moments. How you feel. Everything." He tucks a strand of hair behind my ear. "Also, you deserve to be taken out on a date first.

You know, to make it special and shit. Girls like that kind of stuff."

I smile in spite of the way I'm feeling. He makes some really good points. But still…it sucks. No one ever told me just how much rejection sucks. I try to remind myself he's only rejecting me within this moment. And besides, this gives me ample time to collect myself and really think about whether or not I want to get involved with him. Only a few moments ago, I was convinced we should be friends and nothing more.

"Dahlia?"

"Yes?"

"Will you go out on a date with me?" He winks, letting me know exactly what that invitation suggests.

My smile grows wider. "Maybe," I say. "I'll have to think about it. I'm newly single, you know."

He grabs my ankles, hauling me toward him. I gasp, startled. He leans toward me, his face only centimeters from mine. "Dahlia?"

"Yes?"

"You're going out on a date with me."

"Um, I need to check my schedule."

"Dahlia."

"Yes?"

"I'm taking you to the goddamned Cheesecake Factory, and you're going to love it."

"Well now that you mention cheesecake…"

He presses his lips against mine as I giggle beneath him, but only for a brief moment. As soon as it's over, he backs away again. "Glad that's settled." He reaches for a pillow and lies down on the far end of the blanket and closes his eyes.

I shake my head, wondering what the hell I just got myself into.

CHAPTER NINETEEN

DAHLIA

Waiting for Gwen is making me antsy. There's so much I want to tell her. Everything that happened last night. Everything that *almost* happened last night. My head is still spinning. I need an outlet. I need my best friend. And besides, she made me swear an oath to give her details. I am proud to say I can live up to that promise.

When she walks in through the door, I jump up from where I'm sitting on the bottom step of the staircase. "Gwen, you're here!" *Finally.*

She pushes the door shut behind her, holding her heels in one hand and her purse in the other. Dark circles shadow her eyes. Something is off. Usually she wears her mood on her sleeve, but her face is solid as a stone.

"Everything okay?"

Her eyes lift to mine, as if she's just noticing I'm in the room. "I'm fine." But she doesn't sound fine. Even her voice sounds dead.

She slowly walks toward the stairs, lifeless, and I follow her. "Gwen, I can see that something is wrong." I move around her to block her path, which isn't hard to do since she's moving at the rate of a snail. "Whatever it is, you can tell me. Is this about the internet guy?"

She places one hand on the banister, steadying herself. "Doll?"

"Yes?"

"Do you remember how I asked you the other day why you stopped dressing and acting like yourself?"

I nod.

"And do you remember how you told me you couldn't talk about it?"

"Yes, but—"

"This is one of those things, Doll," she says, swallowing. Pain flickers in her eyes for a split second, and then it's gone again. "I can't talk about it."

"Jesus, Gwen. Please don't use that against me right now." I grab her by the arm. "Tell me the truth, did someone…" I can barely get the words out. "Hurt you?"

She stops and looks at me. I don't think she expected me to jump to that conclusion. "No." She shakes her head. "Nothing like that."

"You swear?"

"I swear, Doll. I'm just…" She looks up at the ceiling, thinking. "Disappointed, I guess. I found out some things I wish I hadn't known."

I watch her, feeling helpless. Not being able to fix what's wrong is killing me, and I hate that she doesn't trust me enough to talk about it.

"I'll be fine," she tells me. "Just give me a day or two, and then I'll be back to normal. But you can't ask me to talk about this, Doll. Ever. Do you understand?"

I don't understand anything. Not the way she's acting. Or why she looks like a zombie. Or what could've happened in one night to change her so drastically. But I nod my head anyway.

"Good," she sighs. "I'm going to bed. See you tomorrow."

It's still early in the afternoon, but I don't ask any questions. Part of me gets it. Some things are too difficult to talk about. It's easier to hide yourself away, spend all day in bed and shut out the rest of the world. The not talking scares me though. The kind of things you can't say out loud are the kind of things that break your soul. All Gwen did was go to a party. To meet a boy. She left here excited, looking for love. What could've been devastating enough to break her soul?

Disappointed now because I won't be spending the afternoon gossiping with Gwen, I don't know what to do with myself. The pit of my stomach twists and spirals until I'm forced to walk it off.

I head outside, curious to see what the grounds look like. Sunlight hits my eyes. It's shining so bright, it's as if last night never happened. The front steps creak beneath my feet. When I look around, my eyes roaming warily over the front lawn, I'm shown the real evidence of last night. And it definitely *did* happen.

Nature has deconstructed our once cheery, manicured lawn, covering it with piles of debris, branches, moss, and leaves. Our round driveway has been narrowed into small patches of white, the fountain in the center of it covered with some monstrous plant. I look back at the house and wince. The poor, tortured oak trees next to my window have broken limbs, some of them scattered on top of the roof. The flowerbeds running along the sides of the house appear ransacked, most of the mulch blown across the yard.

The whole place is one depressing nightmare.

"Hey, gorgeous."

The low rasp of Wesley's voice startles me. I turn around and see him walking toward the front porch, a trash bag in one hand and a rake in the other. He sets the trash bag down and wipes the sweat from his forehead with the back of his hand.

"Um, hi." Yeah, that wasn't awkward at all.

"Bout time you got your ass out here to help." He tosses me the rake. "This is your house too, you know."

"Didn't Harland hire gardeners to do this sort of thing?"

"Yes, but they have the day off, and we're perfectly capable of making this place look like our home again."

Our home. Those two words warm me all over. For the first time since I moved into Kent House, it's starting to feel like a home.

"Don't tell me you're one of those girls who's afraid to break a nail," he taunts me, a wicked grin pulling at his lips. "You afraid of getting a little dirty?"

His question seems suggestive, but maybe it's just in my head. After last night, all I can think about is the way it felt to be pinned down beneath him. And that's why my mind goes straight to the gutter.

"I am *not* one of those girls," I say, yanking the rake with me as I tread across the yard.

I hear him laughing behind me, and it pisses me off a little. He doesn't think I can handle yard work? Please. Just because I live in a mansion now doesn't mean I grew up spoiled. The big houses and servants are part of his world, not mine. I'll have this whole place back in shape before he even finishes with those boards. Then we'll see who's afraid of breaking a nail.

I throw the rake against the ground, sweeping it toward me. Out of the corner of my eye, I catch Wesley watching me, grinning, as he tears off a wooden board from one of the windows. I look away, refusing to pay attention to him, but I continue to feel his eyes bore into my back.

Shaking my hair loose from its hairband, I gather it together again and secure it more tightly against my scalp. Then I really get to work, sweeping the rake back and forth in quick strokes. Behind me I hear Wesley tossing boards into a pile on the ground. Hearing the little noises he's making as he works prompts me to go faster.

Before long, I have half the front yard bagged up into two trash bags. I lug them both over my shoulder, then toss them onto the front porch. Wesley rounds the corner, a pile of boards in his hand. One brow shoots up as he sees all the work I've done. He's impressed, but he doesn't say anything. In fact, it almost looks like he's picking up his pace too.

I go at the second half of the front yard with a vengeance, determined to finish before he does. I spare a moment to look around for him. All the windows are uncovered, the pile of boards next to my trash bags on the porch. Rattling and stomping noises come from above, drawing my gaze up.

Wesley is standing on the roof. He picks up a tree branch and throws it off.

"Aren't you afraid of falling?" I shout to him.

"What?" He leans over the edge, holding a hand by his ear.

I swallow, feeling my pulse quicken. "Be careful!" I say, shouting louder this time. At first I'm not sure he hears me, but then he holds his hands up and sways precariously.

I tighten my grip on the handle of the rake. "That's not funny, Wesley!"

"Oh no," he lilts. "I've lost my balance. Are you going to catch me?"

I'm going to punch him in the damn face. *That's* what I'm going to do. Just as soon as he gets back down here. "Fine, you idiot. Break every bone in your body. See how much I care." I go back to raking the lawn, hoping by ignoring him that he'll stop playing around.

He laughs, and I stiffen at the sound. I almost wish the dumbass would lose his balance.

By the time I'm done with the second half of the yard, I'm sweating. My shirt sticks to my skin uncomfortably, but when I look around, I feel a sense of pride. It looks ten times better than it did when I first walked outside.

Wesley is already done with the windows and roof by the time I'm finished. I frown because for some reason, this is beginning to feel like a competition—which he's clearly winning. When I see him run out of the garage with a broom, furiously sweeping the driveway, I *know* it's a competition. Hurrying, I go inside the house for a sponge and some gloves, determined to clean the fountain before he finishes with the drive.

I pick apart the vines entangled around the fountain, tossing them onto the part of the cement Wesley just swept.

He looks over his shoulder at me, glaring. I let out a small laugh, unable to help myself. We're both out of breath from trying to outdo each other, probably looking ridiculous in the process.

"Here, let me help you out with that."

I turn just in time to get doused in the face with a stream of water. Wesley steers the garden hose toward the fountain, shaking with laughter. "Oops. I missed."

The sponge in my hands drops to ground. Sputtering, I wipe the water from my face, ready to strangle him. Literally. I'm going to wrap my hands around his neck and strangle the guy to death. I stomp over there, intent on doing just that, but in my moment of anger I somehow forget that Wesley is bigger and stronger than me. Before I can even reach for his neck, his arm is around my waist, and he swoops me over his shoulder.

I grunt, startled by how easy that was for him. "Put me down."

All *that* does is make him laugh.

"Why are you messing with me today?" I ask him.

"Maybe I like messing with you."

"Well, dammit. It's not fair. I can't—" An idea occurs to me. "Are you ticklish?"

"What kind of question is that?" He bends as I tickle his side. "Dahlia, stop before I drop you!"

But it's too late. I land flat on my back. The impact knocks the air from my lungs, leaving me gasping for breath. Wesley's mouth opens when he realizes what he's done, but the apologies I'm expecting don't rush out. The shock wears off, and he presses his lips together, trying to keep from laughing. "You okay?"

I'm two seconds from cursing him out, especially because he thinks this is funny, but then I stop and close my eyes. A slow smile works its way to my mouth, and I begin to laugh too. "I hate you," I moan, feeling my body ache all over.

I open my eyes to find him shaking his head at me. "Second time I've witnessed you fall on your ass and end up laughing at yourself."

"I'm allowed to," I protest. "You, on the other hand, are supposed to be a gentleman and offer to help me up."

"No one ever said I was a gentleman." Despite that comment, he reaches for my arm and helps me off the ground. I dust myself off, and Wesley removes a twig from my hair. His close proximity immediately pulls me back to last night. I stop thinking about the yard, his nearness being the only thing I can focus on.

"Dahlia." His dark blue eyes search mine. We stand there, just staring at each other, and I'm not sure how much time passes. I absorb every last detail of Wesley's face, taking in his hardened jawline, his straight nose, and the way his eyes seem to remind me of the night sky, reflecting billions of stars entrenched in an endless blue. I could stare into them forever and never get enough of it.

This feeling is starting to scare me. I've seen it in movies, read it in books, but I think a part of me always thought it was bullshit—exaggerated fluff meant for entertainment. Nothing so incredible could possibly be real.

But here it is.

Something inside this moment tells me I can never turn back. Whatever is happening here, it's too powerful to ignore.

My gaze is only ripped away at the sound of a car horn honking. A red pickup truck pulls up the driveway, a blonde head hanging out the driver's window. The truck comes to a stop, and Tyson jumps out of it. I glance over at Wesley, seeing his confusion. I'm guessing Tyson wasn't expected.

"Hey man, come help me with this keg!"

Wesley runs a hand through his hair. "Shit," he mutters.

"What's wrong?" I ask him.

"We're supposed to throw a party tonight. Here." He drags his hand down from the top of his head and over his face, groaning.

"What's wrong with that?"

"I forgot about it," he admits, turning to face me. "And I planned on taking you out."

I feel my cheeks flush, remembering what he said about how there should be a date before sex. I'm not sure if he planned *that* for tonight too, but it doesn't escape my attention. "Don't worry about it," I tell him. "We can go out another time."

Tyson lets down the bed of his truck. "Are you gonna help me out, bro? Or are you just gonna stand there talking to your hot roommate all day?" He winks at me, and I smile back.

Wesley ignores Tyson and keeps his eyes on me. "I feel like canceling the whole fucking thing."

"No, don't do that," I say, gesturing to Tyson. "Your friend seems really excited."

He stares at me, looking tormented. I believe he would cancel this party to go out on a date with me, and there's something really nice about knowing that.

"Will you come?" he asks expectantly.

"I kinda live here, silly. So yeah. I'll come."

"You know what I mean."

I do know what he means. In the past whenever Wesley threw a party, I stayed hidden away inside my bedroom. Or I'd go to the movies with Gwen to get out of the house. That's the way Wesley and I have always worked. We gravitate away from each other. We're good at it too. It's almost second nature.

Our worlds have shifted, throwing everything off balance. Now it feels like there's a giant magnet hidden inside his body, drawing me closer and closer.

I let out a sigh. "You really want me to come?"

"I don't care if you show up wearing a burlap bag," he says with intensity. "I *want* you to be there, Dahlia."

The way he's looking at me, the pleading lilt to his tone—it's too much. I can't say no. "Okay then." I smile. "I'll be there."

CHAPTER TWENTY

WESLEY

When Dahlia said she'd come to the party, she seemed to mean it. I need her to be here, to somehow prove we've evolved from the people we used to be and the distance we kept from one another.

People file in through the door, rapidly filling up the front rooms, but as each minute passes, I keep looking toward the stairs, hoping to see a chestnut-colored head making its way through the crowd.

An hour into the party, I start to get agitated. She still hasn't shown up yet. It's enough to make me want to go up to her room and drag her ass down here. But I know I won't. She needs to make that decision on her own. She needs to want to be here.

"You look antsy." I turn around to find Charlotte Hart behind me. "Beer?"

"No, thanks."

She stands there, holding out the plastic cup until I finally take it from her and chug some back. "Thanks, Hart."

"No problem. Care to tell me why you keep looking at the stairs?"

Frowning, I wipe the foamy beer residue from my mouth with the back of my hand. She's watching me closely, a knowing look behind her clear blue eyes. "Has anyone ever told you that you're nosy?"

"All the time." She shrugs indifferently. "There's a reason I chose Journalism as my major."

"Because you're good at interfering in other people's business?"

A little smile quirks her mouth. "Because I'm observant. Quit dancing around the question, Wes. Who are you looking for?"

"Why don't you take a guess, little miss reporter?"

Tyson chooses that moment to blast music from the sound system. I see him in the corner of the room, tampering with the volume.

Charlotte raises her voice so I can hear her. "My bet is on your roommate. Where is she anyway? Thought you said you invited her."

"I did." I shrug as if I don't care. "Guess she didn't want to accept the invitation."

Charlotte studies me for a few seconds, tucking a strand of hair behind her ear. I can see why people like her so much. When she gives you her attention, she gives you her *full* attention. Most people appreciate that kind of thing. But right now I wish she'd go find someone else to focus her observant nature on. It's more invasive than I can handle.

"Wow. I think I see what's going on here." Her brows raise, and she continues to stare at me, almost in disbelief. "Can't believe I'm saying this, but Dahlia must've done a number on you."

"What makes you say that?"

"That lost puppy dog look on your face. It's identical to the one I had in seventh grade when I couldn't figure out whether Miles liked me or not."

"Where is your boyfriend anyway?" I ask her. "Shouldn't you be bothering him instead of me?"

She waves her hand toward the other side of the room. "Somewhere getting wasted probably. He gets like that when his team doesn't play well."

"Maybe you should go comfort him."

She ignores my suggestion. "You know, it takes a lot to shock me. But you and Dahlia—I have to admit I'm a little shocked. I don't get it." She sips at her beer. "You must've done a number on her as well."

"If that were true, don't you think she'd be here right now?"

"Maybe. But just because she isn't—" Beer sputters from Charlotte's lips. "Oh my God."

Her outburst seems to come out of nowhere. Then she nods toward the stairs, and I glance behind me to see what she's looking at.

I stop breathing for a few seconds. An almost unrecognizable version of Dahlia is walking down the steps. She's wearing an emerald dress that outlines every curve of her body, her hair left down, framing her face in loose waves. The way she looks takes my breath away. I knew she was beautiful, but I didn't know she could look like this.

When Dahlia sees me and Charlotte, she smiles and heads toward us. Charlotte grabs my wrist and squeezes it excitedly. "Whatever you did, thank you. You brought my friend back."

"What do you mean brought her back?"

"I don't know how to describe it, but it's like she's been in hiding. You brought her out of it."

Hiding?

I never considered that before, but Charlotte makes a good point. Dahlia does go to great lengths to stay invisible. There are never any good reasons why people want to stay hidden.

"Dahlia Reynolds, I have three words for you," Charlotte says as she approaches. "Drop Dead. Gorgeous."

Dahlia fidgets with her bracelet, obviously unused to hearing those kinds of compliments. "Thanks, Char."

"You look amazing," I say, and she looks up at me. "But you can't look like that."

"Why not?"

"Yeah, Wes, why the hell not?" Charlotte adds, placing one hand on her hip.

I keep my eyes trained on Dahlia. "Because I'll have to beat the guys off of you with a stick."

"Oh God," Charlotte groans.

One corner of Dahlia's mouth pulls up into a grin. "Since when are you the jealous type?"

Good fucking question. When have I ever been jealous over a girl? I think about it for a second. "This is the first time."

"Well I didn't do this for any of them," she says, leaning toward me. "I was trying to impress *you*."

My entire body stiffens. "You shouldn't have said that."

"Why?"

I lower my voice so only she can hear me. "Because it makes me want to haul you upstairs and forget about this party."

Her eyes widen for a brief moment, and then her face breaks into a grin. "I'm not so sure I would have a problem with that."

I'm two seconds away from saying to hell with it and throwing her over my shoulder. If I didn't want to do things right with her, I wouldn't hesitate.

Before I can make up my mind, Charlotte steps in and links her arm through Dahlia's, preventing me from acting out on my impulse. "Come on, I'm tired of watching you and Wes drool over each other. You guys live together. Do it on your own time." She steers Dahlia away. As she's leaving she looks over her shoulder and winks at me. "You can have her back later. I promise."

They disappear into the crowd, leaving me standing there, half-dazed. Someone brushes my arm, moving to my side. I look over to see Christine there, but she's not paying me any attention. She's looking in the direction Charlotte and Dahlia left in.

"Hey, Wes," she says. "Who is that girl, the one you were just talking to?"

"Which one?"

Inherently I know she's not referring to Charlotte. Everyone on campus knows who Charlotte Hart is. She's a semi-celebrity in her own right.

"The brunette in the green dress."

"Her name is Dahlia Reynolds." I turn to face her. "She's my roommate. Why do you wanna know?"

"She just looks familiar, that's all." She looks up at me, smiling. "So how have you been? I was disappointed when you didn't visit me the other night."

Most girls would pretend not to care or not to notice. But most girls aren't Christine, and she says whatever she feels.

"Yeah, um about that…" I scratch my jaw, trying to think of something to say that won't offend her. "I just had a lot on my mind that night."

"I was right, wasn't I? It was about a girl."

"Yeah," I answer honestly, my eyes involuntarily looking in the direction Dahlia left in. "I guess you were."

She lowers her eyes, sighing dramatically. "You're breaking my heart, Kent."

"I'm sure you'll be fine," I say, chuckling. And we both know it's true. In the two years since her boyfriend died, Christine has hooked up with plenty of guys without getting attached to any of them.

"My ego *is* deflated though," she laments.

"If it's any consolation, there are a ton of guys here who will be happy you're available."

That makes her smile. "Yes, but none of them are you. There's something different about you…" She reaches for the collar of my shirt, running her fingers down the center of my chest. "I bet you're the type that doesn't know the meaning of ordinary."

I catch her hand before she reaches my lower stomach and gently push it away from me. She smiles innocently, shrugging. "Oh well. Maybe I'll catch you between girls. You never stay with any of them for very long."

"This one's different."

"It's that serious, huh?"

"Yeah, it's that serious." As I'm saying the words, I hear the truth ringing in them. Whatever this thing is with Dahlia, I want it to be more than a fling. We've skipped most of the commitment steps anyway. Like moving in together.

"Well you'll have to introduce her to me. Is she here?"

I look sideways at her, wondering why she wants to know.

She rolls her eyes. "Oh come on, Wes. I just wanna meet the girl who inspired you enough to settle down."

I rub the back of my neck. Part of me wants to keep Dahlia all to myself, at least for a little while. I don't want other people spoiling the newness of it. Right now, what we have is between us, and somehow that makes it more special. Then again, there's another part of me that wants tell the whole world. To let everyone know she's mine.

"Lucky for me, Charlotte's pretty popular." Dahlia circles around me, smiling, and surprising me. "I snuck away while she was caught up in conversation…" She stops when she notices Christine standing there, who is currently staring her down like a hawk.

"I know you."

Dahlia's eyes drift to the floor. "No, I don't think so."

"Yes, I do." Christine stares hard at her, her brows drawing together in contemplation. "You're that girl, aren't you? The one from two Christmases ago."

"I'm not sure what you're talking about."

The way Dahlia stiffens against my side and the nervous look on her face worries me. Just a second ago, she was beautiful and confident. Now she's shrinking into a scared mouse.

I turn my head, leaning close to her. "You okay?"

Christine doesn't seem the same either. The lines by her mouth go rigid, and she moves closer until she's standing directly in front of Dahlia.

"Great choice of girl you made here, Wes. I didn't know you liked the homewrecking variety."

My muscles tense up, my body going into defense mode. "What the fuck are you talking about, Christine?" I wrap my arm around Dahlia's side, almost protectively drawing her against me.

Christine doesn't answer me. She continues to stare Dahlia down, breathing in through her nostrils. "You haven't told him, have you?" she says, keeping her voice low. "Don't you think he deserves to know you prefer men twice your age? Don't you think he deserves to know how you nearly destroyed a family? *My* family."

Dahlia's eyes well with tears, and she swallows. The things Christine says, the things she's implicating…Dahlia is reacting to them like they're true.

"Are you just gonna stand there and not say anything? Go ahead and deny it. I'd like to see you try."

I'm waiting for Dahlia to say something, almost rooting for her to defend herself, but she doesn't. She's crumbling.

"You don't know what you're talking about," she says in small voice.

"Please." Christine snorts. "My mom may believe the shit my dad fed her, but I saw you with my own eyes. I saw you through my bedroom window, begging and pleading with him not to leave you. How could you do that? How could you come to our *house* and do that? Don't you have any shame?"

"Not everything is what is seems," Dahlia says, blinking back tears. She's shaking as she pulls away from me. "I'm sorry for what my presence at your house made you think, Christine, but I didn't have an affair with your dad."

With that said, she walks away. Threading through the crowd, she breaks out into a run and quickly makes her way out of the room. I want to go after her, but I get the feeling she's going to need a moment before I do.

"I think you should probably leave," I tell Christine.

Her face tightens as she looks at me. "You think I'm lying, don't you?"

"It doesn't matter if I do or don't. You upset her, and this is her house. That's why you need to be the one to leave."

She nods, her eyes glimmering. "Fine. I'll go."

She stomps off, the sound of her heels angrily clicking against the floor. Then, changing her mind, she suddenly stops and swings around. She stalks back toward me, her face a stony mask. "Just so you know, I wasn't lying. I'm not the kind of girl who would do that out of jealousy or whatever callous reasons girls do the things they do. Hooking up with you won't make or break me, Wes. There's only one guy I'll ever truly want, and he's buried six feet in the ground." She runs a hand through her hair, looking up at the ceiling, and then back at me. There's something lost in her eyes. Something broken. "The day that girl showed up at my house was the day my family was ripped apart. My mom still won't look at my dad the same way. Everything we used to have, every ounce of happiness, every piece of normalcy, it was all destroyed."

I don't know what to say. I'm not sure if I believe Dahlia is capable of doing the things Christine is claiming, but it's obvious that she believes it. Whatever her reasons...I don't think Christine is lying. And that scares me.

It scares the shit out of me.

"I'm sorry, Christine. But maybe you're wrong. You heard her say that not everything is what it seems. Maybe there's more to the story."

"Believe what you want. Just know that I warned you about her."

She doesn't wait for me to say anything else before turning away. I watch as she makes her way to the door. Once she's gone, I head toward the stairs. I need to find Dahlia.

Thinking of how she reacted, and the way she looked at Christine—it makes my stomach clench. I don't want to believe it's true. I can't believe she would hurt a family like that. She told me she was a virgin. I figured Styler was the only guy she'd ever dated.

But the thing is, I don't know Dahlia that well.

And the things I do know about her don't make me feel any better about the situation. Like the way she goes to Professor Barakat's class even though she's already taken it. And the way she studies him, almost obsessively. And the way she disguises herself to stay hidden. Is that who she's hiding from him? The professor? I swallow, not wanting to believe it. But the more I think about it, the more the pieces fall into place. I hate the way it adds up, the way it all seems to make perfect fucking sense. It feels like someone has slammed a knife into my gut, ripping my insides apart. I don't want to believe those things about Dahlia. I don't want to think she's the kind of person who would do that.

But what if I'm wrong?

It's a possibility. One that I wish I didn't have to consider. But the way she reacted—that's the worst part. Dahlia completely lost it. If she had nothing to hide, the things Christine said wouldn't have bothered her.

I'm not sure what's true and what's not, but one thing is becoming pretty clear. Dahlia is hiding a lot more than a pretty face.

~ ~

WESLEY

I find Dahlia hiding out in the hallway. Her skin is a few shades paler than normal, and she's staring off into the distance. At first I think her reaction is based off what happened with Christine downstairs, but then I notice what she's looking at.

Two people are in the corner of the hall, a couple caught up in a pretty intense moment. The girl gasps in pleasure, wrapping her legs around the guy as he lifts her up. He presses her back into the wall and slams his mouth against hers. In turn, she pulls at his neck, tugging at the collar of his shirt. Their bodies are so entwined, I almost don't recognize them. Then I notice the girl's bronzy skin, her dark hair, and the angled shape of her nose and chin. It's Gwen. I blink a few times, because I recognize the guy too, but my brain refuses to process what my eyes are telling me. Blonde hair, broad shoulders…that can't be who I think it is, can it?

"It's Miles," Dahlia whispers as if she's reading my thoughts.

I reach for her hand and try tugging her back the way we came. "Come on. Let's get out of here before they see us."

"Is that a bad thing? If they see us?" She continues to stare at them with wide eyes. "Every fiber in my body wants to stop them."

"It's not your place." I tug at her hand again, and she reluctantly allows me to lead her away.

Over my shoulder, I spy the couple again. They're really going at it. They don't even notice Dahlia and me leaving the hallway, but I doubt they would notice if the house was on fire.

Unsure of what to do, I lead Dahlia to the other side of the house. We make our way through the twisting hallways with a vengeance, finally stopping in front of my bedroom. I twist the knob, guiding her inside, and then shut the door behind me. Dahlia mutters a string of curses I didn't know she was capable of. She reaches for one of the pillows on my bed, holds it up to her face and lets out a muffled scream.

I go straight for my stash of whiskey hidden in the bottom drawer of my desk. After twisting off the cap, I hand it to her. She lifts it to her lips, chugging back more than I expected.

"Okay. Maybe that was a bad idea," I say, reaching for the bottle.

She hands it over, then plops down on my bed, a miserable look on her face. "This was supposed to be a good night," she says in a small voice, smoothing out the bottom of her dress. "I was hoping for something magical. Not this."

I sit down beside her, my weight sinking into the middle of the bed. Because I don't know where to begin, I don't say anything. I just look around my room, noticing how blank the walls are, how sparse the furniture is, and how lifeless it feels. Dahlia was right. It is boring.

"What do I tell Charlotte?" she whispers. "Or the better question is, am I supposed to tell Charlotte? Would I be doing the right thing?"

I don't know how to answer her. If these were my friends instead of hers, if this were Chase or Tyson, how would I handle it? Would I tell whoever was being played? Probably not. I would stay the fuck out of it and let them deal with things themselves.

"It's not fair," she breathes. "They've always tried to put me between the two of them. I've tried so hard not to get in the middle of their weird feud. That's why I didn't listen to their bickering; the details always get you into trouble, and I refused to take sides." She throws her hands up into the air, letting out an exasperated growl. "But here I am—stuck in the middle! It didn't matter how hard I tried to stay out of it. They've managed to put me in the worst position possible. What am I supposed to do now? Miles is Charlotte's high school sweetheart. They're planning to get married after graduation. Charlotte is supposed to become a local news anchor, Miles a corporate lawyer. They're supposed to have little blonde babies, and their lives are supposed to be picture-freaking-perfect. How could Miles screw that up? How could he do that to her?"

"You don't know what goes on behind closed doors," I cut in. "Maybe they aren't as happy as they pretend to be."

There's one lesson I found out the hard way. My parents seemed happy before my dad left, but I'm not sure how real that was anymore. Obviously there was more going on than I could sense back then. My dad appeared happy to everyone around him, but he must've been hiding how he truly felt. He was damned good at it too. I never once guessed the truth.

"What do I *do*, Wes? What do I tell Charlotte?" Dahlia looks over at me, her eyes pleading with me to give her answers I can't give her.

"I don't have a clue, babe. If it were me…" I rub the back of my neck. "…I would stay out of it. Things have a way of working themselves out on their own."

"Don't you think I have an inherent responsibility to Charlotte? She's my *friend*. That's supposed to mean something. How can I not tell her?"

"Yes, she's your friend, but this is between her and Miles. And besides, no one saw you in the hall. When this comes out—and believe me it will—no one will ever know that you knew about it. Things will get messy between them. There will be bitterness, anger, a lot of hurt feelings. Trust me when I say you don't want yourself attached to that."

She narrows her eyes on me, and I can tell she doesn't agree with what I've said. "What?" I ask her. "You asked, and I told you what I'd do. Doesn't mean you have to do the same."

"Yeah, I guess you're right," she says, looking away.

Dammit if she doesn't seem mad at me for some reason. What the hell did I say? It's not like I'm acting as if it's okay. Cheating is the ultimate betrayal, and I get that. For months I watched my mom suffer at the hand of my dad's choices and how deeply he hurt her. I will never repeat his mistakes. Never.

What surprises me about this whole situation is the way Dahlia is reacting. She's pissed, more pissed than I've ever seen her, which makes Christine's earlier accusations even more confusing. Dahlia would have to be the biggest hypocrite in the world if the things Christine said were true...

But then why did she get so upset? Why did she run away?

Maybe it's true. Maybe she followed in her mom's footsteps, breaking apart a family the way her mom broke apart mine.

God, this is torture. I don't want to believe any of this shit. I need to hear it come from her lips. I need to hear her say it's not true.

"Dahlia," I say, not knowing where to begin. "Downstairs...with Christine. What was that about?"

At the mention of Christine's name, I watch the lines of anger in Dahlia's face fade. Sadness takes over, and she stares ahead without saying anything.

"You can't do that to me this time, Dahlia. I need you to explain what happened down there. I need to know if it's true."

She stands up, her eyes piercing into me. "What do you mean you need to know if it's true?"

I'm caught off guard by the look in her eyes. She never expected me to ask her this. "The way you reacted to Christine, the way you ran off—why did you get so upset?"

"Christine accused me of sleeping with her dad. Wouldn't you be upset?"

"Not if there wasn't any truth behind it."

She slowly shakes her head, staring at me in disbelief. "Oh my God. You believe her."

"I never said that."

"You don't have to. It's written all over your face."

"Then tell me it's not true, Dahlia. Tell me Christine is batshit crazy, and she made every word up. I'll believe you."

"What are you looking for—peace of mind? You can't stand the idea that you've involved yourself with a girl who may or may not be a homewrecker?"

"That's not fair. You're putting words into my mouth."

"No, I'm not. You're asking me to tell you the truth when I've already done that."

I flinch, wondering where this side of her is coming from. When did this room suddenly become a battleground? "You said it to Christine. I want you to say it to me."

"Why?" she asks, tilting her head. "Even if it were true, and I did sleep with the professor, would it make a difference to you? Would you see me differently? Why is it so important?"

"I want to know."

"*Why* do you want to know, Wes?"

"Because your mom did the same fucking thing to my family," I snap without meaning to.

I'm surprised by my own reaction. Standing up, I pace to the other side of the room, and then back again, trying to stay calm. In as calm a voice as I can manage I say, "I know how it feels to be in that situation. I know what it's like to watch your family ripped apart. I don't want to believe you're capable of something like that."

Dahlia goes completely still, holding her breath. By looking at her, you'd think I slapped her across the face. It makes me wonder if she knew. This whole time, all these years, my dad may have kept her from knowing what he did.

"My mom," she breathes. "You think my mom destroyed your family."

"My dad is ultimately to blame, but she certainly had a hand in it. She had to have known he was married when she got involved with him."

"Involved…" Dahlia repeats the word as if she's trying to fit the pieces together. "I can't believe it."

"I'm sorry you had to find out about her this way," I offer, feeling like I should say something. It's not easy finding out your parent isn't the person you thought they were. I know from experience.

She laughs once, a painful sound. "You were right, Wesley."

"About what?"

"You *are* a judgmental asshole."

My head jerks up. When I meet her furious gaze, I realize she doesn't believe me.

"It all makes sense now," she says in a low, choked voice. "Why you hated Harland, why you hated me. The time you wasted hating your dad—it's almost sad."

"What the hell are you talking about?" My defenses go up, and I get the feeling that she thinks she knows something I don't.

"I'm talking about your desire to 'stay out of it', as you put it. It cost you years with your dad that you'll never get back."

She walks to the door, but I get there first, slamming it shut just as she opens it. "I'm about two seconds from losing it, babe. So you better explain yourself. *Now.*"

"Why should I?" She crosses her arms over her chest. "You walk around here, thinking you know everything and believing the worst about people. There is no trial and jury with you. Instead you jump straight to a guilty verdict and sentence everyone you don't trust to your indifference. And now you want me to explain myself after you've already judged me? I don't owe you any explanations, Wes. I don't owe you anything at all."

"Dahlia," I say through clenched teeth. "I watched my mom go through years of pain over the way my dad left her, and here you are implying your mom had nothing to do with it. You *will* explain yourself."

"You should've had that conversation with your dad, not with me. Remember the letter? The one you tossed aside the day Francisco read the will? Your answers were probably in there, but you ignored it just like you ignored him. Luckily, knowing Francisco, I'm sure he has a copy. Ask him for it."

Letter? What the fuck was so important that he had to write it in that goddamned letter?

Dahlia yanks the door open beneath my grip, but stops inside the doorway. "You taught me something about myself tonight," she says without looking back at me. "I don't want to be like you. I don't want to stay out of it. When I tell Charlotte what Miles did, it will devastate her, but at least I will have done something. At least she won't be ignorant. If the situation were reversed, she would do the same for me."

This time I don't stop her as she walks away. I try to tell myself it doesn't matter, that she doesn't know what she's talking about. She wasn't there the night my dad disappeared without so much as a goodbye. I don't give a fuck what his reasons were. He walked away from us, and those actions speak a million times louder than words.

I throw the bottle of whiskey I'm holding against the wall. The glass shatters into a thousand tiny pieces, the noise slicing against my eardrums. I feel like tearing this house apart inch by inch until every last floorboard is turned over. That's what I should've done to begin with. I should've set the damned place on fire and watch it burn to the ground, taking satisfaction in knowing I destroyed my dad's entire life's work.

Restless, I go to my desk and jerk the drawer open. The letter is still resting in its unopened envelope. I take it out, placing it between my fingers. I'm prepared to rip it to shreds, but then I realize something.

Defiance is the only thing fueling my urge to tear it up, and I want to prove that Dahlia's words don't matter. I want to prove that my dad's excuses won't matter. My fingers fall slack, and I loosen my grip on the envelope.

If I read it, I can take satisfaction in knowing I was right. Whatever that man had to say can never make up for what he did.

Slipping my finger under the seal, I pry it open and remove the folded paper. The letter is handwritten, without a doubt my dad's scrawl. I've read too many of his research notebooks to mistake his handwriting for someone else's. Slowly lowering myself down onto the foot of my bed, I begin to read.

CHAPTER TWENTY-ONE

WESLEY

Dear Wesley,

As I sit down to write this, I wonder if your eyes will ever see it. You get that stubborn streak of yours from me. A little stubbornness can be a good thing while hunting down treasure, but in most other aspects of life it won't serve you. Open your mind, son. If you don't take anything else I say to heart, at least take that piece of advice with you. I know you hate me for leaving, and I don't blame you. I really don't. But at least give me one last chance to explain. I'll do my best to help you understand. All I ask is that you keep reading.

Where do I begin? Ha, what a question. To be honest, I've written and re-written this letter so many damn times it seems there is no good place to begin. So I'll just come out with it.

I was sick.

God, that's an awful word. Sick. Maybe that's why I kept running from it for so long. Maybe that's why I couldn't admit it to you. Being associated with a word that represents an all-consuming incapability was the last thing I ever wanted. You and your brother used to look up to me like a hero in one of your comic books. Heroes don't get sick. If they have to die, they go down fighting. Not tied to a bed while a nurse spoon-feeds you your lunch and helps you wipe your own ass. How humiliating. How disappointing. Guess I didn't want it to end that way. I didn't want you boys remembering me like that.

Sooner or later I had to face it though. And son, it wasn't as recent as I've led you to believe. You had just turned fifteen when I started to get headaches so severe they'd keep me in bed for days. I figured they were a result of staying up late reading, and for that reason, I ignored them. Shortly after that came the nausea. Then the blurred vision. That's when I knew something was wrong.

The docs diagnosed me with stage four glioblastoma (fancy word for brain tumor). I'll never forget coming home from that appointment. It was the day your baseball team won its championship. I was so proud of you, but it made me realize I might not be there for any more of those big moments. It took everything I had not to break down right then and there. I smiled and clapped your back, but inside I wept like baby.

A few weeks later I told your mom I was going on a business trip. During that time, I underwent a craniotomy. The doctors removed eighty percent of the tumor, but it wasn't enough. They gave me a year to live. One goddamned year. Believe me, you'll never appreciate life like you do when there's a limit on it. Anyway, that's the year we did all those things you and Sam thought I was crazy for wanting to do, like the Thailand expedition. Looking back on it, riding around on elephants and chasing after legendary treasure leads does seem half mad. But we had fun doing it, and that means the world to me.

My year came and went quicker than any year before that. I figured I was lucky, since I lasted longer than the docs said I would. But about two months after the year was up, things got worse. I had a seizure in front of your mother. Definitely the scariest moment of my life, and I couldn't imagine the fear she felt. The look on her face was unbearable. I knew I had to leave. I loved her too much to let her watch me deteriorate. Whatever months I had left, they wouldn't be pleasant, and I didn't want her seeing it. So I lied. I told her I seized from abnormal levels of glucose in my blood. She believed me, and so I began making plans.

One night a few weeks later, I slipped out while the rest of you slept. I know you think leaving was easy for me, Wesley, but trust me when I tell you it was the hardest thing

I've ever done. In fact, it was so difficult I would've given anything I could to take back my life. When I found out about an experimental program being offered at St. Joseph's hospital in Savannah I jumped on the opportunity. Each week they hooked me up to an IV and pumped high dosages of a mixture of drugs through my veins. The drugs made me weak and depressed, bringing me down to my lowest point. I figured that was it for me. Death was the next stop.

That's when I met Lily. Ah, thank God for Lily. She was a blessing in disguise. She was there battling breast cancer, but every time I saw her, she radiated this unwavering joy, smiling and laughing like nothing bothered her. It was inspiring.

Since our appointments were at the same time, Lily and I kept each other company everyday. She'd tell me jokes and find ways to make me laugh. I'd bitch about how much I missed you and your mother. Sometimes she'd bring Dahlia with her, and I'd tell them stories about you and Sam. Mostly treasure stories. Those were her favorite.

The divorce papers came shortly after Sam died. While I was away, Paul came into your mother's life, and she was looking for a way to move on. And how could I blame her for wanting to? Although I felt myself getting better, I knew I had to let her go. It wasn't fair of me to put her life on hold while I waited for my health to improve. So she moved up to Nashville with Paul while I stayed in Savannah. To this day, she doesn't know why I left. Please don't tell her, son. She needs to live her life without looking back. I'd rather she hate me than to be stuck mourning me.

My recovery did eventually come. The docs at St. Joseph's placed me into remission around the same time Lily gave up on the program. Her results weren't as promising, and she didn't want to waste any of the time she had left in the hospital. This was after Sam died, and you and your mother refused to speak to me. Lily and Dahlia were the only people I knew in Savannah. They were all I had left. So I started visiting the two of them at their home in Tybee Island, and it wasn't long after when I realized I had found a life again. Even though I knew Lily's days were numbered, I asked her to marry me. She refused, of course, and thought I was a fool for asking, but she did agree to let me move in with them. Those last few months with Lily and Dahlia were my chance for redemption. I tried to make her passing as easy as possible, and once she was gone, I asked Dahlia to come back to Florida with me. We were two of a kind, Dahlia and I. We both had lost so much, and we were all each other had. I love Dahlia like a daughter, Wes. She has a kind heart, and an insatiable urge to learn about archeology and history. In many ways, she's like you. Getting close to her made me remember all the things I missed about you and your brother.

Unfortunately, my remission only lasted a year. During that time, I tried to reconnect with you. That wasn't as easy as I hoped, but I don't blame you for turning your back on me either. I turned my back on you, son, and for that I'll always feel remorseful. I'd have been pissed as hell if my old man left the way I left you.

Wesley, I—

I crumple up the paper into a small wad, unable to read anymore. Falling back against my bed, I pound the mattress with my fist. How did I not know? How could I not *know*? I feel like a fucking idiot.

Looking back, it's all so obvious. My dad was never a selfish man. He put everyone before himself. Christ, that may have been his downfall.

Closing my eyes, I fight to keep the pain from ripping out of me. That's what it feels like—like it is literally is ripping me apart from the inside out. In a way, I feel cheated. My dad thought he was saving me years from seeing him at his worst, but I would give anything to have that time back. I would've rather spent that time helping him through it than hating him for leaving.

God, I wish I'd seen it sooner. I wish I would've paid attention. Sam never hated Dad for what he did. He was angry, but he never held the same hate for him that I built up. I wonder if he knew about the cancer. I wonder if Dad told him…

Dahlia was right. Fucking hell, how am I ever going to face her again? The things I said about her mom are almost unforgivable. There's no apology big enough that can make what I said okay. She called me a judgmental asshole, and the shoe sure as hell fits. My dad spent most of my life being a good father and husband. When he left I should've questioned it.

Thank God he had Lily and Dahlia. At least they were there for him when no one else could be. I still think he was dead-ass wrong for pushing his family away, but I understand where it came from. That's just who he was. He wanted the best for us. In his delusional mind, he believed it would be easier for us if we didn't have to experience his illness with him. He was wrong though. So completely wrong.

CHAPTER TWENTY-TWO

DOLL

The air isn't as hot and muggy as it usually is, giving me the chance to study outside between classes. Fall doesn't really exist in Florida. It's mid-September and everything is still green and lush and dewy. But there's a slight breeze in the air today, making the heat bearable. I've always liked the campus grounds anyway. The brick buildings are old and quaint, creating the sense that I'm somehow contributing to decades worth of collegiate history.

Those are my excuses for not going home anyway.

I look down at my cellphone. My next class isn't for another three hours. I could go back to the house...except lately that's not a place I've felt comfortable in. I tell myself I'd rather be here. Outside. Where the weather is semi-nice. Where everything is green and lush and dewy.

Where I'm away from everything that reminds me of *him*.

Two weeks have passed since we've spoken. It shouldn't bother me. Things have gone back to the way they were before. We each keep to our sides of the house, staying out of one another's ways. We don't even see each other in passing. I should feel a sense of normalcy. After all, it's what I'm used to.

And it used to work.

It's what has always worked.

But something's...different.

I can feel it. The energy inside Kent House has shifted, throwing everything off balance. I no longer feel at peace inside my own home. Instead I feel Wesley in every inch of that house. I see him in every wall that separates us. I see him in the staircases and the banisters. Even the library isn't a safe haven anymore. That's where it's the worst.

So I avoid going home as much as possible. I spend all day on campus until it's dark outside, heading home only when I'm so exhausted I know I'll pass out as soon as my head touches my pillow. Harland's will requires me to live there, but he didn't say anything about staying home all day.

Being on campus is easier. I don't think about things. I barely think about him. Or at least that's what I'd like to believe.

A few feet away, I hear a familiar laugh. Looking up from my textbook, I catch sight of Miles in the distance. He's talking and laughing with a few of his football buddies, acting like nothing is out of the ordinary. As if he isn't the scumbag I know him to be.

It pisses me off.

I've been going over this in my mind for days, wondering how to tell Charlotte about what he and Gwen have been doing behind her back. I think I was hoping their little rendezvous was a one-time thing, that maybe it wouldn't happen again, but Gwen is making it obvious that's not the case. She's been so caught up in her dreamy, Miles-infused la la land that she hasn't even noticed I'm not speaking to her. She's always on her phone, twirling her hair with a silly smile on her lips.

It's disgusting.

I finally made plans to tell Charlotte, but getting her to sit down in person isn't as easy as it should be. With the new semester underway, she's busier than ever. She's canceled on me twice already. Relief filled me both times she called to apologize. I guess it's not so strange. Telling her about Miles means watching her heart break before my eyes. How am I going to sit through that? How am I going to get the words out?

I close my textbook, watching Miles break off from his friends. He's heading this way, presenting me with a perfect opportunity. I stand up from the table and quickly stuff my things into my bag. There's got to be a better way. Maybe Miles *is* my better way.

"Hey Miles, wait a sec."

When he hears me calling him, he stops and turns around. Surprise enters his face when he catches sight of me. "Damn, Doll. Look at you. I barely even recognized you."

It takes me a second to realize Miles isn't used to seeing me like this. I'm wearing shorts and a cardigan, without any makeup on. Lately I haven't been keeping up with my disguise. Avoiding Wesley takes up too much time.

"You look like you did in high school," Miles says. His mouth curves into a friendly smile.

I don't waste any time destroying that smile.

"I need to tell you something." I swing my bag over my shoulder, straightening to my full height. "I know about you and Gwen."

In the short time that took to register, Miles tenses up, going on the defensive. He scans the area surrounding us, clearly worried about being overheard. I roll my eyes. This campus isn't that small.

Once he sees it's clear, he grabs my arm and pulls me to the side of the walkway beneath a group of trees. "What did she tell you?" His voice is edged with a sort of fear.

"Nothing. I saw the two of you together at Wesley's party. I'm not even going to get into how wrong I think it is or how repulsed I am by the two of you. What I will say is this, either you tell Charlotte or I will."

He should be the one to break her heart. Not me.

Charlotte deserves to hear it from him. Not me.

Miles rubs his temples, sighing. I watch him closely, seeing a torrent of emotions cross his features. Worry. Fear. Sadness. The emotions look genuine. It's somewhat comforting to know that he isn't taking this lightly. In the back of my mind, I think I knew he wouldn't be the kind to take it lightly. Miles isn't a player. Up until now, I've always admired him. As Charlotte would say, he's one of the good guys. Or at least he was supposed to be.

"I can't tell her, Doll," he says, looking lost. "I'll lose her if I do."

"Did you expect to keep her after this?" I ask in amazement. "You're sleeping with Gwen. You can't have them both."

He sighs, looking away from me. "This thing with Gwen—I didn't mean for it to happen."

"Then why did it happen?"

"I…don't know."

"I'm gonna need a little more than I don't know." I place a hand on my hip, pressing him with a look. "Start talking."

"Doll, I don't know where to begin. You know how Charlotte is…she's stretched in too many directions."

"You're not about to feed me the she's-too-busy-for-me crap, are you?"

"It's the truth!" Miles shouts. When he catches himself, his voice lowers into a heated whisper. "Charlotte isn't the same as she used to be. I'm not sayin' that's a bad thing—college has opened so many doors for her. But she doesn't have time for herself, much less a relationship. I figured once we graduated, we'd have more time together, but I guess I got lonely waitin' for that day to come."

"And where does Gwen come into the picture?"

Miles leans against one of the tree trunks, stuffing his hands into his pockets. I can tell he doesn't want to admit any of this to me, but I'm not giving him the option. "Miles," I repeat more sternly. "How does Gwen fit into all this?"

He lets out a long sigh and meets my steady gaze. "Gwen and I have been chatting online since high school. She never knew it was me, and it started off as just a friendly thing, but somewhere along the road, things turned serious."

I cover my mouth with my hand. "Oh my God. You're the internet guy."

I can't believe it. Miles is *Mr. Sexy Voice.* How is that possible? "Gwen told me his name was Luke," I say, trying to wrap my head around it. "She told me he went to Florida State."

"My middle name is Lucas. In Gwen's defense, she never knew it was me until we actually met. I enjoyed talking to her as someone else. Even though I was lying, I could be myself with her. I know it sounds crazy, but it's how I felt."

"Then why lie, Miles? If she was such a great friend to have, why not tell her who you were?"

If he's being honest, and this whole mess started off innocently, there should've been no reason to lie.

"Because she and Charlotte were always at each other's throats. I couldn't be friends with her and date Charlotte at the same time. They may have allowed you to be neutral territory, but they would've never allowed me the same privilege. I would've been forced to pick a side."

"So you chose Charlotte, but kept Gwen as your dirty little secret. Doesn't sound so friendly anymore, Miles. It sounds like you were getting your cake and eating it too. I'm surprised Gwen wasn't furious with you for lying."

"At first she was."

I think back to the day Gwen came home after she was supposed to meet Luke. I remember how devastated she looked, how empty her voice sounded. "It was the night of the hurricane, wasn't it? That's when the two of you met?"

Miles nods. "I didn't tell her until after the storm started, and by then it wasn't safe for her to leave. She was pissed as hell at first, called me a few names I won't repeat, but there was still an attraction between us. She couldn't deny it anymore than I could—"

"Please stop now. I don't want to hear *those* details."

"What do you want from me, Doll?" Miles looks up at me, hopeless. "What the hell do you expect me to do? Either way I'm fucked. Either way someone gets hurt."

"You have to tell Charlotte."

He shakes his head. "I can't do that."

"Don't be a coward. You owe her the truth."

"She's got too much going on for her this year. What if I ruin that?"

"Trust me, Miles. You're not gonna be the one to break Charlotte Hart. I've known her since elementary school. She's stronger than you think."

"I'll break it off with Gwen," he pleads. "I swear to God, I'll break it off."

I slowly shake my head, for the first time realizing Charlotte isn't the only one who will end up hurt in this scenario. Miles is the first guy I've ever seen Gwen get all glowy about, which has to mean something. For all her dislike of Charlotte, Gwen didn't do this to spite her. She would never stoop so low as to condone cheating for the hell of it. She called the sultan who carved the *Zumina-al-Shimaz* a pig—and he created one of the most romantic pieces of jewelry I've ever seen. She hates cheaters. *Hates* them.

But then why become one?

I glance at Miles, and instantly I know. Gwen enjoys flirting, likes the dating scene, but she won't waste her time and energy on a guy if it isn't carefree and easy. She usually bails the moment things get too serious.

But she didn't bail on Miles.

All things inexplicable can be blamed on love. Oh man. That means Gwen is head over heels for this confused idiot.

"Does Gwen understand that what the two of you have isn't serious?" I ask Miles carefully, almost afraid to hear the answer.

"I don't know." His eyes fall to the ground and he drags a hand through his hair. "We haven't had that conversation yet."

"Then you should have it," I say, getting angry all over again. "You're not just hurting Charlotte, you dumbass."

"Okay," he agrees, nodding. "I'll talk to her."

I turn around to leave, but Miles stops me. "Wait, Doll. Are you really going to tell Char?"

"I'm kind of hoping I don't have to."

"How long do I have?"

I think about his question. Giving him too long to sit on it might not be the best course of action. He might change his mind, and I definitely don't want to be stuck doing his dirty work. "I'll give you the rest of the week. And Miles," I swallow, because I can't believe what I'm about to say. "Make sure you choose right. I doubt you'll get a do-over."

He gets my meaning. Up until this moment, I would've said Charlotte was the right choice. I'm not so sure anymore. Not that cheaters deserve choices. Then again, these are my friends we're talking about. People I care about. Pretending the outcome of this doesn't matter to me is useless. It does matter. They matter.

I leave Miles standing under the trees, making my way back to the sidewalk. Plugging my headphones in, I drown everything out with deafening music and head toward the nearest bench. Tucking my feet under me, I lean back and close my eyes. I've got three hours to kill, and I don't want to spend it worrying about what happens to Charlotte and Gwen.

Sleep comes easily. Even out here in broad daylight, I feel myself drifting off. It's no surprise I'm so tired. The only time I spend inside Kent House is at night, and knowing Wesley is close makes good sleep hard to come by. His face fills my mind, and it's the last thing I see at night. I wish I didn't think about him so much. A crushing pain grips at my heart every time I do.

CHAPTER TWENTY-THREE

DAHLIA

When I wake up, it's dark outside. I look at the time on my phone. *Crap.* I'm twenty minutes late for class.

I jump up and hurry toward the anthropology building. The professor doesn't like it when students are late. Sometimes she locks the door. I'm really hoping she didn't today, because we have a paper due.

As I swing open the door to the building, my bag knocks against the handle, and its entire contents spill out— my books, papers, everything strewn across the ground. I stupidly left it unzipped. Trying not to groan, I kneel down and gather the items as quickly as I can manage.

A sharp twinge pricks my neck. I shoo away whatever is biting me, waving my hand over my shoulder. But my hand goes numb, faltering the movement. It falls slack before my eyes. I stare at it for a long moment, unable to wrap my mind around what's happening. My hand feels heavy…my entire body feels heavy.

Something's wrong.

Flecks of black dot across my vision. I blink several times, trying to focus. My hand isn't the only thing losing its strength. It feels like I'm tethered to a crate of bricks. It pulls me backward, weighing me down. I have no control over it, and that's the most frightening part.

A mosquito didn't do this.

Just as I come to that realization, someone catches me from behind. Fear surges through me, turning my skin clammy. I squint, trying to glimpse the person responsible, but everything blurs. I'm fading too fast.

He grunts as he lifts me over his shoulder. The baritone of his voice sounds familiar, but I can't place it. His footsteps crunch against leaves, and I get the vague sense that he's dragging me out of sight. Away from anyone who can see us. Away from anyone who can help me.

Oh God.

My heart beats wildly inside my unmoving body. I want to scream, fight—do anything—but I can't move a muscle. Whoever has done this to me is getting away with it and there's nothing I can do.

I press to stay conscious, but I can't even fight that.

My world erupts into darkness.

~ ~

A vibrating cellphone wakes me up. My body immediately jerks forward but goes nowhere. I'm bound to something—a chair maybe. I don't know. I can't see anything. There's a cloth wrapped around my head, blinding me, and when I try to move my arms, an abrasive rope cuts into my wrists from behind.

Holy mother of God.

This is the kind of screwed up nightmare you see in movies where the girl is abducted by a serial killer, only to end up getting raped and tortured in some grotesque, twisted kind of way. Imagining the worst, my body starts to shake.

This is exactly why Harland used to go on and on about making sure I was always aware of my surroundings, scaring me with stories of Ted Bundy, and giving me pepper spray to hook onto my keychain. I should've listened to him, but instead I stupidly thought I was invincible and allowed myself to fall asleep on campus after dark. And look where that got me. Tied up to a chair in God knows where with God knows who.

This is it. This is my bitter end.

I shake more violently, feeling tears spring to my eyes. I don't want to cry, don't want to give my abductor the fear he's probably craving, but I can't help it. Bravery is for fairytales.

A phone continues to vibrate from some distant corner of the room. At least I think I'm inside of a room. An air conditioner is blowing from somewhere; I'm definitely indoors.

The vibrating suddenly stops.

"Hello?"

There's that voice again. I feel like I've heard it before, but it's not someone I know well.

"Yeah, she's here," the guy says.

He's referring to me. Oh Jesus. He's referring to *me*.

"No, I haven't gotten a hold of him yet."

The guy goes silent as someone speaks from the other line. "Yeah, okay. I'll have her call him when she wakes up." Another pause. "Actually it looks like she's waking up now."

My blindfold comes off. Blinking rapidly, it takes a few seconds for my eyes to adjust to the dim lighting.

There's a tall figure standing over me. I focus in on the figure's face.

Blond hair. Dimples. Flirtatious smile.

"Tyson?" I croak out.

"Hey, beautiful. Sorry about roughing you up like this, but it had to be done."

Okay. Um. Not exactly the cold-blooded killer type I expected, but I'm still stunned, so stunned that I can't speak. I look around the room, trying to process it all.

We're in some type of office—I think. There's a desk and swivel chair in the corner, but other than that, the room is bare. There are no windows and only one door. We could be underground, possibly a basement.

My eyes shift back to Tyson. Seeing him standing there gives me some of my courage back. He's Wesley's friend. This has to be some kind of weird prank. But for what reason? Initiations? From what I know, Tyson is deeply involved in a fraternity, but I've never heard of anything like this happening. This had to be something he did on his own, and the thought of that freaks me out all over again.

I shuffle against my chair. "Let me out of this thing."

"Can't do that, sweetheart. You have to stay put. I can't risk you trying to escape."

"Are you *insane*?" I screech. "You do know you can go to prison for kidnapping and drugging me, don't you?"

Fear doesn't settle into his features the way I hoped it would. In fact, he doesn't look the least bit put off.

"Don't make me gag you. If you keep shouting like that, I won't have another choice."

Something in his voice quiets me. He's serious. This isn't the charming Tyson I'm used to seeing. There's an edge to him. An intense focus. The way he's acting is almost frightening.

"Why are you doing this?"

"It's nothing personal against you, Doll," he says, rifling through the desk drawer. "You're just the insurance."

"Insurance?" What the hell does he mean by that?

Tyson doesn't clarify anything. He pulls a small object out of the drawer. "Hey that's my phone," I say, recognizing the Eye of Ra painted on the back of the case. I drew it myself with black nail polish.

Tyson punches in a few buttons, making me wish I'd programmed the thing with a security code.

"What are you doing?" I ask, leaning forward in my seat.

"We're going to call your rescuer," he answers without looking up from the phone. "Huh. You don't have Wes's number saved in here."

My entire body goes still. Is Wesley in on this too?

I squeeze my eyes shut, refusing to believe that. He would never do something like this, would he? A small part of me wonders if he wanted me out of the picture. Our last year is coming to end. Maybe he wanted Harland's fortune all to himself.

No, that's *not* true.

If that were the case, he would've let me stay in that shithole condo with Styler. He would've never fought him for the map.

But things have changed since then. We're no longer speaking…we're no longer anything.

I slowly open my eyes, almost afraid to face Tyson. "D-did Wesley plan this?"

"What?" Tyson laughs once. "Naw, but he'll wish he saw it coming."

I release a breath I didn't realize I was holding. He didn't betray me.

I should've never doubted it in the first place. He's not the kind of person who would do something like this, and for the first time in three years, I can honestly say I know him well enough to believe that.

"So what's this about then?" I ask Tyson. "Why do you need me to get to Wesley?"

"You're the insurance, remember? Think of Wes as the payee. Once he pays up, he'll get you back safe and sound."

"Safe and sound…as opposed to what?"

"Dead and silent," Tyson says without batting an eye.

I bite my lower lip. The way he said that seemed way too sincere for comfort. "If you think he has any money, you're sadly mistaken. He doesn't get his inheritance until he gets his degree. You should know that since you're his so-called friend. Although I doubt he'll consider you one after he finds out you're trying to rob him."

"Friendship comes and goes, sweetheart, and it's not money I'm after. Wesley has something we want. Something that belongs to us."

"Who is this *we* you keep referring to? The only person I see here is you."

"I represent one of many, but who we are doesn't concern you. The only thing you should be worried about is making sure Wesley gives us what we want."

He seems so certain and confident. I want to know what's up his sleeve. "You're missing one crucial part of your master plan," I point out to Tyson.

"Oh? And what might that be?"

"Wesley may not be interested in trading whatever he has for me, especially if it's as valuable as you say."

Tyson bursts out laughing, and dammit if he doesn't sound really amused. "Why don't you think you'd be worth it to him?"

For a moment, I debate whether it's in my best interest to tell Tyson the truth about Wesley and me. Probably not, especially since he's counting on him to come here on my behalf. Then again if Tyson is telling the truth, and my life really is on the line, then it's better not to drag Wesley into this too. Although I'm still hurt by the way he believed Christine's accusations, I don't want to see anything bad happen to him. Convincing Tyson that I'm no longer important to Wesley seems like a long shot, but it's worth a try.

"Wesley and I don't speak to one another," I say, carefully choosing my words because I don't want to mess this up. "We're not even friends. I'm sorry to disappoint you, but I don't think he'd risk anything for me."

"Since when? Two weeks ago?"

I blink. How would he know something like that?

"Don't look so surprised, sweetheart. I've watched Wesley dig himself into a hole over you every night for the past two weeks. If he's not piss drunk, he's pummeling his fists into someone's face for no reason. Look at this," Tyson says, pointing to his left eye, which is slightly purple. "This was for telling him he looked like shit—which he did."

I swallow, absorbing what Tyson is telling me. Is it the truth? I figured Wesley was off living his life just fine without me in it. He's never had a problem moving on from one girl to the next.

"You don't know I'm the cause of his behavior," I point out. "Something else must be bothering him."

Tyson shrugs. "Doubt it."

"The Wesley I know doesn't get torn up over girls."

"Yeah, and the Wesley I know doesn't get slapped in the face by some chick at a bar for calling her the wrong name."

I flinch. "What do you mean?"

"I guess he thought he could forget you by hooking up with some random girl. It didn't work. I heard her tearing his ass apart for calling her Dahlia."

"You're making that up," I say, shaking my head.

"Are you trying to convince me…or yourself?"

I stare at the floor without seeing it. My mind goes back to the night I walked out of Wesley's room. The things he said about my mom…and the things he said about me…it hurt, and so I tried to hurt him back. But I never really believed hurting Wesley was a possibility. He's practically untouchable the way he can't be fazed. At least up until now that's what I thought.

My chest feels tighter, constricting. The thought of hurting him, *really* hurting him, doesn't sit well inside of me.

"Uh huh, that's what I thought," Tyson says, watching it all sink in. "You're beginning to see the truth."

"Now what?" A cold, sick dread fills my throat. "You go in for the kill?"

"Thanks to you, this little meltdown of his gave us the perfect timing to set everything up. It couldn't have worked out any better."

"I'm so happy for you," I say, seething.

"Like I said, it's nothing personal, sweetheart."

"You're betraying someone who has been a loyal friend to you for years. What's more personal than betrayal?

And more importantly, what matters more to you than loyalty?"

"That's an easy one. Legacy."

Right now I really wish I wasn't tied up because I'd dearly love to smack the arrogance off of Tyson's face. "Let me guess. Wesley found some long lost treasure, and you want to make a name for yourself."

His lips curve into a slow grin. "You're very perceptive, you know."

"You'll never get your legacy. And if you do, it'll be a lie."

"You wouldn't understand. What Wesley has was never his to take."

"Welcome to the world of treasure hunting. That's how it works, you jackass."

Tyson's grin disappears. "Careful. I don't have to make this easy on you."

He stares me down, but I refuse to be intimidated. "Neither do I."

"You *will* cooperate. You don't have any choice in the matter. Like I said before, you're just the insurance. But don't worry, beautiful. It should all be over soon." He holds my phone up, the dial screen on display. "And I happen to know Wes's number by heart."

CHAPTER TWENTY-FOUR

WESLEY

I'm not sure why I'm here. Maybe I'm fueled by a depraved need to torture myself. Showing up in the one place where I'd be guaranteed to see her, hiding out in the corner of the classroom like some weirdo stalker—it's pathetic.

The seat in the back of the lecture hall where Dahlia normally keeps herself hidden away is still empty. My eyes steer toward the clock on the wall. It's 4:15 p.m. She should be here by now. She comes to Professor Barakat's class every Tuesday and Thursday like clockwork. But every second that ticks by makes it more and more obvious that she won't be here today. I feel as empty as her chair. I hate that something as small as her absence has the ability to control my emotions.

This could be about Christine. Maybe she doesn't feel comfortable coming here anymore, even in disguise. Maybe she doesn't want to risk running into Christine again after what happened at the party.

I tap my fingers against the desk. Without Dahlia, there's no point in staying. She is my entire reason for being here. I should go, but the professor has already begun his lecture, and I'm not sure what it is about him, but something keeps me glued to my seat.

He's going on and on about a fundraiser he runs every year to raise money for a summer expedition. Apparently he doesn't actually go on the expedition; instead he researches locations and raises the money. Dahlia mentioned before the professor wasn't the adventurous type. *I bet he's never been on an expedition in his life*, she said. *He only admires the people who have enough courage to do what he teaches.*

It doesn't make sense though. Why would he fund the same expedition year after year but not take part of it?

As I'm wondering what it's all about, I hear the words *Saiful Azman,* and I snap to attention.

"Every year I encourage my students to look for the Sword of Dreams," Professor Barakat tells the class. "Fourteen expeditions have been completed, and so far, none one of them have been successful. Some people say we're looking for a myth. Some people tell me I'm wasting my time. Those same nonbelievers haven't read the evidence. They haven't seen the sword painted in murals, or heard of it spoken of in legends."

The professor steps around his podium, slowly pacing the floor. "I've been teaching for over twenty years now. I first started researching the *Saiful Azman* when I was a student at UGA. I even did my dissertation on its existence. *I* believe it exists. I also believe I will lead one of my students to uncover it some day. We simply need to be pointed toward the right direction."

The energy in the classroom noticeably changes. Students lean forward in their seats, wearing hopeful expressions. They all want to be that student Professor Barakat is touting. I'm the only one sitting back, tensing up, feeling like I'm wearing a big sign on my forehead that screams, *You're all too late!*

Unfortunately for Professor Barakat, he'll never be able to prove the sword's existence, because I'll never reveal it. It belongs with Sam, not in some stupid fucking museum to be gawked at by people who didn't give their life to finding it. Sam didn't spend the little time he had here researching. He went out there and faced the world. He dug up earth with his own hands. He wasn't a coward.

Barakat doesn't deserve the sword.

Sam does. And I refuse to feel guilty about that.

The rest of the class passes by in a hazy blur of slides and the professor's monotone voice. It isn't until it's over that I understand why I stayed to begin with.

I need to speak to him, face to face.

I need to understand what draws Dahlia to this man.

I need to…I don't know. But I have a feeling speaking to him will give me the chance to figure it out.

People brush by me in a hurry to leave while I slowly walk toward the podium. Some of the students surround Barakat, bombarding him with questions. I stand back until I know I'll get him alone.

"The sign up sheet for next summer's expedition is online!" Barakat shouts. "Check the class website!"

Most of the students break away after hearing that, the crowd dissipating through the lecture hall's double doors. Before long, we're the only two people left inside. He doesn't notice me at first, and I don't say anything. I just stand there and watch him, wondering what the hell I'm gonna say when he notices me. He turns off the projector, then moves to his desk, filing away papers into his briefcase. Once he's all packed up, he turns to leave, but abruptly stops short because I'm standing in his way.

"Can I help you?"

His eyes meet mine, and I freeze. I know those eyes, amber and warm like the setting sun. They're Dahlia's eyes. No one I've ever come across has that same remarkable shade except her…and now this guy.

Fucking hell, does this mean what I think it means?

I analyze his face, noticing the way it slightly resembles hers, the straight slope of his nose, his complexion, his cheekbones, everything. Realizing who he is and what he means to her—it makes me feel sick over the way I questioned their relationship.

"Do you have a question?" It takes me a few moments to realize Barakat is becoming frustrated by my silence. Clearing his throat, he says, "Is there something I can help you with, kid? Otherwise I need to get to my office."

"Dahlia Reynolds," I say, blurting out her name because I have no fucking clue where to start. "You're her father, aren't you?"

Barakat turns a few shades paler. He scans the classroom, then eyes the door before looking at me again. "What's this about?"

"It's true." I shake my head, still in shock. "It's fucking true." Part of me is still in disbelief, even though I can see the evidence with my own eyes.

"Are you looking for money?" he asks, confused. "What do you want?"

"So she's a secret then," I surmise. "What is she—your love child? The wife doesn't know about her? Obviously Christine doesn't because she thinks Dahlia is your girlfriend."

Professor Barakat slowly drops his briefcase to the floor. "You've spoken to Christine? She told you that?"

"She told *Dahlia* that. She saw her come to your house one night, and she assumed the two of you were having an affair."

"Christ, I didn't realize she saw her…" He turns away from me. "My wife knows about Dahlia, but my children don't."

Meaning what? He disowned Dahlia? She's not allowed to be part of their family? "Why is she a secret?" I ask him. "Why don't your kids know who their sister is?"

This guy is really starting to piss me off. I can't figure out why, but he seems more concerned about protecting his other children than Dahlia.

"Who are you?" Barakat faces me again, studying me carefully. "And how do you know so much about my family?"

"You don't get to ask questions until you're done answering mine," I tell him, my tone turning as low and as menacing as I feel. "Believe me, I don't care that you're a professor. I don't care about your precious family. You'll give me my answers, or I'll go to Christine and tell her what you've been keeping from her."

Barakat believes me. He nods and pulls out the chair behind his desk, lowering himself into it. I cross my arms and lean against the side of the podium, waiting for him to speak. I think he's expecting me to sit, but I'm too angry. I need to keep my distance. Otherwise I might end up punching this guy in the face.

"My wife and I had a fight a month before our wedding. At that time, I was confused, wasn't sure what I wanted, wasn't sure if I wanted to get married at all. While we were separated, I met Lily—Dahlia's mother. We dated for a while. She was…different than the Moroccan girls I grew up with. Free-spirited. Out-going. I fell in love with her." He pauses, staring at the wall, and for a second it looks like he forgets I'm there.

"So what happened?" I prompt him. "Obviously you didn't end up with Dahlia's mom, or we wouldn't be having this conversation."

"No, I didn't," he sighs. "My wife came to me a few weeks later and told me she was pregnant. Things were different back then; the Moroccan community we grew up in was extremely traditional. I knew if I didn't do the right thing, our friends and family would shun her. They'd shun me too. So we got married. It wasn't until after Dahlia was born that I found out about her existence. Lily was angry with me for choosing my wife over her. By the time she finally told me, it was too late."

"So you didn't end up with the woman you loved. Big fucking deal. Sounds like you didn't deserve her in the first place. What I want to know is why you're still keeping your daughter a secret."

Barakat scratches his jaw, and I can tell he doesn't want to answer that question. A few seconds tick by before he speaks again. "My wife made me swear never to reveal Dahlia to the rest of our family. We have a powerful name to carry. My older brother was elected to be a representative on The Assembly of Councillors. My wife's father is a prominent military leader in Morocco. It sounds harsh, but Dahlia would've been an embarrassment. All they'd see is the daughter of an American whore."

I flinch at his words.

"It's not how I see her—or Lily," Barakat quickly explains. "But they would've objectified them that way. I was forced to choose, either Dahlia or my family."

I shake my head, too enraged to see straight. "Dahlia *is* your family, you fucking idiot."

"I know," Barakat whispers. "But I had no choice."

"What about her choices?" I ask him. "Why did she come to your house the night Christine saw her? And why was she crying?"

I have a good feeling I already know the answer to that question, but I want to hear him admit it. When he doesn't answer me, I slam my fist down on the podium, rattling the wood. "*Why*, Professor?"

He swallows, unable to look me in the eye. "Her mom had just passed," he answers me in a shaky voice. "Dahlia wanted to get to know me. She wanted to meet the rest of her family."

"And you turned her away, didn't you?"

Barakat only nods.

"So she had just lost her mom. She was new in town, with no other friends or family. And the one person she comes to for help turns her away."

"It wasn't an easy thing to do," Barakat says, still staring away from me. "I wish she could be a part of my life, but it's impossible."

"Did you know she comes to this class every Tuesday and Thursday just to see you?"

Barakat shakes his head. Of course he didn't know. That's why she wore the makeup and baggy clothes—so he wouldn't notice her.

"Well she does. She comes here, probably to listen to your shitty-ass lectures because it's the only piece of you she can have."

Barakat blinks back tears. He's trying to keep it together, but he's not holding up so well. I don't feel bad for him. All I have to do is think back to the way Christine accused Dahlia of destroying their precious family, and the way I practically accused her, and anger reignites my blood all over again.

I take a few steps closer to Barakat, clenching my fists. "You're losing out on getting to know an amazing person. She's smart, she's funny, and she's passionate about archeology just like you…" I stop, my eyes resting on Barakat's briefcase.

The *map*.

I'd bet my entire inheritance Dahlia's map led to the sword. God, why didn't I realize it sooner? She was looking for it too. To impress her piece of shit father. She put her inheritance and her whole life on the line to prove herself to someone who probably wishes she didn't exist. If she ever found out I had it, she'd hate me for it.

Tears are streaming from Barakat's eyes now, but his expression is hollow. I'm not sure if he's even paying attention to what I'm saying anymore. I should probably leave, but I don't right away.

"Don't worry, she won't need you." I stare at him with disgust. "She's going to be happy. I don't know how, but I'm going to make sure that girl is so happy she won't have one damned speck of empty space in her heart for you to fill."

Barakat looks up at me. His voice comes out choked. "Who are you?"

I don't answer his question. He doesn't need to know who I am. All he needs to know is what I've already said. Dahlia doesn't need him. She may think she does now, but I'll do whatever I have to do to make sure she never feels that way again.

My hands are shaking when I step outside of the building. I didn't realize how much anger I was holding back. It wasn't just anger for Dahlia. All the rage and bitterness I felt over the years for Harland is here with me now, brimming at the surface. Even knowing what I now know about why he left, and the disease he kept secret, I'm still angry.

He didn't give me the chance to be there for him. I know I was too stubborn to listen, but he should've *made* me. If I'd have known he was sick...

I wouldn't have lost those last few years.

Instead he gave them to Dahlia and her mother. Not that I'm jealous. I'm glad Dahlia had the part of him I couldn't. She's the one person in this world who deserved to have a father. A real one. But I still wish I could've had mine too.

For so long, I've blamed him. Then when I found his letter, I blamed myself. But we're both to blame. I'm still mad as hell that he pushed me away, and I'd give anything not to be. I'd give anything to let that anger go because after everything he went through, after everything he gave up, he doesn't deserve it.

My phone vibrates inside my pocket, and I've never been so goddamned thankful for the distraction. I pull it out to see Dahlia's name lit across the screen. I answer right away.

"Dahlia, I'm so glad you called. I really need to talk to you."

The phone shuffles for a second, and then I hear a voice I wasn't expecting. "If you want to see her alive again, you'll listen carefully to what I'm about to say.

CHAPTER TWENTY-FIVE

DOLL

At one point or another, I'm able to fall asleep in the chair I'm tied up to. Definitely not the most comfortable sleep in the world, but I'm glad I found a way to pass the time because otherwise I'd be pretty bored. Although when I wake up, I don't feel very rested. My body is so stiff from the awkward position, it makes me want to cry. Tyson only let me loose once to pee in a bathroom directly outside the office. At the time I tried looking around to get clues about where I'm being kept, but there wasn't anything that stood out. I'm not even sure if I'm inside of a house, an office building or some kind of underground basement. The latter seems the most likely, only because there are no windows, no detectable sunlight coming from anywhere. Unless it's nighttime, which would explain the lack of outside light, but I've been going in and out of sleep for so long now that I don't know what time of day it is anymore. It was dark when Tyson abducted me. I'm not sure how much time has passed between now and then.

My stomach growls for the hundredth time, reminding me of how hungry I am. Complaining about it didn't get me anywhere. Tyson said there wouldn't be any food until Wesley showed up. Then he threatened, like so many times before that, to stick a gag in my mouth if I didn't stop bothering him. The existence of this gag of his is questionable indeed. I considered screaming for the heck of it, but I didn't want to push my luck. I'll wait until I know I'm in a place where I have a better chance of being heard. In the meantime, I try to ignore my hunger pains by going back to sleep. It works for a while, but never for very long.

Muted voices carry from somewhere outside the room, jerking me to full alertness. I listen closely, praying for the chance to finally be let outside of this wretched chair. If I ever get out of this mess, I swear I'm going to smash the thing to pieces.

I'm holding my breath by the time the door clicks open. Tyson walks in followed by another guy I don't recognize. I crane my head to look around them, my heart racing. Part of me is praying Wesley will be there, and the other part of me hopes he's not.

My heart stops for a split second, and then he steps inside the room. His eyes dart to mine, his forehead relaxing when he sees me.

Wesley's here. He came. It surprises me how glad I am to see him.

My eyes roam over every inch of his face and body, drinking up the sight of him. He looks like he's been awake all night, his bloodshot eyes ringed with dark circles, and his skin paler than usual. But even though he looks like hell, he's still the most welcome sight I've ever seen. I slowly let out the breath I was holding, feeling a heaviness lift from my shoulders.

"Stop right there," Tyson orders.

Wesley pauses as he reaches for me, his jaw working as he turns to face Tyson. "Then untie her from the fucking chair." I flinch at the cold severity in his voice. I've never seen him so furious. Granted, he's doing a good job of keeping it in check, but it's all there in the tense lines of his body.

"We're not on your territory anymore, Wes." Tyson drops his hand by his belt loop, resting his palm on the handle of a black pistol sticking out from the front of his jeans.

"Look, I told you I'd give you what you want," Wesley says, eyeing the gun. "But not unless she comes with us. You're not taking any risks and neither am I."

"How do we know you won't run off the second you get a chance?"

"Because I want this to be over with. I want you and the rest of Black Templar to leave me the fuck alone."

Black Templar? I've never heard of that name before, but I get the feeling it's the "we" Tyson referred to earlier.

The man I don't recognize moves to Tyson's side. I don't recognize him, but I notice he seems older than the typical college student, his dark hair graying at the sides. He gives Tyson the go ahead to release me, which gives me the impression he holds some authority. "Her presence will ensure his cooperation. We're flying private anyway; they'll be with us the whole time."

Wesley moves to untie me before Tyson gets the chance. The rope unravels from around my wrists, and my muscles scream as I move my arms back around my sides. It hurts, but the pain is the most delicious feeling in the world, and I enjoy every second of it. As soon as I stand up, I kick the chair as hard as I can. It flies back into the corner of the room, turning on its side, but not breaking into the million pieces I hoped it would. "I hate that chair," I mutter in explanation, noticing everyone's stares.

"You'll never have to sit in it again, babe," Wesley tells me, and for the first time since he walked in, I notice the duffel bag attached to his arm.

"Are we going somewhere?"

Wesley doesn't answer my question. Instead he moves in front of me, cupping my face in his hands. "I'm so sorry they've involved you in this." It makes believe the things Tyson said are true. That Wesley never moved on the way I've seen him do with other girls…that he still has feelings for me. I'm trying to process what that means, but stop myself before I get too caught up in my own head.

As much as I'd like to, I can't analyze whatever we are to each other right now. Not with Tyson and his lackey talking about flying private, and the unexplained duffel bag at Wesley's side.

Right now I need answers.

"Who are they? *Really*," I ask, nodding to Tyson. "What do they want from you, and why are they talking about private planes?"

Wesley looks over at them, and then back at me, giving me the impression he doesn't want to tell me this. Too bad for him because I'm not moving until someone starts talking. "They're part of a secret society," he finally says. "Black Templar—basically a bunch of pretentious douchebags who think they own the world."

"You should be careful of what you say," Tyson warns coolly.

"And you should give me some fucking space right now." Wesley steers a hard gaze on him, clenching his fists. "Don't forget how you got that black eye. I'm pretty sure I could give you another one to match it before anyone manages to pull me off of you."

Tyson's lip curls, the rage in his eyes unmistakable. "You've always thought you were so damned special, Wes, but I have news for you. Throwing your fists around won't work here. Being a Kent won't work here either. Your dad's name doesn't mean anything to Black Templar."

The hatred and jealousy in Tyson's eyes is real, and all of it directed at Wesley. Apparently there was another layer he kept hidden beneath his charming party guy façade. How the hell he kept it buried for so long is amazing to me.

"A lot of things don't matter to Black Templar, *friend*," Wesley mutters in disgust.

Tyson stands there for a few seconds, staring Wesley down. The tension in this room is so jolting, it feels like one of them will explode at any second. Then, surprisingly, Tyson backs off and heads to the door. "You have five minutes. The plane leaves in fifteen. Don't even think about trying something stupid."

As soon as they're out the door, my questions spill out in quick succession. "Why is he doing this, Wes? What do they want from you? And you still haven't told me why there's a *plane* waiting. I hope he doesn't think I'm going anywhere with him after keeping me tied up to a chair for hours on end."

"Dahlia, you need to calm down. I swear I'll get us out of this mess." Wesley places his hands over mine, squeezing them, his voice and closeness soothing me in a way that makes me believe him. "Tyson is doing this because he's a backstabbing asshole, and he wants an artifact he knows I have, because he was there with me when I found it."

"Why?" I shake my head, trying to understand.

"It's ancient," he says, shrugging. "And priceless."

"Did he use you to find it? Is that why he pretended to be your friend?"

Wesley nods. "My dad had a reputation. Black Templar knew he had a knack at finding lost treasure, and Tyson got close to me for the sole purpose of using me to get what they wanted. To his credit, I never saw through his act. But what he didn't expect was that I'd hide the treasure. I think he assumed I'd keep it in Kent Library, which, by the way is why that guy broke in on the night of the hurricane."

Okay. I think I start to understand. Tyson probably got another chance to look in the library during the party they threw for Wesley at Kent House. None of us were paying attention to him, too caught up with what was going on with Christine, and then seeing Gwen and Miles. Kidnapping me must be his backup plan.

"So if you didn't stash it in the house, where is this artifact?"

Shuffling his feet, Wesley readjusts the duffel bag's strap on his shoulder. I brace myself, betting anything this is the part where the plane comes in.

"It's not…here. Not exactly."

"When you say here, please tell me you mean it's not in Gainesville."

He shakes his head.

"Not in Florida?" I ask, hopeful.

"Not in this country," he admits, wincing. "It's in Morocco."

I let out a deep breath. "Okay. I can deal with this. Why is it in Morocco?"

"I left it there for safe keeping…with my uncle."

"Why didn't you bring it here?"

"Because I knew I was being followed in Egypt. Not only that, but I had to account for everything I brought back with me after the excavation in Egypt. If I had been caught with the artifact, their treasure laws would've prevented me from taking it. I figured I'd bide my time and go back when I felt it was safe."

I shake my head. Of course he wouldn't have risked getting caught. He's a Kent. When it comes to treasure, Kents don't adhere to legalities; they find ways around it.

"So let me guess. Black Templar wants you to guide them there, right?"

"Yes."

"And now I have to come too?"

"I'm sorry, babe, but I'm not leaving you alone with them. I don't have another choice, since they're refusing to release you until they get their artifact."

"Why do you keep calling it that?" I tilt my head as I try to read his face, sensing he's still keeping something from me. "Why can't you come out and tell me what it is? We've both studied archeology. It's not like I'm some clueless bystander."

He runs a hand through his hair, letting out another deep breath. "I'm not sure why I hoped you wouldn't ask me that."

"Just come out and say it, Wes," I tell him. "I've been through enough already. I can handle this."

The corners of his eyes tighten as he looks at me. "It's the *Saiful Azman*."

The words take a few seconds to register, and when they do, I feel them slam into me like fists. For a second, I wonder if I heard him correctly. I almost want to ask him, just to be sure. My mind could be playing tricks on me. Maybe I've been caught up in this nightmare for so long that my brain wants to keep going with it, extending the torture.

But when I look at Wesley's face and see the way he's looking at me—like he's afraid of my reaction—I know I heard him right the first time.

"Say something," he pleads with me.

Say something?

I swallow, unsure of where to begin. How could I possibly think of anything to say right now? I don't even know what to think, or how to feel. All I can do is stand there in total silence, trying to figure out how to overcome the shock over hearing those words. *It's the Saiful Azman.* They repeat over and over inside my mind, getting louder by the second.

"You really found it?" I whisper, my voice breaking. "The Sword of Dreams?"

When he nods, I feel my throat go dry and my stomach turn in knots. Part of me refuses to believe he's telling the truth. He couldn't have found that sword. Not *my* sword.

I feel his eyes on me, watching me as if he's waiting for me to crumble. "I swear I didn't know you were looking for it until recently. My brother had been searching for it for years. He was chasing down leads in India right before he got into the car crash that killed him. I swore I'd find it for him…I swore his work wouldn't go unfinished."

I nod, taking that in. My gaze drops to the floor, and I cradle my stomach. I feel sick. Countless nights I've spent dreaming of that sword, envisioning it in my mind, picturing it in my hands. All for nothing. And here I am, standing beside the boy who already dug it up, the boy who lived out my dreams and didn't even know it.

"Dahlia, say something. *Please.*"

I almost want to laugh, because there are so many things to say, and yet nothing at all. I can't be mad at him. It's not his fault he found the sword before I could. But I can't be happy either, because it can never be unfound. My hands will never be the first to uncover it. My eyes will never be the first to absorb its beauty.

Of course he'd be the one to find it. He's Harland's son after all; I should've known he'd be looking too.

I want to ask him so many questions, like what it looks like, and if it's really made of solid gold. I want to ask him where he found it, how he tracked it down, and whether it was buried or if it had been stored in some ancient tomb.

So many questions…but I don't ask any of them. There's a painful lump lodged against the back of my throat preventing me from speaking. My eyes and nose sting, and the only thing I want to do is go home, lock myself in my room, and spend the next few days crying my eyes out. But I can't do that either.

Instead I have to go to Morocco and watch Wesley hand over my dream to the members of Black Templar. Before I'm allowed to fall apart, I have to feel my heart ripped out a little more.

"Let's just go," I say, blinking back the tears threatening to give way. I move toward the door. "Do you have my passport?"

"Yes. I asked Gwen to help me find it."

"Good." I reach for the handle, pausing. There's still one thing on my mind. "Why didn't you just call the police?"

"I didn't want to risk it."

"Why not? We can risk it together. The first chance we get, we can try to run. I'd rather do that than watch you give the *Saiful Azman* to them."

Wesley shakes his head. "I'd rather just give it to them. Even if we escape, they'll keep coming back until they get what they want. Before, when it was just me they were after, that was fine. I could handle it. But I won't risk you too.

Your life is too important…" he let's out a heavy sigh. "Dahlia, you're too important to me."

If I had heard him say those words ten minutes ago, it would've thrilled me. But hearing them now is like watching it happen instead of feeling it happen. I can't react to this, not with the shock of knowing everything I've worked for is gone.

"Fine," I say quietly. "Let's just go."

Somehow I stumble out of the building with my composure intact. When I get outside I notice Tyson had been keeping me in the Philosophy Hall—an old abandoned building on campus due for reconstruction. I let out a small laugh. All this time I'd been wondering where I was, and they never even took me off campus.

A black van waits for us behind the building. Tyson opens the door. "Get in."

Wesley and I do as he says. The van takes off at a speedy rate, in a hurry to get us to whatever plane we're being driven to.

"You okay?" Wesley whispers.

I nod, keeping my gaze focused ahead.

But inside I am the furthest thing from okay. Inside I'm wondering how the hell I'm going to get through this.

CHAPTER TWENTY-SIX

WESLEY

Her silence is killing me. There's a million things I'd like to say, but I feel like all of them are the wrong things. I can't imagine how she feels. If it were possible, I'd go back in time and bring her on that expedition with me. I'd lead her to the sword and swear to everyone she found it on her own.

Whoa.

It's true. I really would give her the damned sword if I could. Sam was my brother, my best friend, and I loved him. I would've done anything for him. Searching for the sword was his passion, and he dreamed of finding it, therefore I dreamed of finding it.

But Sam didn't need it. Not the way Dahlia does.

Resting her head against the wall of the plane, she quietly stares out the window, making me wish I had the right fucking words to make this better. I cough uncomfortably, and try and come up with something.

"Dahlia…" Yeah, I've got nothing.

"It's okay," she says without looking at me. "We don't need to talk."

"Don't you think we should?"

"It's just treasure," she says, shrugging. "There's a lot more of it in this world to be discovered."

She's lying. It's not just treasure to her. The problem is she doesn't know that I know what it means to her, but how can I express that without telling her I went to Barakat's class and discovered who he really is? She doesn't want to open up about him, and that's driving me crazier than anything else.

I need to get her out of her own head. I unfasten my seatbelt, click the button on hers and yank her up by her arm.

"Hey—"

"Come with me."

Thankfully she doesn't ask any questions. Tyson and his crew eye me on the way to the jet's restroom, but they don't try to stop me. I steer Dahlia inside, closing the door behind us. Then I flick the lock to OCCUPIED.

"You're being a little pushy," she says, eyeing the door. "What's this about?"

"Go ahead and yell at me," I say, turning to face her. "Get it out of your system."

The restroom's cabin is small, and we're crammed closely together. It's not the most ideal place for this conversation, but since we're on a jet with eight members of Black Templar watching our every move, this bathroom is the only option for privacy.

"Why would I want to yell at you?"

"Because you're angry. And you're hurt. And you need to get it out."

She shakes her head. "No, Wesley, that's stupid. I'm not angry. Now please let me out of here."

I lean against the doorframe, refusing to budge. "Not until you get it out."

"You keeping me trapped in here is the only thing bothering me right now," she says in an annoyed tone.

"Come on, don't be a wuss." I reach out and shove her shoulder. "Scream at me if it makes you feel better."

"Did you just *push* me?" She looks at the spot on her shoulder where I shoved her, and then looks back at me, her mouth hanging open.

"So what?" I shove her shoulder again, more forceful this time. "What are you going to do about it?"

"I can't believe you just did that. Again," she says, her eyes bulging. "You do realize I'm a girl, don't you?"

"It didn't escape my notice."

"So then stop pushing me!" She points a finger at me to emphasize her point.

"If it makes you so mad, then push me back. Get it out."

"No." She stubbornly shakes her head. "I'm not mad, and I'm not your puppet. You can't just expect me to do things because you say so."

"So it doesn't piss you off that I found the sword before you did?"

There's a long pause before she answers. "No."

I narrow my eyes on her, noticing the way her voice went up a notch. "You sure about that? Because if you'd spent more time searching instead of hiding behind your little books, you might've beat me to it."

I'm taunting her, and I feel kind of bad about it, but she's not cracking. I need her to tell me the truth. I need her to trust me enough to do that.

"All you ever did was research, Dahlia. Why didn't you look for it?"

Teeth clenched, she breathes out through her nostrils. "That's not fair. I didn't know where to look."

"Or maybe you weren't *adventurous* enough to try."

Before I know what's happening, Dahlia slams her hands against my chest, shoving me into the cabin door.

Damn.

I didn't know she had it in her. "Thought you said you weren't angry."

"Apparently I lied."

A knock sounds at the door. "Everything all right in there?"

"It's fine. Go away," I growl out. Then, turning back to Dahlia, I push her for more. "Tell me why you're angry."

Tears threaten to spill, and it gives me hope. Her walls are starting to come down. "I hate that you found it before me," she whispers.

"What else?"

Sighing, she waves her hand dismissively. "I don't know."

I turn her chin up, forcing her to look at me. "What else?"

Her whole face tightens. She glares at me, directing all the pent up anger and frustration she tried to hide with one look. "I hate that I should've known better. I hate that you are so much like your dad, and I *hate* that you hate him because he was a good person. The best kind of person." She clenches her hands into fists at her sides. "And I hate what you said about my mother."

Hearing her words feel like a fist to the gut, but I take it all. I know I have this coming. "And?"

"I hate what you thought about me."

"Louder. I can't hear you."

She throws her fist against my chest, her voice rising. "I hate that you believed what Christine said, dammit!"

"Why the hell do you care what I think?" I yell back.

"I don't know." She takes a step back, shaking. "I shouldn't."

"But you do."

She nods. "Before this year, we were ghosts living in the same house. You were nothing to me…I almost wish you were still nothing to me."

I flinch. "You don't mean that."

"Yes, I do!" she cries out. "Everything would be so much easier. I'd rather feel nothing than—"

Before I think about what I'm doing, I grab Dahlia by the waist and pull her against me. My mouth crashes into hers, and without hesitation, she draws her arms behind my neck, kissing me back with a shocking fierceness.

I didn't mean for this to happen. I just wanted to give her space to vent, but now I can't seem to control myself. I can't stop myself from touching her, hoping to somehow erase what she said.

We both slam into the wall of the bathroom door. I lift Dahlia up, sliding her onto the small sink's counter. Her fingers grip my collar, and she pulls me toward her, wrapping her legs around my waist.

I kiss her like a starved man, unable to get enough. Her breath is coming in short gasps, and it thrills me to hear every single one. The kiss intensifies, and I begin to lose myself in the moment.

Another knock sounds at the door.

"What's going on in there?" Someone calls out, rattling the locked handle. "Open up!"

"Ignore them," I order Dahlia, kissing her along her jawline.

"Ignore who?" She looks at me, her eyelids heavy with passion. She grabs my face, guiding my mouth back to hers.

I kiss her again, living in the moment, unfazed by the persistent banging on the door. Neither of us seem to care about anything but each other. The outside world becomes a distant background noise. All I can concentrate on is the warmth of Dahlia's breath against my lips, the amazing way her skin feels, and how fucking good she tastes. I don't want it to end.

"Open up!" a gruff voice shouts. "Or else we're breaking down the goddamned door!"

This time Dahlia stiffens, her mouth breaking away from mine. "Wes?" she whispers.

My forehead drops to hers, and we both try to control our erratic breathing.

"All right," I shout to the person behind the door. "We'll be out in two fucking seconds."

It pains me, literally pains me, but I let go of Dahlia. I turn on the sink faucet and splash my face with cold water. "We should go," I tell her, catching her reflection through the mirror. She's straightening her clothes and trying to smooth down her hair.

"They're gonna think that we were…" She doesn't finish the rest, and it's funny to me that she can't say it.

"Doing exactly what we were doing?"

"Well…yeah." Her face grows a few shades redder. "But it'd be nice if they were left in the dark."

I reach out and tuck a flyaway hair behind her ear. "Who cares what they think, right? They coerced us into this plane, remember?"

"I suppose you have a point."

Someone bangs on the door, shaking the entire cabin. "Dammit, Kent! Open up!"

It's Tyson's voice this time. I swing open the door, and as a result, his balance is thrown off. He stumbles inside, falling to his knees. I lean down and pat him on the shoulder. "Vacant now, buddy."

Dahlia places her hand over her mouth, but not before I catch her grinning. "Just deserts," she says to me on the way back to our seats.

"You've got that right."

~ ~

DOLL

"I was wrong about your mom."

I look up at Wesley, drawing my brows together. That came out of nowhere, and I'm not entirely sure how to react. "What made you change your mind?"

"I finally read my dad's letter," he admits, shifting in his seat. "He never told us he was sick. I never knew…"

"That must've been hard on you." I reach for his hand, entwining my fingers through his.

I get it now. Harland was trying to protect his family, but instead he ended up hurting them. I can't even begin to imagine how Wesley feels. Those last few years with my mom were precious; I wouldn't give them back for the world. Being denied that time with her would've killed me. Harland was a good man, but I think he made a bad choice in not telling his family.

Wesley stares at our hands, a sort of sadness in his eyes. "And I was wrong for not believing you about Christine."

"I know. It's okay," I assure him. "We don't have to do this."

"Yes, we do." His eyes are suddenly focused on me. "I went to Barakat's class yesterday."

Fear ripples through my body, and I go completely still. "You did?"

"Yes."

The way he's speaking creates a tightening in my chest. It's not so much what he's saying, but how he's saying it that puts me on edge. "Why?"

"I think the better question is why do you want that sword so much?"

I loosen my fingers away from his and turn to stare out the window, focusing on the tiny view of passing clouds.

He knows. He's not coming out and saying that he knows, but I get the distinct impression he does.

"Don't do this to me again, babe. Don't shut me out."

"I don't like talking about him, Wes. It's complicated."

"Why is it so complicated?"

I press my lips together, unsure of how to say this. "Talking about him makes it real. I can't explain it; I just feel like it gives him strength over me somehow."

"We can't keep doing this, babe. We can't keep ignoring our problems, hoping they'll disappear. Life doesn't work that way."

"You know who he is, don't you?" I turn to face him, looking straight into his eyes. He carefully nods as if he's afraid to speak.

I stare down at my lap, fidgeting at the frayed strings on my bracelet. There's no avoiding this anymore. There's no hiding from it either. "I wanted the sword because he wanted it…" I swallow, my voice beginning to break. "But it doesn't matter because now I'll never have it."

"Did you think getting it would make him see you differently?"

"Yes. Maybe. I don't know." I let out a long sigh. "I guess I hoped he'd regret everything."

Wesley's voice softens. "Regret what, babe?"

He's making this so easy for me, but the words lodged in my throat are still the hardest ones to say. Not because Wesley's listening. But because I am.

"I'd hoped he'd regret…abandoning me."

"And who is *he*, Dahlia?"

I blink.

Here it is. The moment of truth.

"My father." I lean back against the seat, placing my hands over my face. "God, I've never admitted that out loud before."

My whole body is trembling, and I can't seem to get it together. The strange thing is, I feel better. I feel like I've let something out.

"Dahlia, look at me."

I shake my head, keeping my palms flat against my eyes. Whatever this feeling is, I don't want to ruin it so quickly by judgment or pity or whatever other sad emotion Wesley has reserved for me.

I hear his seat buckle click open. He pries my fingers away from my face, pulling me toward him. Strong arms encircle me, and I'm surrounded with the warmth of Wesley's chest. When I look up at him, there is no pity or judgment in his eyes. He's smiling. "That wasn't so bad, was it?"

"No." I smile back. "It surprisingly wasn't."

CHAPTER TWENTY-SEVEN

DOLL

It's after midnight in Marrakesh by the time we arrive. Tyson wanted to go straight to the sword's location, but everyone convinced him to wait until tomorrow. Apparently it's being kept in the desert, and it takes almost a full day to get there.

"Does your uncle live in the desert?" I ask Wesley curiously.

"No."

"So what's he doing there?"

"A job."

"What kind of job?"

"I don't know," Wesley shrugs. "I didn't ask."

It bothers me that he doesn't know much about where we're going or what to expect when we get there. He mentioned before that his uncle is a geologist, so I guess it makes sense for his work to take him out to the desert. Although I still hate what we're doing, I'm kinda looking forward to seeing it. I mean, it's the Sahara. Who wouldn't want to cross it off their bucket list?

On the way to our hotel, I try to look out the window to see some sights, but it's too dark. Our taxi driver shouts in Arabic at the other drivers, swerving and twisting through the small streets in the same way any American cabbie would. When Wesley says a few words to him in French, his whole demeanor changes. The driver laughs, and they strike up a conversation that lasts the entire drive.

Once we're in the hotel lobby, Wesley argues with Tyson over me being allowed to share the same room as him. As they're arguing, I look over the rest of Tyson's crew. There's five of them, four around my age, and the older one I recognize from back at the Philosophy building. His name is

James, but I'm not sure about the others. They all look semi-recognizable. They could very well be UF students, and most likely are.

Wesley told me on the plane there are more members—a lot more—spread all over the country. They believe they're descendants of Knights Templar, and because the sword was mentioned in one of their ancient texts, they feel entitled to the ownership of it. They share a self-righteous determination that makes me livid about the entire situation. I hate that they're getting away with this. I hate feeling so helpless to stop it.

Wesley's right though; we don't have another choice. They'll never back off until they get the sword. There's something ruthless in their tactics, something sinister in the way they go after people. They were ballsy enough to abduct me on campus property. The lengths they will go to are boundless.

Before I know what's happening, one of the guys pulls me in their direction, a slow smile on his lips. "Would you like to stay in my room?"

I turn my head, recoiling. His breath smells like sour milk, and the tone of his voice makes me cringe. "Thanks, but no thanks." I push at his arms. They're locked tight around my waist, and they won't budge. The harder I push, the tighter he pulls.

Chuckling at my attempts to get away, he says, "Why not? I promise to keep you warm."

"Get your goddamned hands off of her!" Wesley's fist plunges straight into the guy's face, the force sending us both to the floor.

As I'm scrambling away, I feel a hand on my elbow, lifting me up. Guilt immediately washes over Wesley's face. "I'm so sorry—I didn't think the idiot would fall over."

"I'm fine," I say, breathless.

The guy on the floor, however, is *not* fine. Blood drips from his nose, and there's a murderous look in his eyes. The others help him up, looking just as pissed, and for a second I fear they might gang up on Wesley.

A quick glance around the lobby tells me no one is paying any attention. There's a clerk at the front desk talking on the phone, but he has his back toward us. Other than that, there's no one.

Before all hell breaks loose, I march toward Tyson. In the calmest, most serious voice I can muster, I say, "You're either giving me my own room where I can lock the door, or you're sticking me with Wesley. I've put up with a lot of crap from you over the last few days, Tyson, and I swear to God I've reached my limit. If we wanted to escape, we would've done it by now."

A few long seconds of silence pass as we stare each other down. Then Tyson looks at Wesley, and back at me again. "The two of you can share a room," he finally allows. "I'll have someone keep watch outside your door."

"Great. Thanks."

Just when I think everything is over, Tyson signals one of the other guys. Then he snakes his hand around the crook of my arm. "Hey, wha—"

"Let's step outside, Kent."

It's James who is speaking to Wesley now. He's standing directly in front of him, daring him not to comply. I watch the other men go out the back of the hotel, one by one, and instantly I know what they're planning.

My heart begins to pound furiously against my chest. "No," I say, my eyes flicking to Wesley.

His features are stern, but I sense he knows what's coming. He nods once to James. "Let's get this over with."

"Wesley, no—"

My voice is muffled as Tyson draws my face into his chest. "There, there," he whispers into my ear. "Let's not cause a scene."

I'm pushing and fighting him with every ounce of strength I have, but his arms are like tree trunks. Turning my head just enough to get a quick breath, I scream, "Let him go!"

"Shut up!" he hisses. "The more you fight me, I swear to God, the worse I'll make it for him."

Cold metal grazes my side. I feel Tyson lift the barrel of a gun beneath the side of my shirt. Instantly I go still. "You wouldn't," I say, hearing the tremor in my voice. "We're in a public place. Not only that, but you'll never get your sword."

"Don't tempt me. Now that we have Wesley, we don't need you anymore."

"He won't help you if you kill me."

"Let's agree there's no need to find out."

With every precious second that passes, I feel the urge to fight this. To stop them. My eyes flick to the door Wesley and the others went through. Seeing it, knowing what's happening out there and not being able to do anything about brings a heaviness over my chest. There's nothing I can do, and I hate myself for it.

"Now be a good girl and go up to your room," Tyson directs me. "I promised the two of you won't be separated, and I meant it. He'll be up as soon as we're through with him." Tyson puts a key in my hand, then pushes me toward the stairs. "Run along now."

I glare at him, literally feeling surrounded by rage. I've never hated anyone as much as I hate him in this moment. I consider trying to get help, but he rests his hand on his hip bone where the bulge of his gun shows through his shirt, curbing any fight or flight notions coming to mind.

He's leaving me with no choice. I retreat up the narrow flight of stairs, running the entire way.

Waiting for Wesley is pure torture. I sit on the foot of the bed, thinking about when or if he'll come and whether or not I made the right decision in not calling for help. My stomach is in knots, and I feel nauseous. Every second that passes is worse than the last. I can't stand this. It's making me physically sick, knowing this is all my fault. I'm to blame for whatever pain they put him through.

When I hear someone stick a key in the door, my heart stops. I slowly stand, watching the door open. Wesley walks in, and I stop breathing.

His face is battered so badly I want to cry. His upper lip has been split open, blood smeared across his mouth. Both his cheeks have ugly red marks, the left one marked with a small cut above his cheekbone. He's hunched over holding his ribcage, and he walks inside the room with a limp. As usual, the pain is masked in his face, but he can't mask it in the way he's carrying himself.

"Oh my God, Wes. I am so sorry. This would've never happened if I—"

Wesley reaches out, gripping both my wrists in his hands. His voice is low and serious. "Don't you dare blame yourself for this. This isn't your fault. Do you understand me?"

I nod once, a weak effort.

He loosens his grip, searching my eyes. "What happened out there was Tyson those other assholes showing the size of their dicks. We're here because of them. Everything that has happened is because of them. *None* of this is your fault, babe. Okay?"

He stares at me intently, waiting for me to say something. I can't get past his reaction. I didn't expect him to be so upset about me blaming myself. Because I can't stand the idea of putting him through anything else, I give him the answer he's looking for.

"Okay."

He watches me for a long moment, and once he's satisfied, he releases me.

He drops the duffel bag on the chair beside the bed and crosses the room, stopping by the bathroom door. "I'm gonna take a shower. Are you hungry?"

"Yes," I say, feeling my stomach growl on cue.

"I saw a twenty-four hour room service menu by the phone. Why don't you call and order us something?"

"Okay." I turn around and see the menu sitting on the nightstand.

The bathroom door shuts and a moment later I hear the water running. I dial the number to the front desk, relieved to hear the clerk answer in English. I proceed to order enough food to feed five people, hoping Wesley's just as hungry as I am.

Out of curiosity I crack the door open to see if Tyson was serious when he said he'd put someone there to watch the room. Sure enough I glimpse one of his lackeys hanging out at the end of the hall. Frowning, I close the door and lock it.

I'm not sure what to do while I'm waiting for the food, so I search the room in hopes of finding a first aid kit. Luckily there's one stashed inside the closet. Rummaging through it, I pull out things I think Wesley might need, antiseptic, a packet of ibuprofen, Band-Aids, and lay them on the bed.

"There's something I wanna ask you," Wesley says, causing me to jump. He steps out of the bathroom, his hair damp, dressed in a plain white tee and gym shorts. I notice a few bruises on his arms and wince when I see them.

"What if I were to come up with a way that didn't involve Black Templar going home with the sword?"

I sit down on the side of the bed. After what just happened, his question isn't one I'm prepared for. "I don't know if that's a good idea. Even if you came up with a plan that works, you'll constantly have to look over your shoulder. They'll always be looking for a way to take it from you, Wes."

He kneels in the space in front of me, his eyes lit up. "Not if it's reported. Not if *you* claim it."

The excitement in his voice causes my pulse to quicken. "What do you mean?"

"Let's make it public, babe. We can tell the world you found it—you'll be famous. Well, like the fifteen minute kind of famous," he adds with a grin. "But it would still be enough to throw in your dad's face. The one student he wanted to glorify is the same one he shunned. How's that for just deserts?"

"What about your plan to bury the sword with Sam?"

"I think my brother would understand," he says softly. "He would say that you're worth it."

Warmth fills my chest, expanding inside of me. I'm smiling so big it hurts. The things he's saying, the things he's giving up…amazing.

I take both my hands and place them lightly on his cheeks, careful not to hurt him. "That is the absolute most sweetest thing anyone has ever offered to do for me."

"So it's a yes?"

"No."

The surprise on his face makes me laugh. "We can't, Wes. Tyson and the rest of his crew will be furious."

"So what?"

"I don't want to risk it. And besides, I need to let go of wanting my father's approval. I need to let go of trying to be worthy of him."

"That doesn't mean you can't hold the sword over his head while you're doing those things," he grumbles.

My smile grows wider—if it's even possible. "You have no idea how much that means. But really, I don't want it. The satisfaction I'd get from the fame isn't worth risking both our lives."

Wesley stares at me, trying to figure me out. After a few long moments, I feel his mood begin to shift. The look in his eyes slowly changes to defeat, and he lets out a heavy sigh. "Fine. We'll let them have the sword."

I feel really bad. Handing it over isn't going to be easy for him. Earlier when I'd first been hit with the news, I'd only been thinking about myself and how difficult it would be for me. The thought of giving up the sword broke my heart. Wesley put his own blood, sweat, and tears into finding it, and this is going to be just as hard on him. It's not who he is to give up what he's worked so hard for. It's not who I am either, but I don't see any other options.

~ ~

DOLL

Wesley's eyes graze over the various plates we've spread across the bed. "You ordered too much food."

"If it makes you feel better, I charged it to Tyson's card."

He swallows a large bite of rice, smiling. "I take it back. You should've ordered more."

"Maybe I will. Dessert isn't out of the question."

Wesley watches me while I'm eating. His gaze is so intense it makes me feel self-conscious. I readjust my hair and pull it all to one side, then focus on my food, hoping he'll look away. He doesn't. "Stop it," I say, throwing a napkin at him.

"I can't help it. You're so beautiful like this."

"Are you kidding?" I stare at him like he's out of his mind. "I'm wearing sweats, and I have no makeup on."

"No offense, but your version of makeup should be banned."

"Ha ha." I pick up a carrot and toss that at him as well. He catches it in his hand and eats it.

"In all seriousness, I like you better this way," he says between bites. "There's no guard up."

"Guess I don't need one anymore," I say, shrugging. "Then again, with you I never did."

"What do you mean?"

I'm unsure how to put it into words. "You've just always…seen through it."

I think back to the night of Graffiti Bash, remembering the way he saw straight through my disguise. Putting up pretenses with Wesley is impossible. He sees past them. When Styler blackmailed me into living with him, he was right there to bring me home. When I told him I was dating Hayes, he never believed me for a second. He may have ignored me for the first three years of living together, but the last few weeks he's more than made up for it.

"I swear I'm gonna get us out of this mess, babe." He's still watching me, most likely mistaking my faraway look for fear.

"I'm not worried," I assure him. "I just want to get it over with."

"Me, too."

After dinner, we both clear the plates from the bed. Wesley lays down beside me instead of getting in the other bed, but I don't say anything about it. Without a word, he pulls me close to him and wraps an arm around me. I lay my head against his chest. Being this close to him feels so natural, making me feel more at peace than I have in days.

Yawning, I draw my arm across his chest. He grunts, and I immediately move my arm, wincing. "Sorry."

"Don't apologize. Any pain is worth it when you're touching me."

That was cute, but I don't believe him for a second. I'm careful not to touch that part of his chest again. This time when I close my eyes, I fall straight to sleep.

CHAPTER TWENTY-EIGHT

WESLEY

The next day Tyson has two jeeps waiting for us outside. I pass by the guy who groped Dahlia, and he smirks at me. "Nice mug."

I don't give him the pleasure of a reaction. He's not worth it.

Dahlia and I hop inside the jeep along with Tyson and James, and I shut the door behind me.

"Might as well get comfy," James informs us right away. "It's an all day trek into the desert."

Dahlia isn't paying any attention to him. She's drinking in our surroundings, a captivated look in her eyes. I forget how this place looks to newcomers. It's a huge contrast to America, a fantasyland in comparison. Everywhere you look, you find the ancient world meeting the modern one.

Once we get on the road, we pass by a blur of Islamic medieval buildings. Dahlia turns her whole body, trying to see them. I begin to see the city through her eyes, all the things I've seen a hundred times before are suddenly new. We pass by the Medina, and I notice the clambering mule carts, the snake charmers, the veiled women selling their wares, catching the way Dahlia's mouth parts in awe of them.

"It'd be nice if you gave me back my phone, Tyson," she grumbles. "Maybe I could take pictures and actually enjoy part of this experience."

"Nice try." Tyson glances at Dahlia through the rearview mirror. "But it ain't gonna happen until that sword is in my hands."

Dahlia narrows her eyes, scowling. She goes back to looking out the window, a contemplative look settling across her features.

I nudge her side with my elbow. "Everything okay?"

"Yes." Lowering her voice so only I can hear her, she says, "It's just...for so long I identified with my mom's side. White American, grandparents from Pennsylvania, German and Irish descendants—that's who they were. Who *I* was. I refused to acknowledge my dad's side, but now that we're here, and I'm seeing all of this..."

My eyes widen as I grasp what being here in Morocco means to her. I feel like an ass. It never even crossed my mind she would be thinking about those kinds of things.

"He doesn't represent this entire country, Dahlia. He's one person among millions." I reach for her hand, linking mine with it. "Someday we'll come back here and get the full experience."

One corner of her mouth curves into a half-smile. "Don't make promises you don't intend to keep, Wes. You'll break my heart."

"When I say something, I mean it. We'll come back here one day, and we'll do Marrakesh like it was meant to be done."

The sad, lost look disappears from her face, replaced with excitement at the idea of returning. "It's a deal."

Leaving the sights and sounds of the city behind, the drive becomes long and boring. Dahlia naps most the way, her head in my lap. I can't fucking stand her being stuck in the middle of this, but I'm glad she's here with me instead of the hellhole I found her in on campus.

During the drive, the jeep gets stuck in the sand. The tires lose traction. They sink so deep that it takes all three of us to push it out while Dahlia steers it back onto the paved part of the road. This is how I know we're getting close. We're venturing deeper into the desert now, in the heart of Berber lands.

The sun is setting on the horizon by the time we make it to the small village where my uncle is living. Tyson parks the jeep, and the movement wakes Dahlia. She yawns and stretches her arms above her head.

"Oh my God," she says, looking around. "This is like stepping back in time."

She's not exaggerating. The village is comprised of tiny huts, outdoor stoves, herds of roaming goats, children running around chasing each other with sticks, all of which could've been there hundreds of years ago.

"What next, Kent?" Tyson asks me.

"We find my Uncle Rooney."

It isn't hard to find him. He's the only white geologist in the village, and even with the language barrier, the natives immediately sense who we're searching for. We stop in front of his hut, and I find him around back, standing in front of an assortment of labeled rocks. "Wesley, m'boy! Is that you?"

I grin, almost unable to recognize him. He's lost weight and grown a great red beard since I've last seen him covering almost all of his face and neck. "Uncle Rooney."

He reaches out for me, clapping my back. "How've ya been, kiddo?" Leaning back, he rests his hands on my shoulders to get a good look at me. "Hell, what happened to your face?"

Before I can respond, Tyson cuts me off.

"Let's save the reunion for later and get straight to the point."

Uncle Rooney eyes Tyson distrustfully. "Who's this guy?"

"He's uh…" I think about how to introduce Tyson to my uncle, not wanting to say too much. "An old friend."

"Well your friend is rude."

You have no fucking idea.

Dahlia steps around me, holding her hand out for Uncle Rooney to shake. "I'm Doll," she introduces herself. "Also a friend of Wesley's—but much more polite."

My uncle's eyes light up as he takes Dahlia's hand. "Well, well, well. It's nice to meet you, young lady." He lifts her hand to his mouth and kisses it, causing her to giggle.

I roll my eyes. He was always a sucker for a pretty face.

"Kent," Tyson says through clenched teeth.

"I need the sword, Uncle Rooney."

"The sword?" he asks, his voice raising a notch. He takes stock of all of us, his eyes roaming over James and the rest of Tyson's accomplices. His lips thin into a frown beneath his beard. He knows what's going on; he's not a fool.

"Sword's no longer here," Uncle Rooney informs all of us gruffly. "I handed it over to the local government."

"He better be fucking kidding, Wes."

"Shut up, Tyson, and let me handle this." I turn back to my uncle. "Seriously. I know you've got it here, and I need it back."

He lifts his arms in an uncaring shrug. "Sorry guys, but the sword was a valuable piece of history. My nephew was wrong not to turn it over as soon as he found it."

"Uncle Rooney, we've come a long way. I swear it's okay for you to give it to me."

Several clicks sound off from behind us. When I swing around, there's a line of Berber soldiers holding up rifles and pointing them straight toward us. My first instinct is to grab Dahlia and push her behind me. Then I stick up my hands to let them know I'm unarmed. Tyson and the others do the same.

"Guess not everything is ancient around here," Dahlia whispers in my ear.

"Yeah, no kidding."

"What's going on, Wes?" Tyson growls at me, keeping his arms raised above his head.

"How the hell am I supposed to know?"

My uncle speaks to the men in Arabic, pointing at us as he does. I don't know Arabic very well and the dialect is strange. I'm only able to make out a few words, but if I'm hearing them correctly, they sound like directions. *Bind their hands.*

I'm not sure what is going on, but whatever it is, I hope my uncle gets us out of it.

"Wes," he calls to me, then begins speaking in French. "The girl is with you, correct?"

I nod once.

"And the others? They're blackmailing you, aren't they?"

Several thoughts come to mind after he asks me that question. I could lie and say they're not, but he'd never believe me. I could explain what's happening, but my uncle knows me, and he'd never believe I fear for my life. He wouldn't understand why I'm going to these lengths to protect a girl. I peek over my shoulder at Dahlia, who is watching my uncle intently.

Her eyes flick to mine. "He's asking you about them, isn't he?"

I nod.

"Tell him the truth."

"He'll turn them in." I whisper back. "He won't give them the sword if I do."

Dahlia presses her lips together, looking from me to my uncle and back again. Shaky, long seconds pass as I wait for her to say something. A slow smile curves her lips, the fear and anxiety suddenly gone. "Tell him the truth."

My heart leaps at her words, and if I could I would pick her up and crush my lips to hers with an Earth-shattering kiss, but I don't because there are still several guns pointed our way. Instead I speak to my uncle in French, tell him what's going on, and in the next instant he signals the men with guns.

They force Tyson and the others to their knees, binding their wrists with a coarse rope.

"What the fuck is happening, Wes!" Tyson screams. "You fucking set me up! I know you set me up!"

His screaming results in him getting kicked from behind, knocking his face into the sand. They find his gun in his pants, confiscating it. I lower my hands, watching the scene unfold in a state of shock.

Dahlia leans around me, grinning. "Serves him right," she says, looking the happiest I've seen her in days.

James looks over his shoulder at us as he's being taken away. His voice is low and menacing. "Make no mistake, Kent. This isn't the end. You better hope your uncle turned in that sword."

The soldiers drag them toward a group of vans in the distance. "They'll be taken back to the city," Uncle Rooney says to Dahlia and me. "Probably jailed for a night or two, but after that, you're on your own."

I shake my head at that. He isn't use to me being afraid of anything or anyone—he's used to me being prepared.

"Did you really turn in the sword?" I ask him.

"God, no," he scoffs. "I've got it tucked away in my work room. I'll get it for you later. First, we should have some tea."

"Tea?" Dahlia asks in disbelief. "We move on from being held at gunpoint to drinking tea?"

"Of course, m'girl!" Uncle Rooney says proudly. "It's tradition. If you're a guest, you get greeted with tea around the campfire. Besides, it's the Sahara. No one stays shell-shocked for very long here."

"Oh, I'm not complaining. I'm all for tea around the campfire." She turns around to face me. "Can we stay?"

"I don't see why not."

She smiles and my uncle runs off to fetch the supplies. I reach for Dahlia's hand, drawing her beside me. "What was that about back there?"

"What do you mean?"

"You told me at the hotel you didn't want to risk it."

"I guess I changed my mind," she says, shrugging. "I think the desert has made me more *adventurous* than usual." She beams.

"Thrilled to hear it," I say, grinning. "So are you saying you're willing to claim the discovery?"

She shakes her head. "No. I'm still where I stand on that."

"Well we can't keep it. Not now."

"I'm not saying we should keep it either. I've got a better idea."

"What's that?"

"I think we should tell people Sam found it right before he died."

I'm so stunned, I can't speak. Out of all the things I expected her to say, that wasn't one of them.

"Think about it, Wes. His existence won't be just a memory anymore. He won't be a photo tucked away in the back of your closet. He'll have a legacy, even if it's just a small one. People will get to see his name in books...so what do you think?"

"I think..."

I think I'm embarrassed as hell that this girl has the capacity to leave me at a loss for words. Because I can't get my damn voice to work, I take her face between my hands, pulling her lips toward mine. I kiss her with so much emotion that words aren't needed.

After a lengthy heated moment, we break apart. She has to catch her breath before speaking. "I take it you like that idea."

~ ~

WESLEY

"You really care for her, don't you?"

It's a loaded question. I'm thankful Uncle Rooney chose that moment to switch to French because I haven't approached that subject with Dahlia yet. I turn around to search for her, and find myself unable to look away. Firelight dances across her skin, and she's wearing the most peaceful, relaxed expression I've ever seen. She's so fucking beautiful it kills me—I swear she's becoming more beautiful everyday.

"Yes," I finally answer him. "I care about her."

"I can't believe you two spent three years in the same house without talking."

"It's a big house," I say, feeling the need to point that out. "But yeah, I know what you mean."

I'm not sure how I went so long ignoring Dahlia. I couldn't do it now if I tried. Her presence is everywhere inside Kent House. I can't *not* think of her anymore.

"Anyway, I'm glad you've come here in person. I have some exciting news."

I look away from Dahlia, turning to face him. "What is it?"

"The Flor de la Mar." He wags his brows at me excitedly. "The name ring a bell?"

"I don't live under a rock, Uncle Rooney."

"So then you know it's the most valuable shipwreck still lost at sea?"

I nod. My dad told me the story behind it when I was a kid. The ship set sail for Portugal during the sixteenth century, was caught in storm somewhere in the Malacca Straight, never to be found again. Treasure hunters have been searching for it for centuries.

"We think we found it, Wes."

I stare at him for a long moment, thinking it's a joke. He doesn't so much as flinch. My pulse quickens. "You've got to be fucking kidding!" I say this in English, causing Dahlia to glance over at us curiously.

My uncle continues using hushed tones in French. "I have a contact in India, a marine archeologist, who has sent me irrefutable evidence of the ship's whereabouts. He's putting together a team."

I sit up straighter. "Are you going?"

His lips curve into a wide smile as he nods. "Me, a full crew…and you. I convinced him to bring my budding archeologist nephew aboard for the excavation."

"Are you serious? When?"

"A few weeks maybe. However long it takes to get the right equipment together."

I feel my face drop. There's no way I'll be able to go. I'm bound to Harland's will. I'd have to give everything up and put my degree on hold.

"What's the matter?" my uncle asks.

"How long will the excavation take?"

He shrugs. "A few months I suppose. Why?"

"If I go, I'd lose my inheritance."

He stares at me like I'm insane. "Two point six *billion* dollars, Wes. That's the estimated value of the Flor de la Mar. You can't pass an opportunity like this up. Take a semester off and finish your degree later."

"Uncle Rooney, it sounds like a dream come true. But…" I glance at Dahlia. The will isn't the only thing I'm bound to.

"It's the girl," he says, an understanding in his voice.

"That's part of it."

I'm lying through my teeth. She's my only reason. If it weren't for her, I'd say yes in a heartbeat.

"She'll be there when you get back. The treasure won't."

"I know."

"You need to seriously think about it, Wes. This is a once in a lifetime chance. You don't want to let it pass you by."

"Okay," I say, nodding. "I'll think about it."

CHAPTER TWENTY-NINE

DOLL

Wesley's uncle slowly rests the *Saiful Azman* in my hands, careful not to drop it. I clasp my palm over the handle, holding up into the light. It's heavier than I expected. It's also more incredible than I ever imagined. The hilt is made of pure gold, covered in an intricate design of sparkling gems, and the blade has been cut into a perfect curve.

"They say it belonged to Sinbad himself," Rooney informs us. "Makes you believe he existed, doesn't it? Perhaps Sinbad was no more a legend than his sword."

My eyes drink in the beauty of it, leaving me in awe. "I can't believe I'm actually holding it."

"Sure you don't want to keep it, babe?" Wesley asks. He's leaning against the doorframe of his uncle's workroom, watching me. "We can get a better security system installed in Kent House, put it in a glass case on the wall of the library...it'd be a nice addition."

I shake my head. "No. This thing deserves to be in a museum somewhere. It deserves to have thousands of admirers coming to see it daily." I hand the sword back to Rooney, and he carefully places it back in its case. "Thanks for letting me see it."

"Well it belongs to you and Wesley now."

"We're gonna say Sam found it," Wesley tells his uncle. "Finding it was his life's dream. I think he'd like having his name attached to its discovery."

Rooney, who by his expression must've been close to Sam, smiles sadly. "He would love that."

Wesley nods and looks away. The pain clouding his eyes is heartbreaking. Talking about Sam isn't easy for him. I hope this helps him gain some peace. That kind of peace is worth it—and it's why I go to the Pretty in Pink Ball every year. I need that time to make something good come from my mom's death. Maybe Wesley has needed the same thing all along for Sam.

"Before you go, I want to give you something." Rooney rifles through the cabinet under his desk. "Here it is."

He reaches for my hand. In it, he places a small, circular stone. "I always make sure I give my guests a parting gift, especially the pretty ones," he says with a wink. "It's turquoise—the first stone ever crafted for jewelry by the Egyptians."

"It's lovely," I say. "Thank you."

"You're very welcome."

"Where's my gift?" Wesley complains, a note of humor in his voice.

"I said only the *pretty* ones," Rooney scoffs. "Pain in the ass nephews don't fall under that category." Despite his words, he moves in to give Wesley a bear hug. "It was nice seeing you, kiddo. And don't forget to think about what I said."

Wesley nods. "I'll give you an answer soon."

As soon as we're in the Jeep and driving away from the small village, I ask Wesley what decision his uncle was talking about.

"It's nothing," he says, shaking his head. "Just an expedition he wants me to go on."

"What kind of expedition?" I ask curiously.

He glances away from the road to look at me for a moment, pushing his sunglasses up the bridge of his nose. "It's uh…a shipwreck he believes has been found. The Flor de la Mar."

My jaw drops. "The *Flor de la Mar*?" I echo in disbelief. "How can you say that so calmly?"

I suddenly remember Wesley's outburst last night, and the excited mood he was in while talking to his uncle by the campfire.

"That's what the two of you were discussing last night, wasn't it?"

Wesley nods, staying quiet.

"Why the face?" I ask him. "You should be thrilled beyond belief right now. I think I heard it was worth over a billion dollars."

"Two point six, actually."

I shake my head, dumbstruck. "Then what's the deal? Why don't you seem more excited?"

"I can't go." He shrugs. "They want to start excavating in a few weeks."

I turn in my seat to get a good look at Wesley. "You'd lose your inheritance," I say in understanding. "But wouldn't you make more off the expedition?"

"Most likely."

"Then what's stopping you from breaking the terms of the will?"

"I don't know…I haven't said no yet. It's just a lot to think about. I'd be gone anywhere from six months to a year."

"Oh."

Six months to a *year*.

Just thinking about Wesley being gone that long makes my heart sink. Living in Kent House would go back to the way it was before. Lonely.

My next words are lodged in my throat, but I somehow manage to get them out. "You should go."

"Really?" Surprise thickens his tone. "You want me to go?"

Of course I don't *want* him to, but I can't say that. Telling him to stay for my own selfish reasons is just plain wrong. Exploring is who he is. Treasure is who he is. So I do my best to put on a very reassuring smile. "It sounds like one heck of an opportunity, Wes. If it were me, I wouldn't let anything get in my way."

He frowns, then looks back at the road, his reaction confusing the hell out of me. "Yeah, that's pretty much what my uncle said."

"Harland would be okay with it, you know. In fact, I think he'd be thrilled for you." I look down at my lap, thinking about what else I can say to reassure him. "And besides, we're friends now," I point out. "Which is what I think Harland really wanted. Screw education. I'm sure he didn't give a crap about that."

I grin, but it quickly fades when Wesley doesn't laugh. He doesn't even crack a smile.

"Friends?" he asks me. "Is that all we are?"

"You know what I mean, Wes. He wanted us to be close."

"I don't believe in being friends with girls. I told you that already."

"So you don't consider me someone worthy of giving your friendship?" I ask, hurt.

"No, that's not what I…" He lets out a frustrated sigh. "You'd be a good friend, Dahlia—if I didn't want to have sex with you every time I look at you."

My cheeks grow hot. "But still…there's friendship behind the attraction, isn't there?"

He looks over at me again, then back at the road. Long, awkward seconds pass before he finally agrees with me. "Yes, there is."

I gaze out the window for a long time before speaking again. When I do, my voice is heavy. "Wes, can I ask you something?"

"Anything, babe."

"Do your reasons for not wanting to go include me?" I immediately feel stupid for saying that, wishing I could take it back. "Not that I think you'd ever turn down a once in a lifetime chance for something so new—you know what? Forget I even asked."

The car slows down. Wesley pulls over to the side of the road, puts the Jeep in park, and turns to face me. "You are absolutely one of my reasons. Don't sell yourself short, babe. I don't care if this is still new or not. Every other fucking thought in my head is about you. If I had to leave you, I'm pretty sure I'd lose my mind."

I'm so stunned I can't breathe. His words work their way straight into my chest and squeeze me so tightly, making it impossible to breathe. He's just summed up exactly how I feel.

Wesley looks away from me. He bangs on the steering wheel, cursing. "Yes, I want to go. *Of course* I want to go," he says. "And if there was a way to bring you with me, I'd do it in a heart beat. But since I can't, I feel...against it."

"Wesley, I..."

I'm at a loss for words. Tears are building in my eyes, and crying is the last thing I want to do. I force myself to take a deep breath.

"We're twenty-one, and we have our whole lives ahead of us. If you don't go, you're being untrue to yourself. A job like this is what you were meant for."

"Don't tell me that," he says angrily. "Don't act like you don't care. I know you do."

"That's not what I'm doing." I shake my head, pressing my lips together. "The problem is that I do care. I care too much. Don't get me wrong, I love what you just said to me, and I feel the exact same way. I don't want you to leave. But I couldn't live with myself knowing I let you walk away from this. Don't ask me to do that, Wes."

He lets out a long sigh, resting his head back against the seat. "So what do we do? Do we end it before it ever really began?"

"I don't know," I say, shrugging. "You would be gone a long time. Maybe it would be less painful for both of us if we did."

Wesley turns away, looking out his window. "Fine." He shifts the gear out of park, steering us back onto the road. "If that's what you want."

He's angry with me. I open my mouth to say something, but close it again. I don't like that he's upset, and

I certainly don't like being the cause of it. I don't know why I even agreed to ending it in the first place. It's not what I want. It's not how I feel.

Even so, I can see the purpose of staying away from each other. The more I feel for him, the harder it's going to be to watch him leave. And the more he feels for me, the more he'll want to stay. I'm not going to be that girl, the one he'll regret years later. I'm not going to be the one he blames for missing out on one of the greatest opportunities he'll ever get a chance to take.

So I won't say anything. Maybe it will be easier for him if he's angry. He's upset right now, but maybe there will come a day when he's grateful for this moment. I hope that's possible.

Because I know I'll live to regret it.

CHAPTER THIRTY

DOLL

One week later...

There's a persistent knocking at my bedroom door that refuses to stop. I keep thinking to myself, if I don't answer, maybe whoever it is will go away. And just when I think the unwelcome visitor has given up, the knocking starts again, relentless.

After what seems like the ten millionth knock, I groan into my pillow.

"*What?*"

"Doll? It's me, Gwen...can I come in?"

I sit up in my bed, rubbing my eyes. I haven't thought about what I was going to say the next time I saw her. I don't know if I can do this right now.

Before I can answer, my door swings open. Gwen walks in, shutting it behind her. "I realize under the boss-employee relationship, this may seem inappropriate. But I'm not here as your employee. I'm here as your best friend. And as your best friend, I want to tell you that you can't keep ignoring me. I need you."

I tuck my pillow over my stomach, hugging it to me. "Can we do this later? I just got back."

"Doll, you may not realize what day it is because all you've been doing is sleeping, but you've been home for five days now."

"I'm jet-lagged," I grumble, silently counting back the days to see if she's right. Have I been home for that long? It's possible. I remember blowing off a few classes because I was so tired.

"Are you okay?" she asks, tilting her head. "I'm not sure what happened in Morocco with Kent, but I'm worried.

You look like you've been living in a garbage can. I almost prefer the crazy makeup and hoodie over this."

Looking down at myself, I notice the ketchup stain on the T-shirt I've been too lazy to change out of. Gwen has a point.

"I'm fine," I sigh. "I'll be back to normal soon. I just need some time to recoup."

"Recoup from what?" She makes her way to the edge of my bed, sitting down on it.

I shake my head. "If we have to have this conversation, let's get to the point."

She lowers her gaze, staring down at her lap. "I love him, Doll. What I did was horrible and awful and wrong, but I love him. I always have." It takes her a few moments before she can look me in the eyes. "Do you hate me for it?"

"Sort of," I answer honestly. "I hate what you did to Charlotte. Does she know yet?"

Gwen nods. "Miles broke up with her a few days ago."

"You're stupid if you think that's how it went down. He probably told her everything, and then she broke up with him. You're most likely the consolation prize. Congratulations."

"He told me about your conversation, Doll. He told me about how he planned to end things with me, and make it right with Charlotte."

"What changed?"

"He figured out he's in love with me," she says, shrugging.

"I'm so happy for you."

Gwen winces. "You have every right to be mad. I would be, if it were me. I can't stand cheaters, and in the mix of all this, I became the other woman. I'm ashamed of that, but for that alone. I've been in love with Miles since we were kids, Doll. When Charlotte found out I planned to ask him to the seventh grade dance, she beat me to it. Why do you think

I've hated her so much over the years? That's what started it all."

Really? That's what began their ongoing feud? I shake my head, unable to believe all those years of hating each other was caused over a date to the seventh grade dance.

"Forgive me if I don't think you can compare that to what you did to her," I mutter angrily. "We're adults now, Gwen. You're supposed to act like one."

She nods sadly. "You're right. I hated her based on what she had—what I thought she stole from me." She stands up and walks away, pausing by the door. "I'm sorry for putting you in the middle, Doll. It wasn't fair to you."

I nod, acknowledging her apology. Out of all the pain she's caused, I didn't think she recognized what she put me through as a result of it. I think I needed to hear it.

"If you don't want me to work here anymore, I'll understand."

I hug the pillow closer to my chest, unable to look at her. It's breaking my heart, and I want to stay mad. "You can keep the job."

"Okay," she says, wiping away a tear from the corner of her eye. "I'm glad." She turns to leave, then stops again. "Do you think you'll hate me forever?"

I press my lips together, wishing I could say yes. She deserves to lose a friend over what she did. Coming out the winner seems unfair. I don't even want to think about what Charlotte's going through. But if I said yes, I know I'd be lying. My life wouldn't be the same without Gwen. I hate what she did, but I don't hate *her*.

"No," I finally admit. "I just need some time."

The corners of her lips curve into a semi-smile. "That's really good to hear...I miss you."

"I miss you too."

"How much time do you need?"

"I don't know. A few weeks."

"That long?"

"I'm still angry, Gwen. Really angry. You hurt my best friend. I'd feel the same way if Charlotte did it to you."

She nods. "Okay. I can wait."

Once she's gone my room feels painfully quiet. Going back to sleep is tempting. You can't think or feel anything when you're asleep. Well you can, but only in dreams, and you've forgotten them by the time you wake up. Gwen isn't the only reason I've been keeping myself holed up in my bedroom. I think I've been waiting for Wesley to leave before starting my life again. I don't want to walk around this house, knowing he's still here. I might change my mind if I do. I might ask him to stay, and that's the last thing he needs while preparing to go on the expedition of a lifetime.

But I can't do this anymore either. Sitting here and being depressed isn't helping anyone—and it's killing my grades. Wesley is living his life in a big way, and I should be doing the same.

Besides, there are things I need to take care of. One of them being Charlotte. She may have hundreds of friends to console her, but I know she's going to need me to get through this. If I'm any kind of friend at all, I have to be there for her.

I stand up, looking around my messy bedroom, then down at my body. First things first—a shower. Then I'll find Charlotte.

CHAPTER THIRTY-ONE

WESLEY

"Dahlia wanted me to give this to you."

Francisco hands me a typed document. As I look over it, I realize it's a contract. Dahlia's signature is at the bottom.

"What is this?"

"Once you leave, the full inheritance will fall to her, provided she graduates. She asked me to draw this up for you. In it, she agrees to give you half of all the money and valuables she receives."

I keep reading for myself, unable to believe she would do this. "Not just half, Francisco. She's agreeing to relinquish anything I ask for."

Francisco coughs uncomfortably. "That's correct."

Looking up from the document, I stare at him incredulously. "Why is she doing this?"

"In her words, it's only fair. She said you've earned this, and she wants you to leave with the peace of mind of knowing that no matter what you dig up out of that ocean, you'll still have your inheritance."

I crumple the paper up, handing it back to Francisco. "No way. I'm breaking Harland's terms. She's supposed to get everything."

Francisco stares at me like I've lost my mind. "We've already processed this through the courts, Wes. You can't say no. It's already done."

"So undo it."

"I can't. It's her choice."

"Well then tell her I don't want it. I don't want anything from her."

"I can tell her that, but I doubt she'll change her mind." He eyes me with concern. "Is everything okay, Wes?"

"Everything's fine," I snap.

Immediately I feel bad. Francisco isn't to blame for my problems. Taking it out on him won't help either of us.

"Sorry," I say. "I'm in a bad mood, that's all."

"You should be on cloud nine." He claps my shoulder. "Get it together, son. You have no idea how lucky you are."

"You're right," I say, without meaning it.

Because I don't feel lucky. I don't feel anything.

The next few days pass by in a blur. During the day, I spend my time getting everything organized by packing, dropping my classes, booking my airfare, and keeping myself as busy as humanly possible.

It doesn't really hit me that I'm leaving until the day before my flight. Chase shows up at my house to hang out before I leave, surprising me, because I hadn't been sure if he and Tyson were co-conspirators.

As soon as I tell him what happened, I know he had no involvement.

"Everything makes a shit-ton of sense now, Wes. Think about it—we had a tail on us the whole time we were in Egypt. The guy who stabbed you must've been in on it with Tyson. He had to have been tipping them off."

"Yeah, I figured that out as soon as he told me he took Dahlia hostage."

Chase shakes his head. "We're done," he says, sighing. "I'm fucking done with that guy. What he did to you makes me sick, and I swear to God the next time I see him, I'm gonna beat the shit out of him."

"Don't bother. He's not worth it." I feel a grin tug at my lips. "But I appreciate the thought."

"Well, if it makes you feel better, I came over with good news. Where's your remote?"

I'm confused, but I grab the remote off the side table and hand it to Chase. "What's this about?"

"The professors have been buzzing about it all day." He flips to a news broadcast. "They're doing a feature story on your sword."

"Seriously?"

He nods, looking at his watch. "Just a few more minutes and it should be on."

We watch the broadcast together, and my heart stops when I see Sam's picture displayed on the screen. The news anchors refer to him as one of the most clever treasure hunters of our time. My heart swells with pride—for myself and for my brother. If it weren't for him, I never would have found it.

After it's over, Chase turns around to face me. "I bet he likes this better than being buried with it."

"Yeah. I think so too."

We drink a few beers, hang out and play video games for a while before it starts to get late. Chase stands up to leave. "I still can't believe you're leaving."

"You and me both."

"It's not gonna be the same around here." He leans in to hug me, slapping my back. It shocks the hell out of me because Chase has never been much for showing emotion.

"Take care, bro."

"You too."

Once he's gone, I look around me and it really starts to sink in. I'm leaving. Tomorrow. My gaze drifts to the right wing of the house, knowing Dahlia's up there somewhere. I saw her car parked out front.

I hate that she's handling this so well. "*We're twenty-one*," she told me, and for some reason that really got under my skin. What does it matter if we're twenty-one or forty? What I feel for her, I've never felt with anyone. Who is she to say it will pass? Maybe it's easy for her to forget, but I never will.

I'm getting angry all over again, and I hate that she has the ability to affect me like this. I try to tell myself by tomorrow it will all be over. I'll be too pumped to think of anything else but of getting on that boat and starting the excavation.

But it's a lie.

If I don't see her at least one more time, I'm going to be looking back instead of focusing on what's ahead. Before I change my mind, I run up the stairs.

CHAPTER THIRTY-TWO

DOLL

He leaves tomorrow.

I overheard Francisco talking about it on the phone while I was in his office. I wish I didn't know. It would've been better if I had woken up tomorrow, and he was gone. Now I have to get through tonight knowing he's leaving in the morning.

I'm pacing the space in front of my bedroom door, every so often stopping to stare at the door handle. Should I go find him? There's so much I want to say, but I don't know if telling Wesley the day before he leaves is a good idea.

I glance at my reflection in the mirror over my dresser, as if the girl in it will give me answers. I'm wearing a dress, my hair left down in loose waves that hangs over my shoulders. And I'm wearing makeup. Flattering makeup—not my usual stuff. I actually don't look half bad. But it doesn't give me the courage I need to go find Wesley.

I start pacing the room again. He's probably excited and nervous and busy packing. Distracting him is the worst thing I could do.

I should leave it alone, dammit.

But the thought of Wesley leaving without knowing how I feel doesn't sit well in my stomach. I stop to stare at the door handle again, determined to make a move. I lift my hand to open it, but there's a knock.

I swing it open. Wesley is standing there, his hand raised mid-knock. "That was fast."

"I was just about to come out."

We stare at each other for several seconds, each of us staying completely silent. My eyes rake over him as if I haven't seen him in years. He looks good—too good. His general attractiveness mixed in with how much I've missed him make for an intoxicating combination. I can't look away, can't get enough of him. Or maybe I'm doing it because I know this is the last time I'll see him.

"There's something I need to say to you before I leave," he says, his tone determined.

"Me too," I say. "But you go first."

"I'm in love with you."

Wait—what? That was supposed to be my line.

Hearing him say it though is so damn nice. It calms something inside of me, alleviating a fear I didn't know I had. I didn't want to be the only one who felt this way.

"I don't care if you think we're too young or if what we have is too new. You're it for me, Dahlia. I mean it, you and no one else. Ever. And whether we're apart for one day or a thousand, I'll still be missing you at the end of it. You're all I'm ever going to need again for the rest of my life. So you better get used to it because—"

I place the palm of my hand over his mouth, cutting him off. "I love you, too."

That's all it takes. The weight in his eyes disappears, and I can visibly see the shift in him. Just like me, he simply wanted to know he wasn't alone.

Wesley kicks the door closed and reaches for me, brushing his lips against mine. The warmth from his lips travels through every cell of my body. There's a sweetness that has never been there before—an emotion I've never felt from him.

An uncontrollable need to keep going consumes my mind and body. If this is supposed to be my last night with him, I want it to be memorable. I don't want regrets.

I back up from Wesley, sliding my dress sleeves off each shoulder, letting the material fall in a puddle on the ground. I step out of it, kicking it aside. I stand there before him wearing only my bra and panties, feeling more exposed than I ever have in my life, but somehow I gather the courage to look at him.

His eyes travel over every inch of me in a very slow, caressing way. "Are you sure?" he asks uncertainly. "That's not what this is about. I didn't come up here for this."

"I know."

Swallowing, I gather the courage to reach behind my back and unclasp my bra from its hook. I toss it behind me, keeping my eyes on Wesley. Then I bend over and slip out of out my panties as well.

I walk toward him, and he sucks in a breath. "It's okay. I want to," I assure him, resting my hand on the front of his belt. "I want this. With you."

He dips his head, pressing his lips against mine and kissing me as softly as possible. Like he's afraid I might change my mind. I deepen the kiss while tugging on his belt, not wanting to break away and give either one of us too much time to think about what we're doing. Unbuckling his jeans, I pull them down.

Wesley yanks the shirt over his head, then lifts me up and carries me to the bed, easing himself down on top of me. He breaks away from the kiss again, pushing himself up to stare down at me. "Last chance," he says, his breath uneven. "It doesn't have to be tonight. I can wait for you."

I take his face in my hands. "Maybe you can wait, but I don't want to."

"You should know that after this, I'm never giving you up," he says, swallowing. "I won't listen to any more talk of ending things or reasons why we should keep our distance." He leans down to kiss the side of my neck, slowly trailing a path of kisses over my jawline. I shiver, feeling a thousand tingles dance over my skin. "After tonight, you'll be mine. Completely. I want to hear you say it."

I nod, very willing to agree to those terms. "I am yours, and you are mine."

Wesley nods, gaining the permission he needs through my acceptance. Now that we've come this far, there is no going back. I'm perfectly fine with that. With all reservations gone, he kisses me hard and passionately. Now that he's made up his mind, he wants to see it through just as badly as I do.

When I feel his hand slide up my inner thigh, my breath catches in my chest. His fingers find their way between my legs, gently slipping inside of me. He moves back, and I keep my eyes locked with his, helpless to control the tiny spasms and tremors running through me. With each movement of his hand, my body convulses a little more. The need he's forming within me consumes every thought. I reach up to grip his shoulders, digging my fingers into his flesh. "Wesley, I…"

He moves away from me, and I hear him shuffle for his jeans, pulling a condom out of his wallet. The intensity of the mood breaks for a moment.

"Really?" I grin, unable to help it. "In your *wallet*?"

"This one has been in here since the day I met you—the real you. I haven't been with anyone since then, and there won't be anyone after."

His words touch my heart in a way I didn't think possible, relaxing my mind and body. In that moment, I know I'm ready for this, and for him.

I part my lips, hearing the condom rip open as he kisses me. When I feel the hardness between my thighs, I don't shy away from it. I let my legs fall open for him, closing my eyes.

My muscles tense as he pushes inside of me, and I brace myself for whatever pain is to come. He slows, kissing me tenderly.

"Look at me, babe."

I do what he asks and look up at him, seeing the way he's holding back, and I see it's taking a huge amount of effort for him to do so.

He presses inside of me a little more, and I gasp.

"I've never done this with someone I love," he whispers, kissing the side of my face. "I think this is how it should be. How it was meant to be. With you."

I nod, biting my bottom lip.

"Breathe, baby."

Doing what he says, I open my mouth to breathe, feeling most of the pain dissipate after a few short seconds. Wesley eases up, and then gently presses down again. This time, the pain fades to the background. My hips arch around his, and the next time I feel him push into me, I cry out, the sound muffled against his chest.

He begins to move faster and harder, rocking in and out of me as a bead of sweat films over both our foreheads. Each time he fills me, I want him closer and deeper than the last. Waves of pleasure course through my body, building a constant need for more. My breath goes still, and I arch my back as one last powerful wave crashes through me.

Wesley grips my hips, his movements turning rigid as he pushes into me deeper than before, molding his body to mine. Shudders convulse through him, and he goes still, the release making him groan against my ear.

He drops his head beside mine, his breath feathering against my neck. I feel his rapid heartbeat begin to slow against my skin.

"I love you," I whisper into the air, needing to say it again. I feel like I need to thank him for making that experience so heart-wrenchingly perfect.

He leans up and looks into my eyes, then kisses me fiercely, and I feel like I've just been branded. Maybe I have. In this moment, he is branding me for all time by giving me his heart, his soul, and a piece of him the rest of the world will never get to see. Knowing it belongs to only me gives me the most beautiful peace.

~ ~

WESLEY

The next morning Dahlia gently nudges my shoulder. She peers up at me, the morning sun gleaming in her soft amber eyes. Seeing her like this, in bed next to me, she's the most beautiful thing I've ever seen.

"If you don't wake up, you're going to miss your flight."

My flight? She can't mean…

Fear instantly washes over me. I stiffen, slowly lifting my head from the pillow to look at her. "What you said last night…it was all a lie?"

She furrows her brows, giving me a funny look. "What are you talking about? Of course it wasn't a lie."

"Then why are we still talking about me leaving?"

A frown pulls at her lips. "Wesley when I agreed not to end things, and when I told you I love you—I meant it." She reaches for my face, pressing her lips against mine for one short kiss, then leans back again. "But if you don't get your ass on that flight, you are not the man I love."

"How the hell are we supposed to make it work with you here and me halfway around the world?"

"We just will," she says, sounding positive about the whole thing. "You'll have to call me as much as you can. If not, we can email or talk online. We'll *make* it work, Wes. I have no more fears about us. I know that we can do this. If you trust me in the same way, you'll know I'll be patiently waiting for you to finish one of the most exciting jobs of a lifetime, so that you can hurry up and find your way back to me."

My chest tightens, warmth spreading over me. I do know that. I know she'll be here, and I know we will make it work. And deep down I know if she weren't forcing me to go, she wouldn't be the woman *I* love.

I grip her face, crushing my lips across hers. "Thank you."

She smiles. "Anytime. Need a lift to the airport?"

I look down at my watch. "Fucking hell," I mutter and jump out of bed. "I'm gonna have to get ready fast."

I hurry about her room, gathering up my clothes. Glancing up, I catch the sad look on her face, and I immediately drop my clothes to the floor.

"Oh don't let this deter you," she says, pointing at her face. "I still want you to go, but…I'm going to miss you like crazy."

In a few short strides, I'm back beside the bed. I lean over to kiss her again, pushing her down against the mattress. Gently sucking on her bottom lip, a soft moan escapes. Sliding my hand under the sheet, I run my fingers across her bare leg.

"Wes," she gasps. "I thought you said you were running late."

I break away for a second, my mouth curving into a slow grin. "Then we'll have to make this fast. Because I'm about to show you how much I'm gonna miss you too."

CHAPTER THIRTY-THREE

DOLL

Three months later…

There's a sense of awe that comes over me as I enter the ballroom. Waterfalls of drapery cascade from the ceiling to the floor in every shade of pink imaginable, from a blushing rose to a bright magenta. Tables glisten with soft candlelight, and there's a band center stage, permeating the place with upbeat music.

"I'm transferring out of here at the end of the semester," Charlotte says to me as we take our seats.

The news hits me like a bomb. "Are you serious?"

She nods, looking away. Since she and Miles broke up, she hasn't been the same. I don't blame her for wanting to leave, but not when she's so close to graduating. People surprise me. I figured Charlotte would rebound quickly. She's strong like that, but something has changed inside her. She's not the same person she used to be.

"You have one more semester left, Char. You've got the sorority, your academic achievements—you're really gonna give all that up?"

"I quit the sorority, Doll. Couldn't take it anymore." She twists the napkin on the table uncomfortably. "Ever since Miles…you know, I've been realizing more and more that this life isn't me. Yeah, I've made a name for myself, and yeah I have a lot of achievements under my belt, but it's not what I care about. It's not who I want to be."

The pain in her voice breaks my heart. "Who do you want to be?"

"Someone with real friends. Real relationships. I want to do things that are important, but at the same time not be so busy."

She looks at me, and I get what she means. I don't want her to go, but if this is what she wants, I'll support her. "In that case, I hope you find what you're looking for." I rest my hand on top of hers. "But you're not allowed to forget me, okay?"

"I won't." She offers me a weak smile. "You're one of the only people here I care about."

"So where will you go?" I ask curiously.

"Oh I don't know." She shrugs. "I'm thinking down south. Miami, maybe."

"I can deal with that. As long as you're not moving across the country."

"I considered it," she says sadly.

I hate that she said that.

"So how are you doing?" I ask, concerned.

"I'm okay. It's getting easier." Her eyes drift to the dance floor. "This kinda stuff is hard though, seeing all the happy couples dancing, smiling and kissing. It makes feel sick to my stomach. Are they really happy? Or are they all hiding behind a lie?"

I see where she's looking, noticing one of the couples holding each other as they sway to the music. Seeing it makes my chest tighten. "I know what you mean...sort of. It's painful for me too, but in a different way."

Charlotte swings around in her chair. "Well you, my friend, may get a happy ending after all."

"What do you mean?"

She nods to the space behind me and stands up. "I'm going to get some food while the two of you enjoy being reunited.

Confused, I look behind me.

My heart slams against my chest. Wesley is standing there, decked out in a tuxedo and looking absolutely gorgeous. I throw my arms around him, hearing him chuckle.

Gripping his arms, I back away, refusing to let go just yet. I need to look at him. All of him. I want to make sure he's real. "What…why…how?"

He laughs again. "I was able to get three days off. It took me twenty-seven hours to get here, and it'll take another twenty-seven to get back, which means…" He glances down to look at his watch. "I have another ten hours to spend with you."

"So instead of taking a break, you came all this way to spend *one* night with me?"

He nods.

"Why?"

"You're worth it."

I take his face in my hands, pulling his lips to mine. Kissing him sends sparks throughout my body, making me groan against his lips. Feeling him, touching him—it all seems like I'm in a dream. "You have no idea how thrilled I am that you're here."

"I have another surprise," he says, reaching into the inside of his jacket. "One Gwen thought you might like."

He pulls out a box, opening it for me to see. Inside is a giant sparkling ruby cut in the shape of a heart—the *Zumina-al-Shimaz.*

I place my hands over my cheeks. "You're letting me wear it?"

"No. I'm giving it to you. It makes sense that you should have it. You own my heart, Dahlia. You should have this one as well."

I shake my head, unable to stop my eyes from watering. "This is too much. You being here makes me happy enough."

Wesley pulls the necklace out of the box. "You're gonna put this necklace around your neck, babe, and you're gonna enjoy it."

"Okay." I grin in spite of his words. It didn't take much convincing.

He clasps the necklace around my neck, looking me over, and giving his nod of approval. "Beautiful."

"So ten hours, huh?"

"That's right."

"We should make the most of those ten hours then."

"I agree."

I reach for the crook of his arm tugging just slightly. "Will you dance with me, Wesley Kent?"

"I'd be happy to, Dahlia Reynolds."

"Good." I smile and lean close to his ear. "One dance. And then afterward, I think we should go home."

He nods, the idea appealing to him. "That has a nice sound to it. Home."

THE END

Thank you for reading! You can visit me at:
http://www.shannaclayton.com
Facebook
Goodreads
Instagram: @shannaclaytonbooks
Twitter: @shannaclayton

33685189R00181